Terence Blacker was born in 1948 and was educated at Wellington and Cambridge. His first novel *Fixx* was published in 1989 to considerable acclaim, the *Guardian*'s Robert Nye describing it as 'overwhelmingly comic'. He has also written several books for children and his story *Ms Wizz Spells Trouble* was shortlisted for the Children's Book Award of 1989. He has contributed weekly columns for the *Sunday Times*, the *Independent on Sunday* and *Publishing News*. He lives in London.

Also by Terence Blacker

FIXX

and published by Corgi

The Fame Hotel

Terence Blacker

BLACK SWAN

THE FAME HOTEL
A BLACK SWAN BOOK : 0 552 99550 9

Originally published in Great Britain by
Bloomsbury Publishing Ltd

PRINTING HISTORY
Bloomsbury edition published 1992
Black Swan edition published 1993

Set in 11/12pt Linotype Melior by
County Typesetters, Margate, Kent

Black Swan Books are published by Transworld Publishers Ltd,
61–63 Uxbridge Road, Ealing, London W5 5SA,
in Australia by Transworld Publishers (Australia) Pty Ltd,
15–25 Helles Avenue, Moorebank, NSW 2170,
and in New Zealand by Transworld Publishers (NZ) Ltd,
3 William Pickering Drive, Albany, Auckland.

Printed and bound in Great Britain by
Cox & Wyman Ltd, Reading, Berks.

To Sarah-Jane Forder

The following document shall be known as

EXHIBIT A

This, at least, is the way I saw the death of Ollie Sincton.

Doubtless, were the man himself here to tell the story, he would impose on it some kind of dignifying shape, transforming the rough material of the real world into a neat, marketable fantasy. In a Laura Nicholl novel it would be an uplifting parable of modern consumerism in which good, elemental things (wealth, sexual virtuosity, fame) finally triumph. A tabloid version, Nightclub Naughty Suzi Ashbourn Tells All, would present a cloying mix of snobbery and squalor, a bonkologue with heart.

But this is my version. Whispers, the scratch of pen on notepad, the soft whirr of the camera, secondhand words. I was in the right places, asking the right questions, noting it all down, reconstructing.

Trust me. I'm a policeman.

Part One

1

London had stalled on the day Robin Nicholl kissed his wife goodbye, stepped blinking into the sunlight of the Gloucester Road and made his way to the small, discreet service flat in Mayfair where the body of his best friend had recently been found. A heatwave, the annual invasion of ugly tourists and a series of random transport strikes had sent the city's discontentment rate soaring. No-one was happy. Office workers bitched and gossiped, dreaming of their holidays. Commuters leapt out of their cars and brawled with one another in the middle of the road. Marriages cracked in the heat and, although it was far too clammy for a civilized affair, people slept together out of spite or boredom. The legendary, fear-based qualities of the English – tolerance, manners, a polite lack of curiosity into the lives of others – had gone missing. In a month's time, London would return to normal; until then, it would be sticky, dissatisfied, pointless.

Robin Nicholl sat in an underground carriage, uneasily, like an uninvited guest. It was crowded, mostly with foreigners, but there were a few sullen natives, swaying, sweating, eyes half closed. Not so long ago, Robin would have given up his seat. Now the gesture had become redundant; it seemed vaguely insulting to suggest that a woman needed to sit down more than a man did. She had to be old, crippled or pregnant; the etiquette was complicated. How old was old? What if the pregnancy turned out to be mere obesity? Nervously Robin glanced in the direction of a plump woman standing in front of him. No, it wasn't worth the risk.

He smiled at a small Japanese child who was sitting beside his parents on the seat across the aisle. The child looked away, but his father leant forward.

'Excuse,' he said. Robin had the sort of face which invited approach; hustlers, hookers, tourists, they always chose him. 'Excuse, please,' said the Japanese man more insistently.

'Yes?' Robin smiled, the hospitable Englishman.

The man stabbed a finger at a map of the underground that he was carrying. 'Please. Why is Buckingham Palace?'

'Sorry?' Robin was momentarily confused. 'Why is what?'

'Why is Buckingham Palace?'

'Ah, yes.' Robin nodded apologetically. 'Change at South Kensington –' He pointed to the map. 'Take the District Line to St James's Park.'

'Thank you sir.'

'And it's "where" not "why".' The fat woman shot him a withering don't-encourage-them look. '*Where's* Buckingham Palace?'

'Change South Kensington,' replied the tourist, puzzled. Was asking the very question you had just answered yet another aspect of British protocol not mentioned in the guidebooks? 'Take District Line to St James's Park,' he said politely.

The train drew into Hyde Park Corner station. 'Have a good stay,' said Robin, standing up. The woman fell into his empty seat like a fat girl playing musical chairs. Robin noticed that the bag she was carrying was from Mothercare.

'Sorry,' he said weakly. The woman scowled.

So much hostility, Robin thought sadly as the escalator took him towards daylight. What had happened to London? Last week, on this very line, an old man in a raincoat had been stabbed by a youth whom he had unwisely asked for money. That was how people expressed irritation these days – with a blade

14

through the ribcage. Having wiped his knife on the victim's coat, the young man had stepped off at the next station and disappeared into a crowd of commuters.

A waft of hot summer air caught Robin by surprise as he surfaced above ground. You didn't expect London to smell of sweat and people. He turned into Half Moon Street, passing a news-stand. Ollie Sincton was no longer news. Yesterday there had been a few lurid tabloid stories — 'KINKY FRIEND OF STARS MURDERED IN LOVE-NEST' — but, after the police had announced that the dead man was not, on the day of his death, meeting an actress, a politician or a newsreader, interest had slackened. It was just another London crime; newswise, Ollie's murder lacked legs.

Robin had never been good at expressing feelings. The twenty-four hours since he had heard about Ollie's death had been accompanied by a strange empty nausea in his stomach, as if he were on his way to some dreaded event: an interview, an exam, a departure.

No more Ollie. He didn't want to talk about it.

In this, as in many things, Robin differed from his wife Laura, who had managed to respond to questions from the press with the correct air of stunned disbelief. Like many of her friends, Laura was adept at feeling the right things in the right way. They felt bad about what they ate, the clothes they wore, how much money they had or didn't have, Planet Earth, the weather. To Robin, a sunny day was a sunny day, not the beginning of the end of the world.

He entered the block of flats where Ollie Sincton was said to have conducted secret sexual business. A doorman seated at a table in the lobby glanced up at the tall, curly-headed man and then returned to his paper, seeing that the visitor was neither winner nor loser enough to merit his attention.

Flat 56. Robin took the lift to the fifth floor and walked the length of a long corridor until he reached the door of Oliver Sincton's love-nest where, that Saturday afternoon, I was waiting to interview him.

He was not anyone's idea of a romantic-novelist's husband, Robin Nicholl. Lanky, dishevelled, a goofy, worried look on his perspiring features, he had the slight stoop of a man embarrassed by the amount of space he occupied. There was something of the schoolmaster to him, the good-hearted stalwart with a silly nickname and a bad record for keeping order. He was the type of man who cut his own hair.

'Detective Inspector Potter, Robin Nicholl, sorry,' he said, hovering uneasily at the front door.

'Glad you could make it,' I said. 'Coffee?'

'Erm.' Robin seemed taken aback by this hospitality at the scene of the crime but followed me into the kitchen where DC Dexter was standing over a kettle like a TV cook.

'Detective Constable James Dexter, Mr Nicholl,' I said. 'We can't stretch to milk, I'm afraid.'

'If you knew how unlike Ollie this is,' Robin said.

'Your first visit here, is it?'

'No-one knew that Ollie had this place. He lived in Putney.' Robin wandered into the sitting-room. 'It's so tidy.'

'A tart's flat, that's what it reminds me of. Bottle of wine in the fridge. A few clean sheets and towels in the airing cupboard. Prints on the walls.'

'Yes, it's strangely impersonal.'

'In my experience—' I allowed myself a lightly ironic *aperçu* '—folk rarely decorate the flats they use for illicit affairs with shots of the family. It seems to strike the wrong note.'

'It might not have been for that,' said Robin gloomily.

I looked down at my notes, then at a copy of the statement taken from Nicholl the previous day. A 42-year-old American with a dodgy private life found dead in a small service flat. In the general scheme of things, it seemed a scummy little crime.

'And the last time you saw him was on the night of his death at this—' I put on a bit of a pantomine here '—this Groucho Club.'

'Yes. My wife and I had been to some sort of dinner to launch a magazine.'

'You say Sincton asked you to be his literary executor should anything happen to him.'

'He was slightly the worse for wear, but it was an odd remark.'

'Which is why you're here.'

'When you told me he hired a flat, I thought there might be something of interest.'

I sipped at my black coffee. 'Murder's always interesting,' I lied. 'It's amazing how some folk seem to latch on to it. Gives their own lives a lift, a thrill.'

'I take my responsibilities as a literary executor very seriously.'

'So you'll be wanting to see the papers.' I walked across the small hall to the bedroom. Robin followed.

The room was tiny and occupied almost entirely by a double bed which had been stripped down to the mattress, on which Forensic had chalked an Ollie-shaped line, spread-eagled.

'How long had you known the American gentleman?' I asked, as we stood staring at the bed.

'Twenty years or so. We met at university.'

'And he stayed on in England.'

'He wasn't close to his family.'

'So it seems.'

'He thought it was civilized here.'

'Handcuffed to the bed, his private part decorated with a doughnut, then stabbed through the neck.' I glanced at the stained mattress. 'He certainly seems to have entered into the spirit of the place.'

'He liked the way it worked,' Robin said bleakly. 'The chat, the networks, the scene.'

'I see.' Already I was getting a bad feeling about this case. What at first sight had seemed straightforward – idiot with dodgy libido gets involved in a spot of muckiness, the muckiness goes too far, the idiot dies – was acquiring ramifications. This was not your average tosspot; he was a media tosspot, a tosspot with words, with celebrity friends.

'The papers are in here?' Robin asked.

From the kitchen we could hear Dexter washing up the coffee cups. I turned to the large wardrobe behind me and opened it with a flourish. In contrast to the tidiness of the rest of the flat, it was crammed with scuffed and dog-eared magazines.

I picked one up and flicked open a page. ' "I'm Rita, I'm raunchy. Go anywhere, do anything. Can entertain. O and A levels. French, Greek, S/M, switchable." ' I gave the magazine to Robin. 'Marvellous thing, education,' I said.

'Readers' Wives.' He spoke as if in a trance. 'This can't be Ollie.'

'He used them. They're marked, like a racing formbook.'

'It's so . . . vulgar.'

'Still waters.'

Robin turned to go. 'Ollie wasn't deep,' he said. 'That was his great strength.'

It took more than an encounter with the law and the revelation that his best friend had been in the habit of meeting contributors to *Readers' Wives* to throw Robin Nicholl off balance.

Now, as he walked from Half Moon Street towards the gallery where he had agreed to meet his wife, he was intrigued. While Ollie had been widely known, he was hardly the type to acquire enemies or inspire jealousy. His was not a name to be dropped at the literary salon, in the Green Room before an egghead discussion on television. He was fringe, a fixer. When

18

projects hit a problem (an overextended biographer, a blocked novelist, a word-blind celebrity), Ollie, the good ghost, would somehow materialize at the right moment. With his help, the biographer miraculously found time to fulfil contracts signed in greed and haste, the novelist recovered her flow, the celebrity discovered articulacy.

It was his style with women too. Robin had never quite understood the secret to Ollie's strike rate. Even at Cambridge, where male undergraduates regularly used to commit suicide out of virginal frustration, he had cleverly ignored the girls of Girton and Newnham, whose sexuality tended to be going through a tiresomely Lawrentian phase, and worked his way through the cream of the foreign-language schools until, out of sheer university pride, the girl students joined the queue.

Here was the mystery. What was a man whose looks, charm, discretion and availability ensured sexual ease and variety any time he chose doing with grimy sub-pornographic magazines and readers' wives? What was his game?

Robin hesitated outside the gallery in Cork Street. Inside were denim and dark suit, creatives hobnobbing with the superior kind of punter who not only paid thousands for the wild daubs displayed on the walls but could explain why. Through the glass doors could be heard the familiar symphony of well-educated conversation, punctuated by occasional feminine laughter. As he opened the door, he heard a woman say loudly, 'I did *not*, Henry, *God* you're foul.'

This kind of event had its own geography; the important guests at the centre, the run-of-mill party-goers forming an inner circle around them. Robin normally found himself in a corner passing the time with some hanger-on – a publicity girl or a security guard.

For a few moments he watched as, across the room,

Laura Nicholl, bestselling author, reputed million-airess, perfect wife, talked to three men, her eyes alight with interest. He had become used to seeing men of all ages falling in love with her as she sparkled and made each of them feel witty and alive. His wife's social magnetism neither disturbed nor excited him; it was simply part of her character.

Robin pushed through the crowd.

Without taking her eyes off the man who was addressing her, Laura extended a hand backwards, like a sprinter receiving the baton, and drew Robin into the circle. The conversation dwindled and died, the men's fascination with Laura being tempered by the presence of her husband, and they drifted away.

'How was the inspector?' she asked.

'Depressing. I'll tell you about it later.'

'Darling!' A plump middle-aged woman embraced Laura, placing herself squarely between Robin and his wife. 'God, I enjoyed your book. You know, I read it aloud to my husband in bed.'

Laura squeezed Robin's hand and let it go, an expressive marital gesture combining affection, apology, exasperation and dismissal. He weaved his way towards the outer circle.

'In bed with your husband,' he heard Laura saying. 'Exciting. How was I?'

Other people's misfortunes cement a marriage. Sometimes, after dining with a couple whose relationship was clearly dead, Robin and Laura would return home in silence, united by sympathy and deep gratitude that they had one another. The closer the friends, the more surprising the failure, the better they felt. Since Ollie's death, it had been particularly good. In different ways, they had both envied him. Robin contrasted his own daily round of unadventurous domesticity with Ollie's eventful and ever-changing romantic life. Laura admired his facility with words, the apparent ease with which he was able to complete

20

projects that had defeated better, more interesting minds. Now he was revealed as a restless, unhappy bachelor who had indulged in pathetic, sordid adventures at a secret flat. A loser, in fact.

As they drove home in Laura's Mercedes, she talked about the fools she had met at the gallery. Robin closed his eyes, swore to himself that he would never again attend one of her parties, and thought about his own good fortune, his secure and happy marriage.

Poor Ollie, he thought. Lucky us.

2

There was a crime party going on outside but the atmosphere at Vine Street police station, my place of work, was relaxed. Men in shirtsleeves sat on the edge of desks or leant against filing cabinets, chatting, laughing, flirting with their female colleagues, drinking from plastic cups. In one corner of the large open-plan office a telephone was ringing, ignored. Every year it's the same: the sun comes out, bringing to bloom all the nasties on God's earth, and half the force is away enjoying a lager binge on some hapless Mediterranean island.

It was Sunday afternoon. Already much of a weekend I would happily have spent in suburban bliss with Joy and the kids had been occupied with the affairs of Oliver Sincton, whose homicide had sufficient publicity potential to catch the eye of Superintendent Norman Biddle.

The super was at home. I was in my office, assessing the case. Detective Constable James Dexter was in front of a word-processor studying the notes of Oliver Sincton. That was how it worked at our shop.

I stood up and looked through the glass partition separating my office from James and his colleagues. He was sitting bug-eyed before the screen like a loony undergoing some form of weird TV therapy. Whatever he had found on Sincton's little word-processing disks seemed to be absorbing his full attention.

It would be just my luck if this murder had to be taken seriously.

Policing's a career much like any other. Only, where

the rest of the world has its deals and fiddles and marketing opportunities, we have fraud, theft, assault, homicide. They're rungs on our ladder. One man's murder is another man's career break.

So, while certain misdemeanours in the hierarchy of crime (broken heads in Cardboard City, domestic violence in Southall, bloodshed at a crack-house in Brixton) are hardly worth the shoe leather of the luckless noddy taking statements, others can bring all sorts of rewards in terms of publicity, unofficial finance or gold stars on the personnel file.

We live in an age of visibility. In murder cases there's a moment, not long after the body has cooled, when a decision has to be made. To wit, is this one a goer and, if so, what's in it for me?

I returned to my desk and picked up the telephone.

'Norman, Simon here. Sorry to bother you at home.'

'Right. What's new?' Sarcasm was wasted on the superintendent.

'The Sincton case.'

'Yes.' I could imagine Biddle sitting there in his head-of-the-household armchair, a stern decisions-decisions expression on his heavy, bland features. 'What gives?'

'By all accounts our friend put himself about a bit. The contact magazines we found were marked. No-one knew about the flat.'

'Bit of a swordsman, was he?'

I wondered vaguely whether Biddle's amiable, churchgoing wife was in the room with him.

'The post-mortem suggests there was no sexual activity on the night of the murder.'

'Apart from the fact that he was spread-eagled naked on a bed with a doughnut on his dick.'

'Apparently, he was wearing that before he was killed. It wasn't a finishing touch on the part of the murderer.'

'Sounds iffy to me, Simon. Why not leave it to Dexter?'

I paused before casting my line upon the water. 'Could do, Norman. It's just these computer disks he's left. It seems Ollie was well connected. As you know, he had a few friends in the media world.'

'Yes.' Biddle, who had an all-pervading weakness for the excitements of public life, sounded thoughtful. 'Perhaps you and Dexter had better run with it for a while. Keep me posted.'

Putting down the phone, I sighed. Few of us are naturally telegenic but even my unexceptional looks (imagine a weary solicitor at the end of a long day, receding sandy hair, pale eyes) make me more suitable than Norman to the occasional cameo role in public. Something odd happens when the camera turns on him: the head's too big, the eyes sink into the face. The overall effect is not reassuring.

Me and Dexter. I walked out of the office and peered over my colleague's perfect, square shoulder like a caring schoolteacher. James Dexter, I admit, possessed certain qualities, personal and physical, which I found unendearing. His handsome, dark-featured integrity, for example, bordered on the unprofessional. That stubble-chinned enthusiasm for work, the trim optimism, those brown eyes smouldering with a sense of civic duty; none of it pleased me. But it was his hair, the sort of mop which delights girls and hairdressers, that annoyed me most. I thought of my own visits to the barber and the futile rearrangement of my sadly thinning locks that they involved.

He noted down a name on a pad beside the word-processor. 'What's troilism?' he asked in a distracted voice.

I glanced at the screen. 'Why'd you want to know that?'

'Ollie Sincton refers to this troilism thing now and then.'

'*Ménage à trois.*'

James looked up at me, a picture of boyish confusion.

'Three in a bed,' I said.

'Oh.' He returned to his pad. 'That.'

Girls rang James every day. He ignored them, placing the pursuit of society's wrongdoers before any idea of personal pleasure. He could take his pick, and probably did, when he had time. Doubtless he graduated in troilism while still at school, even if he didn't know the correct terminology.

I picked up his notebook and read a list of names, mostly those of women.

'Is it all like this?' I asked.

'Sex and showbiz.' He reached for a few sheets of paper on the desk beside him. 'I thought you'd like to see something from the Jane Goodenough file since she was one of the last people to see him alive. He met her through Russ Targett.' James gave a little laugh. 'Do I whaaaat?'

A less worldly detective inspector than myself might have doubted his sanity at this point but, my wife being something of an *aficionado* of popular television, I understood the reference to a minor comedian and his asinine catchphrase. 'Very good, James,' I said. 'Get that list of Sincton's contacts to me by the morning, will you?'

I gathered the sheets of paper. Back in my office, I sat down to read.

You know the Bunch of Grapes in Hans Crescent? Sure you do. Anyone who ever pulled blind knows the Grapes. Time was when Quasimodo could score there on a Friday night (in fact, knowing the regulars' taste for the exotic, Q could take his pick). As closing time approached, you could cut the sexual tension with a knife. Where is she, the restless young suits were thinking; the secs were crossing and uncrossing their legs like vaudeville. Where the fuck is he? I'm not going home alone, my god. And none of us did, then.

Now it's cooled down. You can find anyone there, even losers. People hang out to sip spritzers, rub Filofaxes, do meetings. The Devil Disease has driven the flying-fuck brigade underground. There are pick-ups, of course – there'll always be pick-ups – but nothing's clear-cut any more. Those legs at the corner table might be on, but then they could just be here for conversation. This celibacy thing has fucked up even life's simplest pleasures.

Anyway I'm here on business. An interface with Russ Targett, the alternative comedian who now fronts a quiz show, a celeb nouveau who fancies doing what all celebs nouveaux are doing: get the cash and credibility of a book published under your name without the hassle of engaging the brain or putting pen to paper. Russ is hot for a ghost. Enter yours truly, warm smile upfront, calculator in back pocket.

Russ talks. I listen. A light-hearted autobiography is what he has in mind, something brimming with zany anecdotes and candid insights into the life of the stars, Russ portrayed as a regular guy with a certain small talent – 'Hey, Russ, c'mon,' I go, 'not that small', Russ shrugs modestly – OK, a certain talent for entertaining other regular guys. He'd love to write it himself but he has this cerrazzeee schedule at present.

All the time he's talking, Russ is checking himself out in a nearby mirror or darting anyone-recognize-me glances around the room. That's when he sees a girl sitting alone, small, straight-haired, fragile, with those perverse thin lips the English do so well. She looks intelligent, which I like, and – to an expert eye, at least – restless. Russ puts the bullshit on hold, like someone cut the autocue, as he tries the highly amusing 'Who me?' grimace that works so brilliantly on television.

She turns away. Now I really like her. Unfazed – Russ's taste, I happen to know, runs to pea-brained teenies with streaked hair and downwardly mobile lips – he returns to his favourite subject.

So I move into full tarting, friend-of-the-stars mode. Russ looks thoughtful and promises to talk to his people, finally breezing out of the bar with a purpose-ful, no-autographs-please air.

That's when the girl catches my eye. In an odd, doll-like movement she raises her empty glass and tips it unsmilingly. I take my bottle over to her table, and fill the glass.

'Hi there,' I go, Mr All-American Boy.

She raises an eyebrow like she's in some idiot movie with nix dialogue and loads of meaningful looks.

'Party time?' I say with that pre-coital catch in the voice I'm told is absolutely irresistible.

She folds her copy of The Times *and puts it in her briefcase.*

We don't finish the wine.

There's an etiquette to the one-night stand these days. No, not between the sheets, stupid – there only politeness is impolite – but in the warm-up, the cool-down. Down here among the sexual underclass, it's regarded as the height of bad form to assume that you're invited for the night.

Sex with me? Sure. Sleep with me? Now hang on a minute, you saucy minx.

Because allowing a stranger to sleep with you or, worse, to watch you sleeping is a far greater intimacy than a mere fuck. Spending the night has overtones of relationship – the very last thing in the world on the mind of the healthy one-night-stander. It involves time, conversation, rather than simple lust and need. You could end up talking about your hobbies, your family, the way you vote, for god's sake. And then where would you be?

Do it, relax, do it again. And, after a decent interval, slip back into the night from whence you came. That's the way it is these days – in England, at least.

Of course, for losers, this can be confusing. They were brought up to believe that sex on the hoof, the post-coital split, was rude and insensitive. A certain amount of time and fake tenderness was the price you were obliged to pay. When losers figure out the change in the rules, if they ever do, they don't know whether to be pleased or insulted.

Jane and I knew the rules.

Her flat: very smart, very ordered, very bachelor girl. I'd have laid money that this girl was the type who, after a serious talk about contraception and commitment, folded her clothes carefully on the chair before going to bed with someone. So did he, probably. Lovely clean sheets, cute little plumped-up pillows and, on his and her chairs, two tidy stacks of clothes. I wasn't going to have any of that shit.

These were my thoughts as I paced her sitting-room while she fixed me a drink in the kitchen.

She brought me a whisky which I downed in one. It was no time for cocktail chat. Some of them want teddy, daddy, mummy, and I can do that if required. But not tonight.

'Let's go,' I said.

And she gave me that look that nice girls give you when they're just about to forget that they're nice girls, haughty and horny at the same time. 'D'you always behave like this?' she asked.

'Yup.'

We both laughed and she led me to the bedroom.

For all this country's many and various qualities, it has to be said that England is not the natural home of the blow-job.

The great English breakfast, sure. The great English muffin, maybe. The great blow-job, forget it. Yet, god knows, I've tried. These last twenty years have been a personal crusade – the search for a half-decent English gobble has been my Holy Grail.

I guess it's the education that instils this prissiness,

this heavy-hearted sense of duty in English girls who enjoy most anything else. Here, home of the quaint and historical, the one tradition that matters – the great oral tradition – seems to have gone missing somewhere along the way.

They try, of course, either worrying away at you like a dog with something it wants to kill ('gamming' and 'plating' are their revealing terms for it) or, the nice girls, daintly bobbing about with eyes squeezed shut as if confronted by a horrid, horrid pudding.

And when, after a few painful or dull moments they pop back up with a golly-I'm-glad-that's-all-over look on their faces, and you really do have to insist (English girls can be embarrassed into doing virtually anything), they descend reluctantly, grimacing, tense, punishing you cruelly with their teeth. Yeech. I swear that my efforts to convert this country's womanhood to the joys of the oral tradition have left me positively corrugated.

Now, since I was in one of my masterful moods that night, I kept myself icily in check, resisting the temptation to push her on to the bed for a sharing experience. That would be for later. I sat on a chair in front of her dressing table and said, 'Take your clothes off.'

Jane made to switch off the bedside light.

'Leave it,' I said.

She went to draw the curtains.

'And them,' I said. For the first time, she seemed faintly shocked. 'The neighbours deserve a treat.'

My bedside manner is not always this crass, by the way, but – maybe it's the blood of my poor colonized ancestors coursing through my veins – the English upper middle classes tend to bring out the beast in me.

Satisfyingly crestfallen, Jane stood in the middle of the brightly lit room and peeled off, revealing her trim, pale, slightly under-nourished bachelor body (we get the body we deserve).

Then – unasked! – she dropped to her knees before me and – well, you can guess the rest. My ascendancy was destroyed, my quest was over. What a surprise that was.

'Are you absolutely sure you're English?' I asked later.

Jane reclined against a pillow, sipping her wine, naked and dignified. 'Of course,' she said. 'Why?'

'I bet there's a bit of French in there,' I said.

'Excuse me, we were only in the bloody Domesday Book.'

'The what?' Christ, I laughed. It seemed a weird moment for family pride.

'We were,' she said, comically affronted. 'No ... what? We were. You can check.'

It was different from then on. We spent the night laying waste to her bed and, in between times, talking.

That's right. I stayed, when the socially correct thing to do was to kiss and run.

'Anyway what was the name?' I asked as the birds began to sing outside the window.

'Name?'

'In the Domesday Book.'

'Goodenough.'

I could understand James Dexter's confusion. The American's clammy account had the feel of fantasy about it; yet the names were real, Jane Goodenough existed. I picked up the phone and called Dexter. He staggered in, bleary and red-eyed from Ollie's adventures.

'How many of these disks are there?' I asked.

'Three, sir.'

'Get Jean to copy them, will you. That bloke Nicholl, the literary executor, could probably use them. Go round and give him one of the originals you've looked at.'

'Wouldn't that be giving away evidence?'

'You might say that. It's a risk worth taking.'

The detective constable, who holds my strategic powers in some respect, nodded knowingly.

'We just let him have a disk then,' he said.

'Correct.'

'You don't think this executor fellow could be involved in some way?'

'Somehow I doubt it.'

I smiled at the thought of Robin Nicholl dancing around Ollie Sincton's bedroom, a doughnut in his hand. Now that was fiction.

3

At one-fifteen the following day Robin stood outside La Magritte restaurant in Soho, his arms around a large cardboard box, hoping that someone would open the door. At last, a waiter inside noticed him.

'Cheers,' gasped Robin, squeezing by.

'Have you booked, sir?'

'Guest of Mr Gyles,' said Robin, his chin resting on the top of the box. 'I couldn't just leave this some-where, could I?'

He checked in his package, brushed some plastic shavings off his brown tweed jacket and, running a hand through his uncombed curls, was led to a corner table where an authoritative little man in a dark suit was waiting for him. 'Phew,' said Robin, taking his seat. 'Sorry I'm late.'

'You look like a fucking gamekeeper,' said Alan Gyles coldly. 'They know me here.'

It was on occasions like this that Gyles found it difficult to believe that he and Robin were partners in what had once been a profitable little business. During the five years that Can-Do Children's Productions had been in existence, the two men had grown apart. Once a mere accountant, Gyles was now a voguish media entrepreneur, a man who understood both cash and creativity; Robin was still the same old Robin, only more so.

'Dare I ask what's in the box?' said Gyles.

'A computer.'

'Not bought on the firm's account, I hope.'

'Good lord, no. Plastic card.'

'Yes, how is Laura?' Gyles smiled nastily.

'Very amusing. She's fine. Going to the first night of this musical tonight. *Perfectly Frank.* You going?'

'I'm one of the principal backers. And it's *Absolutely Frank.*'

A waiter approached and asked whether they would care to enjoy an aperitif before their meal.

'No,' said Gyles. 'We'll eat straight away.'

Robin attempted to decode the menu before ordering the only dish with the word 'chicken' in it. 'Of course, we're both very cut up about Ollie,' he said, after the waiter had gone.

'Sure, sure,' Gyles said quickly with a frown that managed to express both sympathy and a determination not to allow the conversation to be diverted down a non-productive route. He had know Sincton slightly – who hadn't? – but the man was dead, no longer on the agenda. He opened a slim briefcase beside his chair, took out a sheet of paper and gave it to Robin. 'Our latest accounts,' he said. 'Not a pretty sight.'

Robin glanced down a list of figures most of which had brackets around them. 'Looks like a small cash-flow problem.'

'No flow,' said Gyles. 'No cash. We're a one-asset company and that asset's a stiff.'

Robin tried a smile. 'You're not talking about Max, I hope,' he said.

'Who else?'

Max Beanbag. Robin had only had one real idea as a children's merchandiser and, luckily for Can-Do Productions, it had been a good one. Max, funny and wobbly, squat and naughty, Max Beanbag, the kiddies' favourite, star of TV, books, T-shirts, posters, confectionery and assorted fancy goods. And now the merchandising spree was over. Max, a has-beanbag.

'I warned you,' said Gyles. 'Six months ago I told you we needed product, input.'

'Input, yes.' Robin stared across the restaurant as

33

Gyles spoke urgently. How had this charmless, dead-eyed accountant become the acceptable face of money among the media set? he wondered. In the briefcase, still open on the floor, there was a book, no doubt the novel to be seen with, this month's fiction accessory.

Gylesian words – futures, technologies, incentivisations – drifted into Robin's consciousness. When Alan Gyles talked business, nouns became verbs, singular became plural, as if the language, like everything else, needed to be changed and expanded, even at the expense of clarity.

The waiter returned, bearing a microscopic portion of gaily coloured toy food. Robin could see why this kind of meal suited Gyles and his friends; fast, decorative and indigestible, it would send them back to work leaner and angrier than ever.

'It's interactionals the market's hot for,' Gyles was saying. 'Give me some scribe and concept boards – something at least so that I can potential steers on our futures.'

'I have no problem with that,' said Robin, trying gamely to enter the spirit of the thing. 'I'll scribe something over the next week or so.'

Gyles rapped the table as if bringing him to order. 'Robin, we're talking yesterday.'

Robin sighed. 'I have a lot on my mind,' he said. 'Will you be going to Ollie's funeral?'

'I'd like to but I've got a meeting.'

'A lot of people will have meetings tomorrow.'

'Life must go on.'

'I'm his literary executor. I have to sort out his papers. See if there's anything publishable.'

Gyles looked at him murderously. 'Executor? The man was a ghost, for Christ's sake, not Johnny fucking Updike.'

'The police delivered a computer disk to me this morning. Ollie's notes. There are others apparently.

Maybe he left something worth publishing. That's why I upgraded my technology.'

'Let me just get this right.' Alan Gyles was smiling, never a good sign. 'I have just outlined—' he smoothed the tablecloth '—the current scenarios involving Can-Do Productions. If I may summarise them in terms which even you might be able to grasp: we are fucked. Unless you come up with an idea ASAP we may as well both pack up and go home, me to my other companies, you to count your wife's money—' He paused for effect. 'It's hardly the moment to start delving into the secret life of a dead hack.'

'I'm doing it because I was his friend.'

'Very moving.' Alan Gyles looked distantly over Robin's right shoulder, tapping the table with his left hand. It was a device he used at meetings that were over-running. 'I only wish I could help but, you see, I'm not creative like you. I just work. Give me a problem, I go into an office, I pick up a telephone, kick a few arses, get out my calculator and solve it. I blame my upbringing. This old-fashioned idea of working for a living really depresses me sometimes.'

'I work too.' Robin looked around helplessly for a waiter. 'Sometimes.'

'You think that background is enough, don't you?' Gyles dabbed the corners of his mouth with a napkin.

Never trust a man with entirely straight hair, Laura had once said; never trust a man without a sex life. Robin wondered what Gyles did about that; something abrupt and time-intensive, no doubt.

'You think you can get away with staggering in here looking like someone from Cardboard City complete with his mobile home just because of your charm or who your wife is. Sorry, Robin. It's not like that any more. The party's over.'

'I see.'

Gyles glanced up as the waiter walked by. Within

seconds the bill was in front of him. Gyles checked it carefully, then signed.

'Now you're going to have to excuse me, old chum,' he said, leaning down to close his briefcase with a click. 'I'm needed back in the real world.'

Robin carried his computer through the streets of Soho, relieved that the ordeal of lunch with Alan Gyles was over for another month. That Gyles was unmoved by Sincton's death had been entirely predictable, as had been his indifference to the notes Ollie had left behind. The posthumous work of a dead ghost was unlikely to make a Hollywood film or a West End musical, after all.

In my line of work one becomes all too familiar with the change that comes over some folk when the bedroom door closes. Thugs frolic like schoolgirls, whey-faced tax inspectors become mighty raging bulls, society hostesses trade in gentility for every kind of sluttishness.

All the same, Oliver's version, The Secret World of Jane Goodenough, was rather too obvious a male fantasy to be plausible. Respectable country girl who hangs out in singles bars? It was pure video-land.

So it was without any due sense of optimism that I made my way up the Mall that Monday afternoon and into the large modern building which houses the Ministry of Defence. After a certain amount of fussing about by Security, I was directed down a long corridor to Jane's section.

'Detective Inspector Potter?' A man in his late twenties – tall and bony, with rather more wispy hair than one would expect in a defence establishment – greeted me. 'Christopher Hudson-Black. I'm Miss Goodenough's assistant. She's in a meeting at present but won't keep you long.'

The man showed me into an outer office where there was a desk behind which he sat down, not giving me another look. In an adjoining room were two middle-aged female secretaries, working in a brisk way that suggested they could be here all night if the Ministry required.

There was a copy of the *Spectator* on the corner of Hudson-Black's desk. I picked it up with a muttered 'May I?'

Hudson-Black glanced up and gave me the slightly insulting smile of a young Tory MP meeting a constituent. 'Of course, Inspector.'

Ten minutes she kept me waiting in that ante-room. That's unusual. In my experience, those in authority are uneasy about policemen loitering outside their offices. Jane, apparently, did not have to worry about impressions.

Eventually the door opened and three Ministry men emerged, talking among themselves. After they had gone, Jane appeared.

'I'm so sorry, Detective Inspector,' she said. 'Meeting went on a bit.'

'Life's a meeting,' I said. 'It was good of you to see me at short notice.'

She gave a humourless little laugh. 'Quite.' With the distracted air of one who has better things to do, she led me into a large, bright room with military prints on the wall. 'Let's sit over here,' she said, gesturing towards a corner where there were some leather chairs and a low table. 'Unfortunately, I have to be away in twenty minutes' time.'

'This is no more than a preliminary meeting.'

She frowned, clearly not pleased with the idea of future dealings with the police, and I allowed a few telling moments of silence, as if collecting my thoughts.

'So how can I help you, Inspector?' she asked eventually.

Jane was, as they say in Whitehall, entirely appropriate. The sensible haircut, the pale face unblemished by make-up and the sober dark suit were irreproachably professional. When she looked at me, it was with the cool and easy confidence of a manager.

'As you are aware, I am investigating the death last Thursday of Mr Oliver Sincton,' I said, pulling myself together. 'I was wondering if you could fill in a few background details for me.'

'Of course.' Jane's face was composed with the polite gravity required by the occasion. 'I'll do what I can.'

'Perhaps you could tell me about the last time you saw Mr Sincton.'

She hesitated. 'I saw him the night he died. We had dinner at the Groucho Club. We used to meet once a week, normally Wednesdays.' She spoke as if Sincton had been dead for years. 'We met at the club at about eight. I left at ten-thirty because I was working the next day. He stayed.'

'That was normal? He didn't—' there was no avoiding the innuendo '—take you home?'

'I have my own car.'

'How was he that night?'

'Same as ever. Funny, charming. He was drinking rather more than usual.'

'He didn't seem worried in any way? Work, women?'

'Oliver was never really the worrying kind.'

'Tell me about how he earnt his living.'

'He was a ghost-writer. He helped people with their books.'

'People.'

'The sort of people whose books you see in the shops at Christmas time. Celebrities, if you like.'

'He'd what, sit down and write these books with them?'

Jane laughed. 'Ollie? No, he'd get them to talk into a tape recorder for a few hours. Then he'd do the rest. It was an arrangement that suited everyone.'

'Must have given him a certain power, all those famous people baring their souls to him.'

'He wasn't interested in power. He was what we in Whitehall call "pro-active" – not merely responding to things but initiating them.'

'What was his attitude to money?'

'Normal.'

In most interviews they tell you too much. Only lags, ex-cons, tend to be as carefully economical as Jane was being. While I half-listened to her talking about Ollie and his career, I found myself thinking of his notes – that first meeting at the Bunch of Grapes. Was it possible? I wondered. Was it conceivable that she should go home, apply some colour to those delicate, palely forbidding features, and skip out, in less entirely appropriate clothes, to a singles bar?

It was time for me to move in a little closer. 'Of course,' I said, 'Ollie wasn't always just a friend.'

'No. We had a relationship.' She might have been confirming an item of government policy.

'Lovers.'

'If you want to put it like that. It lasted a couple of months. It was going nowhere.'

'Where did you first meet?'

'At a gallery. An old schoolfriend of mine was exhibiting her photographs. Ollie was there. We had a drink. That was that.'

I smiled. 'Fast mover, our Mr Sincton.'

Jane took a deep breath, as if to keep herself in check. 'It's not like that these days, Inspector. Fast movers went out some time ago. A week or so after our first meeting, we extended our relationship. By mutual agreement.'

'Did you know he kept a diary?'

'You mean his disks?' Jane smiled tolerantly. 'That was fiction. In certain circles, Inspector, it's regarded as very important to be working on your novel. Even if it's never finished, it provides a badge of seriousness. Ollie took the rather mundane plot and characters of real life and goosed them up to make something altogether more sexy and exciting.'

I couldn't help noticing that, for the first time, there were signs of colour in Jane's cheeks.

'Ollie's novel.' She laughed again. 'It was something of a joke among his friends.'

'Did you read it?'

'He read certain passages to me. I told him I'd sue. It was therapy for him.'

The interview had yielded little. As I wrote a few notes in my pad, I asked, 'D'you know the Bunch of Grapes?'

'No. What exactly is it?'

'Some kind of wine-bar, I gather. Oliver Sincton was seen there a few times.'

'I don't like bars. And I've never heard of the Bunch of Grapes.'

'You've been very helpful,' I said, standing to leave. 'I will, of course, be in touch if I need any further information as our inquiry proceeds.'

'Naturally. Do you have any leads?'

'It looks like he was meeting people at a flat in Mayfair. Blind dates, you know?'

'Dangerous thing, the male menopause,' she said, extending a hand.

I smiled politely. 'So they say.'

Was it another day of 'unofficial action'? Had an epidemic of sunstroke decimated the staff of London Transport? Maybe the tracks had simply expanded in the heat. Whatever the reason, it was a long and unpleasant journey back to the suburbs that night.

Eventually a train arrived at Westminster station. I fought my way into a carriage in which I was obliged to stand in closer proximity to strangers than any Englishman finds acceptable. By the time we reached the main-line station, I understood why heat and violence so often go together.

With sharp elbows, I gained a seat on the 6.33 where, in a compartment of evil-smelling commuters dozing over their evening papers, I was able to compare my impressions of Jane Goodenough with those of Oliver Sincton.

The ambition in that girl, jeez, it's terrifying. At first she tried to disguise it – to be prepared to do anything to get on is something to which a cute yuppette in sensible shoes will not readily admit – but, after I had tossed her a few hot little items from my own blue book ('Ugh, Ollie, how could you?'), she opened up.

The fact is, Jane's doing very, very well at the Ministry. She came third in the Civil Service entrance exam (the winner has since committed suicide). The guys at her level are five to seven years older than her. She's just barrelling her way to the top. There's no stopping her.

But professional success isn't enough for Jane. She cheats, she cuts corners. Over time, she's become a mistress of the destabilizing memo, the career affair. She just loves to use her divine, baser assets.

According to Jane, there's personal and professional sex. Shortly after we had enjoyed some of the personal, she confided that she was spending one afternoon a week in an intimate, professional interface with the head of her department, a jerk called Davies. It's not pleasant, says Jane – the man has blow-torch halitosis – but he's a frightened little creep who'll help her career along in return for sex now, discretion later.

Before that – Jane believes in careful scheduling, although overlaps do occur – there was a Conservative MP who referred to sex as 'horizontal jogging' and whose post-jog debriefings – there was always plenty of time, this guy being more of a ten-yard-dash man than a jogger – were particularly valuable. Before that, a French arms dealer, an American CIA man and, a deeply unpleasant experience, a red-faced lobby cor-

respondent on The Times. *It occasionally turns the stomach, this part of Jane's Ministry work, more often it's crushingly dull, but it eases her progress up the one slippery pole which matters to her.*

Then there's playtime with strangers. She doesn't even like it – says her. It sneaks up on her, nags at her, makes her life a misery until, just to get back on an even keel, she gives way to it. For a day or two beforehand she's tetchy, aware of a growing sense of anticipation that will not be denied.

She sets out for the Grapes, never failing to take with her that essential prop, a copy of The Times.

The Times? *It keeps away the riff-raff, says Jane. It establishes a tone.*

The morning after, jerk ejected with minimal politesse, she scrubs the flat, a housewife whore, and feels ashamed yet oddly purified. She arrives punctually at the Ministry, smelling faintly of cleansing agents. *Well that's that out of the way.*

Dangerous as it is, Jane's life accentuates the positive, she says, eliminates the negative. Supremely efficient, it involves no courtship, no love and few words. It has a beginning, then, swiftly, an end. She does not mess with Mr In-Between.

Jane hates relationships. She hates talk. Words bring her down. She's discovered that men who hang out in bars, restlessly eyeing the clientele over glasses of white wine, are rarely champs when it comes to conversation. Out-of-towners, married bastards off the leash, sexual hoodlums of one type or another – none of them is there to shoot the breeze.

Afterwards, of course, it's different. Grimly, inevitably, they slip back into character. *So many boring men, says Jane. What makes them think that just because she's fucked them she wants to talk to them, to hear their vapid, flatulent, banal confessions, that she's interested in their goddamned grey little lives? Getoutahere, please.*

* * *

Singles bars, sado-masochistic civil servants, horizontally jogging politicians; and, among them, making notes, Oliver Sincton.

It all seemed a long way from Purley.

4

Robin was easily distracted; doggedness was not part of his character. There were times when simple duties, like making a bed, buying a shirt, thinking of a birthday present for his wife, seemed to require teeth-gritting efforts of motivation and muscle power that were frequently beyond him. Yet now, as he sat before his word-processor at ten o'clock that Monday night, he was ready for his new project.

The idea of mining something of worth from Ollie's notes had begun to take hold. Since the days when they had been students together, Robin had admired the American's ambition and appetite for new experience, his dangerously developed social skills. In a world of sexual confusion – everywhere he looked, Robin's friends were falling in and out of love, cheating on their spouses or lovers or both, discovering, woefully late in life, that they were, or weren't, gay, that all this time they had been paddling up the wrong creek – Ollie's love life had a heroic, all-embracing simplicity.

After university Robin had lost contact with Ollie until marriage to Laura had brought them together again one evening when he had been attending the annual Christmas party of the *Soho Review*, a style magazine for the literary élite. The wine had tasted filthy, the cameras had flashed, affairs had blossomed in the warmth generated by red-hot gossip. Reviewers with publicity girls, racy female novelists with editors, TV researchers with presenters; recently, illicit sexual adventure seemed to have become an essential part of the creative process. And there, at the centre of it all, was Ollie Sincton, moving from one group to another, hugging, laughing, slightly drunk. His hair was shorter than it had been at university which, oddly, made him look younger than Robin remembered.

'The same old Oliver Sincton,' he had said to Laura.

'You know Ollie?'

'We were at university together. How do you know him?'

Laura had stared across the room to where Ollie stood in conversation with a smiling, dark-haired woman, his right arm casually resting on her shoulders.

'Oh, everyone knows Ollie,' Laura had said without particular affection.

Robin's office was at the top of the house so that, even as darkness closed in, it was still hot from the day's sun.

He pressed some keys on the keyboard. A list of names appeared on the screen.

Laura Nicholl knew how to behave at a first night. From the moment when she alighted from the dark, shiny limousine rented by Alec Frewen, her publisher, taking care not to be caught by the paparazzi showing too much thigh or cleavage, she was entirely at home. Although she had been famous for only five or six years, she had paid attention, worked at it, so that, to an outsider, to the ordinary people in ordinary clothes who strained to catch a glimpse of her, she seemed a natural celebrity. She had style, presence.

Because minor royalty had agreed to attend the opening of *Absolutely Frank*, a brave but misguided attempt to put the life and loves of Frank Harris to musical form, it was an occasion for the aristocrats of the gossip columns. There was the all-girl singing group with their indiscreet, star-studded love lives. There was the boyish cabinet minister with his latest actress. There was a pocket hunk from Hollywood, morose and unshaven, a galaxy of soap-opera stars, more blow-dried disc jockeys than any teenager could dream of. And, of course, the consorts, the lovers, the walkers, the alibis, the mistresses, the toyboys. Famous, or famous for being famous, or famous for fucking the famous, they were all there.

The crowd's response to Laura, as she took a photo-call on the pavement outside the theatre with her charming, ugly publisher, was more affectionate than awestruck. She was what's-her-name, you know, on the telly, funny on chat shows. They liked her; she was almost one of them. She made the media tarts who fluttered and gasped in the lobby seem insubstantial, as if the hours of work they had put into this evening (shiny lipstick, skimpy frocks, viciously eccentric hairstyles) were no more than an exercise in pointless vanity. They masqueraded as vamps or *femmes fatales* or courtesans when really anyone could see that they were just girls on a night out.

Laura, on the other hand, was the real thing. Her manner, as she paused in the foyer to give her coat to an attendant, suggested that she had been born to celebrity. Royalty, the cameras, evening dress; this was everyday life to her. No-one, seeing her tonight, could be surprised that her publisher insisted on using author photographs on the front of her novels as an essential part of the package.

This bimbo backdrop showed Laura at her best: her skin pale among the vulgar Riviera tans, her dark hair curling without a hint of streak, her figure that of a grown-up, generous and knowing. There was nothing fake about Laura's wholesomeness. She looked the sort of woman who might be a talented gardener, an effortlessly brilliant cook, a warm-hearted mother; the fact that her garden consisted of paving stones, she resolutely refused to spend time in the kitchen, and was entirely indifferent to the idea of having children hardly seemed to matter.

After the publication of her first novel, Laura had

been approached by advertising executives selling everything from cornflakes to shampoo. She was, they thought, the English rose grown up, a fantasy wife who represented honest and old-fashioned sex before it became sexuality – laughing, healthy, roll-in-the-hay sex. She had briefly considered the offers, then turned them down.

There was something else as she took her seat for the performance that night: a hint of colour in the cheeks, a blush, as if, having prepared for the party, she had looked so gorgeous, so irresistible, that someone had just had to give her one before she stepped out of the door.

Someone? Her husband, of course. Asked by journalists, with whom she had an excellent relationship (cracking carefully indiscreet jokes, remembering names), where she found her ideas, Laura would say, 'My husband, he's the brilliant one – all my books come from him.'

Now and then, goaded by a newspaper editor who just knew that there must be specks of grey in Laura's blue sky, a reporter would hunt down the genius husband and ask, 'Is it true that Laura's ideas come from you? Where do they come from? How do you work together?' while thinking, *him?* With Laura Nicholl? Bloody weird.

Robin, who was uncomfortable in the role his wife had given him, would tell some unconvincing lie. The more they probed, the less they discovered. Some of them may have wondered why so brilliant a man should be at home merchandising fatuous kiddy products but none articulated the question. They returned, more or less empty-handed, to Laura who would come up with an absolutely smashing quote. Laura gave great press.

There was one question which journalists never failed to ask Laura Nicholl. Take away the mealy-mouthed waffle about research methods, it was simply this: 'Have you really done all the wild, filthy things you describe so graphically in your books?'

And Laura would laugh her famous laugh (if it were emanating from anyone else, it would be positively inelegant) and tell them to speak to her husband about that.

After *Absolutely Frank* had run its unhappy, tuneless course and the curtain had fallen to restrained, polite applause from the invited audience, Laura and Alec Frewen stayed a while at the reception, accepting a few more photo-opportunities before walking off into the West End night where, over dinner with a handful of friends and colleagues, it was agreed, with much innocent pleasure, that the musical was hilariously bad and would inevitably close within the month.

It was half past two before Laura came home.

'Robin? Are you still up?' Laura picked her way through the debris of her husband's office towards the corner where he sat, his face illuminated by the glow of the word-processor screen. She stood behind his chair, her hands resting lightly on his shoulders. 'What on earth are you doing?'

'Bought a computer,' said Robin.

'Why?'

Robin relaxed against the warmth of his wife, breathing in the smells of the real, social world. 'Ollie kept notes,' he said.

'Ah. And they're worth staying up for?'

'Take a look.'

Laura peered at the screen. 'Ugh,' she said after a moment. 'Is it all like this?'

'More or less.'

'Makes your job easier, I suppose. Not much to trouble a literary executor there.'

'Maybe not.'

'Looks like male fantasy-land to me,' said Laura sleepily. 'Ollie in Bimboland.'

'Perhaps. How was the show?'

'Awful. Hysterically. Wonderful. Are you coming to bed?'

'In a minute.' Robin watched as Laura swayed towards the door, her long dress rustling as she went. She swore as something crunched beneath her feet. Even drunk, his wife was seductive.

Sighing, he turned back to the screen.

Just after three in the morning, Robin stood up and switched off the word-processor. His eyes ached from staring at the screen. Bimboland. Perhaps Laura was right.

He wandered down to the bedroom where, uncharacteristically, Laura had left her clothes in a pile on the floor. The bedside light was still on but she was in bed, sleeping the sleep of the slightly pissed.

Robin made his way to the bathroom, pushed a toothbrush around his gums for a few seconds and stumbled back to the bedroom. Ollie may have had his wild night with Jane, but this was home. He peeled off his clothes and slipped into bed beside Laura.

He looked at her for a moment with the warmth he never quite dared express when she was conscious. Who needed adventure when your bed was shared with someone like Laura? Lips slightly parted, she was actually snoring. Robin smiled; it must have been quite a party. He wasn't sleepy, but then he never was these days; insomnia had crept up on him unannounced. Not so long ago, a few pages of a bad book or a few minutes of tender, economical sex with his wife would have done the trick but now bad books merely irritated and sex was rarely an option.

In this, as in practically everything else, Robin felt out of step with the rest of the world. He didn't care. He had become accustomed to a life of virtual celibacy, to the gentle marital rejections. Lying beside his beautiful wife, watching her as she slept, was worth a hundred of Ollie's erotic adventures. All the same – maybe it was reading about Jane – he felt restless. Briefly he considered imposing himself on Laura in a stealthy dreamlike way, but then he thought better of it. How undignified, how loathsome, to slip into his wife while her back was turned.

Slowly he lifted the sheet and looked at her body, rising, falling, in perfect repose.

He moved lower in the bed. He even liked the smell of her. Tracing a finger down her backbone, he breathed in deeply, then stopped. Something was wrong. He sniffed again. Robin was used to his wife returning late whiffing of stale cigars or wine, but tonight there was something altogether different.

Lying still under the sheet, he tried to think of logical reasons why Laura should smell like that. A new washing powder? Some sort of exotic marine dish for dinner? With a sleepy moan, she rolled over on to her back. The waft of warm air left no more room for doubt.

Robin, wakeful, sick to the stomach, sat up in bed, turned off the bedside light and stared into the darkness. It had been a long time, but that uniquely intimate smell was unmistakable.

Oh my God, sex.

5

Funerals are not a fruitful area for investigation. In my early days in the force, I used to hang around chapels and crematoria in the innocent hope that, at the final, poignant moment, barriers would be down, truths revealed. Nowadays I tend to avoid them. Death is dull; it's banal. You're more likely to get a lead at a wedding.

'Will we be going to the funeral, sir?' James Dexter asked me on Tuesday morning. Whatever hour I managed to reach the station, Dexter was there first.

'I rather think not,' I said, glancing down at his notes. 'Funerals depress me.'

Dexter looked disappointed. 'All the same, it would be interesting to see who turns out.' He hesitated. 'Of the people mentioned on the disks. Martin Coleman, Suzi Ashbourn, Russ Targett.'

'James,' I laughed. 'We're policemen, not groupies.'

He shrugged. 'I thought it might be useful to see which of Ollie's friends were prepared to pay their last respects.'

'What time does it begin?'

'Eleven o'clock. West London Crematorium.'

'All right.' I turned towards my office. 'Don't forget your autograph book.'

'I believe that you have been seeing another man.'

Robin Nicholl stood in front of the bathroom mirror, tousled, unshaven, wearied by a night during which he had been tortured by thoughts of his wife, then of Ollie and eventually of them both. He looked into his eyes, the eyes of a cuckold.

51

No. Not seeing another man. It was no time for euphemisms. Directness was needed. 'I happen to know that you have been unfaithful to—'

Wrong. Ludicrous. Absurd. Robin felt his confidence waning. Of course she was unfaithful. What on earth did he expect when all he could offer was tepid, ineffectual niceness? It had been so long since Robin had occupied the high moral ground in his marriage that, almost by force of habit, he found himself slinking into cringing self-doubt and defeat. In the world where Laura felt most at home, everyone was a hands-on achiever, everyone was a darling, and the dividing-line between a darling you took to lunch and a darling you took to bed was notoriously unclear.

Hands on. Robin gripped the side of the basin at the thought of his wife being caressed by another man.

'You've been fucking someone else, haven't you?'

That was it. The literary set liked that word. Fucking well fucking some other fucker, you fuck.

She would go pale, back away before her husband's anger.

'Wh – what makes you think that?'

'Because—' He would say this between gritted teeth, fists clenched at his side. 'Because last night you came to bed reeking, yes *reeking*, of semen.'

'Seamen?'

Oh God, he was losing it. Don't let the adulterous bitch defuse the situation with her famous repartee.

'Stinking of seed.'

The colour would have returned to her cheeks by now. 'Seed, darling?' She might even laugh.

'Spunk!' said Robin out loud.

'Mmm?'

Robin turned to find Laura leaning against the side of the door. She looked pale, wrecked, hung over, adorable.

'Are you all right?' he asked.

'Tea?' Laura winced as if the word had set off a series of explosions in her brain.

'Of course.'

She hesitated. 'Why were you saying "spunk" to yourself in the mirror?'

Robin shrugged. 'Just . . . psyching myself up for the day.'

'Wha?' Laura squeezed her eyes shut, then tottered back to the bedroom.

Tea. Yes, the foul adulteress should have tea, brought to her by her ever-loving, ever-faithful husband.

Despite his night of pain and anger, Robin was already slipping back into character. Of the many ways of extracting revenge on a cheating wife (self-righteous rage, icy dignity, strategic violence to treasured household objects, a suicidal alcoholic binge), he chose the least effective: niggling, self-lacerating sarcasm.

'What's a matter wi' you today?' she asked as he brought her breakfast in bed.

'Me? I'm *particularly* well. I'm absolutely *fine*.'

He drew back the curtains so that the sun beat cruelly on her aching eyeballs. Pretending to mistake her hangover for flu, he scurried to the medicine cupboard for vitamin C tablets.

'No,' the adulteress whispered as her husband propped her up roughly and held a pill to her lips. 'Leamelone, plea.'

'Poor darling,' he said loudly. 'This will make you feel better. You've been overdoing it.' Reluctantly, she took the pill and Robin went downstairs, allowing her to prepare for the day.

He strode around the kitchen, tidying, almost throwing dishes into the dishwasher. Oddly, it was he who felt guilty, for worming his way under the sheets, pathetically sniffing around.

He paused mid-chore. Perhaps she was at it all the time, had been for ages. There was a thought.

It was ten o'clock before, pale and beautiful in her dark suit, Laura made her way unsteadily down the stairs, the picture of a grieving friend. It was fortunate that her only duty today was to bid a final farewell to Ollie Sincton; the white skin, the dark shadows under her unfocused eyes, would serve as marks of grief and shock, not the aftermath of a drunken, adulterous orgy.

'Brown shoes,' she said as Robin took her arm. 'Should be black.'

He looked down. He had managed to find his old, mis-shapen dark suit but his brown shoes, scuffed and marked mysteriously with white paint, were hardly appropriate for a funeral.

'Yes,' he said. 'It's important to keep up appearances, isn't it, darling?'

Laura shrugged. 'Forget it,' she said.

It was a bad day for a funeral. Robin and Laura drove northwards in silence, past parks full of people lying awkwardly in the sun like victims of some strange disaster. The traffic was sluggish, too. Robin sweated in his dark suit while Laura, eyes closed, frowned as if she were trying to remember something. Heat, hangover and a funeral; she wished she had stayed in bed.

There was a good crowd outside the crematorium and at first, when they arrived, Robin thought that his prediction to Alan Gyles that many of Ollie's associates would be unavoidably called away on business had been unduly cynical. Then he noticed another, smaller group standing a few yards away.

'There seems to be more than one funeral,' he said.

'Queue,' said Laura. 'Better make sure we go to the right one.'

They got out of the car and walked slowly towards the mourners, Laura adopting the stunned expression of one too grief-stricken to speak. Yet, among the guests at Ollie's last party, there was more embarrassment than grief as they waited in the morning sun, glancing occasionally at the larger party nearby as if they were likely to rush the crematorium, to nip in first.

'Laura, Robin. So glad you could make it.'

They turned to see the Reverend Martin Coleman, a career cleric with whom Laura shared a publisher. A small, neat man, his grey hair curling over his ears, Coleman was wearing a light, well-cut suit over his dark shirt and dog-collar. 'I'm doing the honours for poor Oliver.'

'I'm sure he would have been pleased,' said Robin.

'I thought a quick service,' said Coleman cheerfully. 'Nothing too downbeat or—'

'Religious?' Laura smiled.

'Ollie was never exactly High Church.'

'Was he any Church?' asked Laura.

'Oh, sure, in his way. Something of a sleeping partner, of course, but the investment was there all right.' Coleman gave a chilly little smile. 'How's work, Laura?'

'Fine.'

A man emerged from the crematorium, which might have been the head office of a slightly vulgar estate agent, and nodded twice.

'Looks like we're on,' said the vicar with an apologetic wince. 'Any chance of a chatette when we're through, Laura? A friend at the Beeb has come up with something I thought might be of interest. Perhaps we could toddle down the road to my place for a drink.'

Turning to the crematorium like an actor who had just been given his cue, Coleman missed the look of queasy distaste which crossed Laura's face. She had an old-fashioned view of the Church and disapproved of Coleman, with his portable telephone and Paul Smith suits, his appeal to the young and moneyed to take out shares in faith, to make God part of their portfolio.

Ollie, who had worked with him on his first book, *Talking to the Chairman: Faith-Management for the*

Eighties, had seen through him immediately, but its success had established Coleman's reputation as an acceptably contemporary religious personality. These days, he was rarely out of the studios and wrote a column on God, Sex and Your Career for one of the tabloid newspapers.

'Poor old Ollie,' Robin said. 'He deserved better than this.'

Down the driveway, not far from where Dexter and I sat in our unmarked vehicle, a group of comically lugubrious pallbearers who were gathered around the hearse stubbed out their cigarettes, straightened their ties and brushed the dandruff from their shoulders.

'I've always wondered why those people seem to smoke so much,' I said.

'Sir?'

'Funeral operatives. As soon as they have a break, they light up. Something to do with the job, I suppose.'

'Yes. Why?'

'Smoking? Cremation?'

'Oh, right.' Dexter looked gloomily towards the crematorium. 'He's smaller than I thought, that Coleman bloke.'

'Television does that.' The mourners were making their way into the building. 'Not much in the way of glitterati, is there?' I said, thinking of my wife Joy.

We heard the tip-tap of high-heels and, moments later, a slim blonde figure, wearing a skirt rather more revealing than is usually seen at funerals, hurried by the car.

'Strewth,' said Dexter, a man not normally given to libidinous thought.

'Suzi Ashbourn,' I said. 'Suzi, making her entrance.'

'You know her?'

'You could say. We go way back. The last time I saw her was in the interview room, discussing her brief but

56

well-publicized relationship with Eddie Tubbs, the bent bookmaker,' I said.

'She's gone up in the world since then. Hobnobbing with the royals.'

'That's what they call it these days, is it? Hobnobbing.'

'Ollie only mentions her once on the disks. It seems he didn't, you know, go to bed with her.'

'Must make him almost unique among her friends.'

We watched and waited in the car after the coffin had been borne into the crematorium. It was getting hotter. One of us, or both, needed a bath. At that moment I didn't give a twopenny toss who had stabbed Mr Oliver Sincton through the neck.

At last, after about ten minutes, the doors to the crematorium opened and, with palpable relief, the mourners walked out into the sunlight. I stepped from the car and, followed by Dexter, approached Robin and Laura.

'Mr Nicholl,' I said. 'I've not missed the ceremony, have I?'

'Yes, I'm afraid you have.'

'You missed a treat,' said Laura.

Robin said, 'This is—'

'Inspector Simon Potter, Mrs Nicholl.' I shook her hand. 'My wife's a great admirer of your work.'

'I'm so glad,' she said, as if her life had been empty until she discovered that she was appreciated by Joy Potter of Purley.

Turning to Robin, I said, 'More material for the literary executor, I'm afraid. D'you have the disk, James?'

Dexter reached into his pocket and handed the second Sincton disk to Robin.

'Nothing much there for us. Maybe it has some literary worth,' I said, and Laura smiled.

I noticed Suzi Ashbourn, her face fixed in what she assumed was the correct expression of sorrow, talking to Martin Coleman, and wondered vaguely what the two had in common. The bimbo and the cleric; they probably had the same agent.

Leaving Dexter with Robin and Laura, I wandered over. 'Hullo, Suzi,' I said. 'It's been a long time.'

Suzi managed a smile. 'Were you a friend?' she asked.

'I'm the investigating officer.'

'Hanging around at a funeral.' She looked away. 'Very nice, I must say.'

'I hadn't known you were one of Ollie's set.'

'We worked together.'

Martin Coleman winced. 'I'm not sure this is quite the place—'

'Of course not, Reverend,' I said. 'Just passing by to pay our last respects.'

As I went back to collect Dexter, Suzi muttered something about poor taste. It was quite a comment, coming from her.

We walked to the car.

'Was that Jane Goodenough there?' Dexter asked.

'No,' I said. 'She wasn't.'

6

Picture a perfect English scene. Hedgerows neatly trimmed, fields of wheat (this year not a blade had been flattened by rain or wind), the occasional combine harvester trundling amiably through the gold, houses – grey, weathered houses which look as if they've grown out of the landscape as naturally as the oaks and beeches which surround them – and birds, summer birds which swoop, chatter and generally celebrate the glory of England in August.

Nearby, a bald man clips his hawthorn fence, red-faced and happy (the summer was kinder to country folk than it was to Londoners), a gardener mows the lawn, children exercise their ponies by the quiet, meandering, gentle country roads, past hazel trees, orchards, bushes which will soon be heavy with blackberries. Groups of drinkers, enjoying a long lunch break, laugh outside a pub as a young woman flashes by in a white Saab, turning heads, bringing smiles of approval to faces. Absolutely perfect.

Jane Goodenough liked the Cotswolds. She felt good when people looked at her as she drove past like an advertisement for something expensive and unattainable. Here was order, decency, so different from the surly, randy unruliness of London. You knew where you were in the Cotswolds. The people in large houses owned the land or did significant jobs in the City; those in farmhouses worked the land or did insignificant jobs in Banbury or Chipping Norton. The cottages belonged to labourers, weekenders, teachers. Here she relaxed, became herself. Every day, in London, strangers told Jane what they would like to do to her.

Building workers shouted it across the street; men in suits ranged up beside her at traffic lights and mouthed it, revving their cars hungrily; waiters murmured it as they served her in restaurants. Her car caught the eye too. It was nine months old and already three times pedestrians had walked past it, scratching it, gouging its shiny white surface with their keys. London, the home of the priapic leer, the envy scratch. No wonder Jane needed to visit the Cotswolds now and then.

Many of Jane's friends had settled for this, the Amandas and Julias of her schooldays. She saw them occasionally, using their plumply predictable lives as a touchstone by which she could judge her own progress, their spreading rumps and ruddy disappointed faces to remind her of her own flawless figure, her pale, unlined complexion. She visited them for weekends in their converted farmhouses, played with their over-confident children, parried with a smile the fumbling, drunken advances of their husbands. (Flirtation seemed to be big in the country, the middle classes caught up in a permanent state of socialised foreplay leading nowhere; the more Jane saw of domestic sex, the less she liked it.) It was rare when she had not returned to her orderly flat in Islington with a deep sense of relief.

Jane turned into the drive of her father's house and felt the old weariness, the familiar tension, creeping over her. Roses, fig tree, the immaculate lawn with the inevitable bloody croquet hoops in precisely the right places. Although she had only visited Roseclare as an adult (an army child, she had never stayed anywhere long enough to call it home), the house reminded her of childhood, family, duty, all the things she liked to believe she had outgrown.

Her father had always made her feel inadequate; he could undermine her sense of self more effectively than any Permanent Under-Secretary. Perhaps that was something they taught you at Sandhurst: wordless demoralization. She talked, he listened, and, behind the smiles and polite questions, Jane could feel the sadness. She wasn't married. She wasn't like her mother (or maybe she was too like her mother); she wasn't a son. Somehow Daddy – dear, fussy, celebrated Daddy – did it every time.

Brigadier Harry Goodenough, a tall, good-looking man with carefully combed silver hair, came to the front door and stood open-armed in a self-conscious, almost ironic gesture of greeting.

'Darling,' he said, mixing reproach with affection. 'Here you are at last.'

'Sorry, Daddy –' Father and daughter brushed cheeks like marionettes. 'Terrible traffic.'

'Poor darling,' said Goodenough, ushering Jane into the house with a vague sweeping movement of the right arm. 'Come and have a drink. I'm sure you need it.'

In the hall a small, muscular man in his fifties greeted Jane politely. Colin (once Thompson, then Corporal Thompson, now demobbed and with a civilian Christian name) understood the protocol: welcome the daughter of the house, serve Pimm's in the drawing-room and return to the kitchen.

Goodenough smiled, sipping his drink. 'What a nice surprise this is,' he said.

The room in which they sat was restful, antique, almost like an old-fashioned tea-room. A stranger might note that there were flowers everywhere: on the piano, by the silver drinks tray on the sideboard, up and down the wallpaper, through the french windows which opened on to the garden. A critical, negative, observant person (the late Oliver Sincton, for example) might have reflected that the flowers had a certain imposed orderliness to them, like well-drilled soldiers on parade, but most visitors to Roseclare were simply charmed. Such colour, such gentle, natural good taste that one might have detected a feminine hand at work were it not for the knowledge that this was the domestic headquarters of Brigadier Harry Good-enough, war hero, divorced.

'Well,' said Jane, not yet ready to discuss the reason for her unusual midweek visit. 'It really does look as if a promotion is on the cards.'

'Darling. I *am* proud.'

'The word is that Davies, my awful head of department, might be kicked upstairs.'

'At last.'

'And since I've kept my nose clean . . .' Jane smiled guilelessly.

'My daughter, the Whitehall warrior,' said Good-enough.

For a moment they sat there, like strangers. Conversation was never easy between Jane and her father. They expressed affection or concern with a bantering sense of self-parody, as if they were in a drawing-room comedy in which he played the part of the silly old worrier, she the gushing daddy's girl who had never quite grown up.

Yet there had been times, as he grew older, when Goodenough had seemed more approachable, as if he regretted the polite lack of feeling that had marked his relations with his daughter. It was twelve years now since his wife, Jane's mother, had left him, packing a single bag and moving in with a restaurateur from Amersham with whom she later relocated to France. During the week that Jane had spent at Roseclare after her mother's departure, Goodenough had forgotten his fear of appearing vulnerable or weak-willed long enough to share his bitterness and confusion with her.

Jane had listened, longing all the time to return to London, her career and sanity. She had inherited her father's distaste for clutter.

'Have the police been in touch?' she asked, breaking the silence.

'Some detective fellow rang after breakfast. Potter. Seemed a nice enough chap.'

'Yes, he came to the office yesterday. Apparently Ollie had been seeing unsuitable women.'

Goodenough placed a hand on his daughter's arm. 'I'm so sorry, darling,' he said.

'We weren't that close towards the end. In fact, I rather played down our relationship.'

'Very wise.'

'The Ministry can be so stuffy about that sort of thing. Did Potter mention anything about computer disks?'

'No.' Goodenough paused. 'I thought they were just notes for his books.'

'They were, Daddy,' said Jane, fixing him with her clear blue eyes. 'Notes for books.'

'Strange chap.' Goodenough stood up. 'How about a round of croquet before tea?'

7

As if the seedy details of Ollie Sincton's life somehow contained the secret of why Laura had taken to cheating on him, Robin spent much of that week reading the disks we had given him.

'I never realized he had meant so much to you,' Laura said to him on Thursday morning.

'I need to understand.'

Laura laughed. 'Understand what? He did a lot of words. Maybe he enjoyed a bit more sex than most people. Big deal.'

Robin looked at his wife as she checked the mail in the hall, putting all but one letter, a bill, in her brief-case, a woman of importance about to go to her office, leaving her husband shuffling about the house in his slippers.

'Words and sex,' he said. 'Is there anything else these days?'

Laura kissed him lightly on the cheek. 'Forget Ollie,' she said. 'Startle Alan Gyles with a brilliant new product. You weren't meant to be a literary executor.'

After she had left Robin climbed the stairs to his office. Distantly, he heard the voice of Ollie Sincton. 'Hey, don't knock words, Robin,' he had once said. 'Words are important.'

They had arrived at Cambridge together. During those early terrifying days, Ollie had stood out, a laughing, confident American who seemed to have read all the right people: Frost, Manley Hopkins, Gertrude Stein, Auden; he could quote from them all.

Although Ollie never spoke about his education in

America, Robin had imagined an East Coast school full of Sinctons reciting Whitman on the way to baseball games, luring peach-skinned cheerleaders into bed with metaphysical conceits lifted from John Donne. It was only much later, when they were friends and it no longer mattered, that Robin discovered Ollie had been granted entry to Cambridge as part of an earnest attempt by the university to prove, to itself at least, that by giving bursaries to a group of reasonably bright Americans it was no longer an extension of the English public-school system. Of the eleven imports, only Ollie and a Massachusetts medical student who went to Girton survived the first year.

It was an odd friendship from the first, but it had worked. Perhaps, beneath that brash exterior, Ollie was uneasy about the peculiar English way of life at Cambridge. As a guide to an alien culture, with its little quirks of irony, its jokes, its mania for self-deprecation, Robin was more than adequate.

Words provided Ollie with a good Cambridge. Not for one moment did he attempt to fit in with the locals. He played up the American background which his contemporaries found exotic and exciting. He talked his way into Footlights where he lifted old Sid Caesar sketches, into the student magazines where, without achieving anything in particular, he became something of a luminary, and, of course, into countless beds. Tall, with that straight dark hair and the wit to take the steam out of difficult situations, Ollie was a role model before the term had been coined. Boys stopped wearing black when Ollie went for the breezy, outdoor look. Girls wore their hair long and uncombed because that was how Ollie (and therefore everyone else who mattered) was known to like it. Once, out of playful spite, he had himself photographed with a solid briar pipe clenched between his teeth; within the week pipes were all the rage.

Words on the page were more of a problem. He came

down with a Third, along with the dunces and nervous cases.

Not that it made any difference: Robin's Upper Second was, to Ollie, a source of mild amusement. So *that* was how you spent your days at Cambridge, you little swothead you.

Ten years later he made an important discovery. Written, spoken, so long as the world needed words, Ollie Sincton would never go hungry.

Robin sighed, feeding the second of the two disks into the machine. Before long, he found what he was looking for.

Jeez, am I a lucky boy. Sometimes I think that no-one has found a job more suitable to his talents than Oliver D. Sincton. On the move, in demand and, of course, caring. I'm providing a service that gives untold pleasure to a few admittedly privileged people. I should get some kind of government handout for what I do.

Ghost. It doesn't sound much, does it? Who'd be something as transparent, as goddamned shifty as a ghost when more substantial options are available? But ghost is the wrong word. A ghost may be scary but it's not what you'd call active; it's an observer, an outsider powerlessly watching real life as it unfolds. Not me. I'm a ghost with go, a spook that calls the shots.

I'm rarely in the spotlight and, oh boy, that suits me fine. Almost uniquely among my celebrity-crazed peers, I have absolutely no interest in fame. I do my beautiful work unnoticed but not unthanked. I'm a bent historian, if you like, re-inventing the past to fit the present.

There's my strength, my power. Fools believe that it's the present and the future that's the problem. They worry, write tragic, bleeding letters to care-columnists on the tabloids. What's going to happen? I don't know where to turn. Tell me what to do, who to see, please. And the hard-faced, chain-smoking harridans switch on their sympathetic money-for-old-rope smiles. Calm down; it's all going to be fine. The past may have been bad, the present may be shit, but the future – possibly the distant future – will be just great. It's all going to change.

And it never does. One thing in this life is sure: if yesterday's infected, today is sick and tomorrow's dead. The problem is not the future but the past. When Sympathetic Cynthia says, What's done is done, the question is how to make the best of it, she's absurdly, wildly wrong. What's done is not necessarily done. If you happen to have outgrown your past, as many of us have, it can be re-shaped, re-styled, to suit your present needs. It's not easy – it involves putting yourself in the gentle, discreet but never cheap hands of Doctor Ollie – but it can be done. With me, you can be born again, supplied with the personal history and personality you always wanted. Fix the past, lay those ghosts, and the rest of your life will take care of itself.

Take Russ Targett. Class dunce overcomes innate disabilities (asthma, drunken father, dull school, lumpen defeated mother, no brains worth mentioning) to become prime-time TV's favourite teeth-and-smiles jerk-off artist, a triumph of ambition over talent. That's reality; if I were unfortunate enough to be Russ, I'd hire a ghost to tell something approaching the truth, perhaps holding back on the nose job and the interest in high-school bimbos, but not Russ. He wants me to present him as Mr Quietly Sensitive, a man with such a deep love of words that his present job, grinning frontman for a superlimp game show, is but a mere stepping-stone on his way to a career in serious writing. Plays, novels, his mum and dad always had faith in him, they used to love his little stories, maybe invent a crusty but inspiring English teacher. And write it nice, all right, Ollie? Sure thing, Russ.

Or the brig. Sensitive, intelligent, a man blessed with a distinguished career and a lovely daughter. Why the need to write it all down, spell it out, risk revealing those ambiguous little moments that are part of every life to a ghost like Ollie Sincton? Search me.

There were so many people, it seemed to Robin, who had entrusted their secrets to Ollie and who had something to gain from his death. He would make some calls.

Pushing the papers on his desk aside to reveal a dusty grey telephone, he picked up the receiver and dialled.

Harry Goodenough received many demands on his time these days. Something of a political activist, he raised money for the local Party, kept the council up to the mark, chivvied his MP – a smooth, alarmingly young former banker – about a bypass or open-cast mining. Ill at ease with the new brand of Conservatism, Goodenough saw himself as a civilizing influence, a Macmillan man putting the brakes on its more vulgar schemes. Then there were old army friends – officers, men even – who still wrote to him. More and more, he found himself sending letters of condolence to the wives of old soldiers who, often within moments of retiring, had quietly toppled off the perch. He had been working on one of those letters, deploying the economical phrases with a practised hand, when he was interrupted.

After the call he felt unsettled, irritated. Leaving his desk, he walked to the hall, took a pair of secateurs and, frowning, went out to the garden.

Across the hall Corporal Colin Thompson pressed the speaker button on the telephone extension and stared into space. The room where he sat was not elegant. There were tin ashtrays on a square, ugly sideboard and the two armchairs in front of the large television set, which was showing racing from San-down Park, had dark, shiny headmarks on them. It was dusty, uncared for, like the waiting-room of a country railway station.

Behind him, on a plain white wall, were two pictures, one a long regimental portrait, the other a photograph of Corporal Thompson standing with two of the men while on active service in Malaya. Brigadier Harry (although he was a colonel then) was just in front of them, and they were all looking into the distance, as if identifying an enemy position. The photograph had been posed for the regimental magazine, but it brought back memories. It had been good then.

Colin Thompson took a long, thoughtful swig at the can of beer in his hand. 'Prat,' he said.

'Robin rang.'

'What?' Laura sat up in bed, holding the sheet to her chest as if her husband were likely to burst through the door at any moment.

'He called the office this morning.'

'Shit.'

'Could be business, I suppose.'

'Robin? Business? That'll be the day.'

'I'm sure it's nothing.' Nash kissed her gently on the shoulder.

'What on earth could he want?'

Laura was in her agent's bed in her agent's studio on the top floor of Nash Literary Associates, her agent's offices in Soho. She and Nash would meet once or twice a week, usually in this large airy room which was entirely uncluttered by the debris of everyday life. (Nash had no time for debris, and not much for everyday life.) In one corner, bright in the afternoon sun, was a wide, low double bed. At the other end of the room, acres away, was a desk with chrome legs upon which pages from a manuscript were neatly piled. The office downstairs, designed on

69

the California model, was disconcertingly paper-free.

Theirs was a cool, civilized affair. That afternoon, which not even the news of a call to Nash's office from Robin could spoil, had been one of languid pleasure; clammy, gasping, bruising passion had no place here. Even the first time, a couple of years ago, had been a decorous, almost subdued event.

On the white table beside the bed stood a bottle of champagne and two glasses which Nash had just replenished. Laura lay face down, chin on hands, as London's most feared literary agent massaged her back, the strong hands easing the tension away. 'Nice,' sighed Laura. She gasped as Nash poured a few drops of cold white lotion down her spine. 'I just wish that stuff didn't smell so disgusting.'

'Never mind the smell.' Nash carefully replaced the bottle on the bedside table. 'You'll feel great after this. Cream of sturgeons' eggs. It's all the rage in LA.'

Laura laughed. 'That's fine, then,' she said. 'He's behaving so oddly these days.'

Nash, who had come to accept that listening to Laura praising her fearfully dull husband was the price to be paid for their affair, said nothing.

'Something's happening to him. He spends all his time reading Ollie Sincton's notes.'

'He's not working then.'

'No, he appears to be utterly bored by work.'

'Most people can't afford to be bored.'

'It's strange – he's so sarcastic, polite. The other day I caught him saying things to himself in the mirror.'

'Things?'

'I think it was "spunk".'

'What?' Nash laughed and ran a hand casually up Laura's thigh.

'All he can talk about is Sincton.' Briefly Laura lost concentration. 'I thought this was meant to be a massage.'

'Deep massage.'

'All the rage in LA.'

'Precisely.'

In Laura's neatly compartmentalized life, guilt played little part. First of all, by some way, Robin. Then her career. Finally, the little rewards she gave herself for being professionally successful and a moderately good wife: nights out, harmless sexual diversions.

So it was partly true what she told her interviewers. She did have a perfect marriage. There was a warmth there, a level of communication, missing from most relationships.

Now and then a renegade journalist, some sour, awkward bastard, would attempt to tarnish the image of Laura Nicholl, whose wildly erotic writing was belied by her cosily unadventurous private life, but on the whole there was little prying into her marriage. She was what her public wanted: the sensuous wife, the unspoilt success, the domestic celebrity. To shatter that image would truly have been a scandal.

Before Nash, there had been occasional insignificant others: lunchtimes spent in a hotel bedroom with an ex-boyfriend, a night with a fellow journalist while abroad on some travel jaunt. It added a touch of the unexpected to her life, a spot of pillow talk, some laughs, a bit of pleasure.

She turned over and ran her fingers through Nash's hair. Quite a lot of pleasure, really. Her agent was a good lover of the restrained, authoritative school.

The telephone by the bed rang softly. The Coast, it had to be: everything stopped for the Coast. Nash picked up and, resting the phone on Laura's stomach, conducted some business. 'Yes.' A long pause. 'No.' 'Then we walk.' 'Forget it.' The voice at the other end became more urgent and the agent smiled, twiddling absent-mindedly with a lock of Laura's pubic hair as if it were an executive toy. 'Good, yes.' The tone of the conversation changed. 'We're comfortable with that. Fax me a draft contract.'

'I ought to go soon,' Laura said, after the deal was completed.

'Not yet. I'm an agent.' Nash put the telephone back on the table and placed a finger gently on Laura's lips, then down, slowly tracing a line south, over her chin, her neck, between her breasts. 'Enough is never quite enough.'

Laura laughed, then caught her breath. 'Oh Claire,' she said. 'What would I do without you?'

Robin was no sneak; spying was not his style. Yet, over the two days since his wife had come to the marital bed smelling of intimate, alien substances, it had become oddly important to him to discover whether she was unfaithful on a part-time, amateurish basis or whether something more serious was happening.

But how do you tell if a woman's cheating? They are so much more cunning than we are. Deception's no big deal to them (Joy, poker-faced, can halve the price of a new dress; heaven knows what else she lies about). If, in an unlikely moment of daring, Robin had leapt on to the merry-go-round of infidelity, he would return home with his socks inside out, his shirt hanging out at the back, maybe even with that another-busy-day briskness that betrays so many male adulterers. He would talk too much, blundering from transparent lie to inept alibi.

Laura, who moved in a world where truth was trimmed to fit the moment, was different. For all her openness, she was careful, guarded, even with her husband.

It was becoming an obsession. Robin watched carefully as she was reading her mail or answering the telephone. Jotted notes torn in two before being thrown away he pieced together as soon as she left the room.

Did she have the look of an adulteress, the voice, the posture? No. There was colour in her cheeks, of course, but there was nothing unusual in that, nor in the fullness of her lips when she returned at the end of the day, or an evening, or a night, kissing her husband, asking him normal, friendly questions.

Body language then. Last night Robin had thought he was on to something. Preparing for bed, Laura put on a dressing-gown before taking off her underclothes, as if she were in some public place. Lying in bed, eyes narrowed, Robin moved in for the kill.

'Why so shy?' he asked.

Laura drew back the dressing-gown and pinched some imagined flesh around her waist. 'Diet time again,' she sighed, walking to the bathroom.

The white skin of her back had seemed uneven in colour.

'What are those red marks on your back?' he asked when she returned.

Laura looked over her shoulder, the sides of her mouth pointing downwards.

'Massage,' she said. 'I went to Oasis after work this afternoon.'

Hmm. Robin wasn't sure.

He had checked her diary, but Laura's professional life was so busy, and such a mystery to him, that the meetings, the initialled lunches, might have represented a thousand trysts for all he knew.

Then, late that Thursday afternoon, Robin's behaviour went beyond the acceptably paranoiac; he decided to check the laundry basket.

Quietly he made his way to the bedroom, pausing only to ensure that the maid Consuela was working downstairs in the kitchen. He approached the basket cautiously, as if something might leap out at any moment.

He raised the lid and, muttering quietly to himself, began to riffle through the clothes Laura had worn the previous day – the underclothes.

Soon he had convinced himself that he had his

evidence. Clue one: there were three pairs of knickers lying in the basket. Three in one day? Too many, surely. Clue two: it had been one of Laura's late nights. Clue three: one of the garments was not only new but expensive, silk, red.

Red! My God, the woman had no shame.

Slowly, carefully, he lifted the first pair to his nose. Sweet essence of wife. Briefly aware of his own absurdity, he dropped them back into the basket. The second pair. He breathed deep. Nothing. With a sudden movement, he grabbed the whorish red things and, groaning, buried his face in them.

It was as he stood there, draped in red, a man with a knicker nose-bleed, that Consuela walked in. They both froze, like actors in a French farce waiting for the laughter to die down. Then the maid gave a little sound – a cough, or maybe it was a suppressed giggle (these *Englishmen*) – before leaving the room.

'Yes,' said Robin loudly. 'Yes, they definitely need cleaning, Consuela.'

Ignoring the maid's knowing smile, he pushed past her and ran up the steps to his office.

'Damn!' Robin swept a pile of disks from his desk. They hit the wall with a clatter.

On the ground lay a silver key.

8

Be afraid. Be very afraid. We are about to enter the social world of Jane Goodenough: the drinks, dinner parties and charity functions where the latest generation of upper-middle-class folk become their parents. It's not pleasant, this journey into the cold interior of London life, but it has its significance.

For the most part, Jane's life was a model of organization. There was her job at the Ministry, which fully occupied her between the hours of eight-thirty a.m. and seven p.m., weekend work on a report or White Paper being an occasional necessity. The career affair of the moment would take up one evening or afternoon of the week (and, if a few hours out of the office were required, Jane scrupulously made up the lost time, working late, a small price to pay). As for duty visits to her father, one weekend every six weeks or so was quite enough for both of them.

So there was time to spare. She read *The Times*, or her favourite glossy magazines, she watched television. And, because it was important to keep in touch with one's contemporaries, one's muckers, she was part of an informal, undemanding social set.

That Thursday she arrived for work earlier than usual. When Christopher Hudson-Black brought in her mail at nine-fifteen, she told him she would be out that afternoon for a meeting in Knightsbridge, news that mildly surprised her assistant as Tuesday was normally the day for afternoon meetings out of the office.

At half past three she took a taxi to a dull, anonymous street in Pimlico, where she alighted outside a tourist hotel named the Chester.

'Mr Williamson is expecting me,' she told the receptionist.

'Mr Williamson would like you to go straight up.'

'Room number?'

'Room 351, madam.'

Jane thanked her.

Seeing her Permanent Under-Secretary Hugh Davies in this way neither thrilled nor disgusted Jane: it was simply part of life. True, the first kiss – she closed the door, put down her thin black briefcase and smiled – was a small ordeal on account of the bad breath for which he was well known (there were jokes in the office about chemical warfare) but, after that initial impact, she became acclimatized.

'Sorry you couldn't make Tuesday,' he said, holding her. They laughed guiltily like teenagers who had bunked off school.

'Family business,' said Jane, kicking off her shoes.

In many ways, it was a perfect affair. Davies, married for twenty years, unfaithful for nineteen, was in his early fifties, with the tired, grey looks of a man who had spent most of adult life in an office. He was a competent, unexceptional lover who made love with the same good-humoured efficiency with which he chaired meetings: long enough to make it all worthwhile without becoming tedious. There was rarely any other business.

The life expectancy of an affair based almost entirely on convenience is shorter than most. Jane had been meeting Davies in this hotel room for over a year. Useful as the arrangement had been, she had recently become irritated by the way he would talk about his family while in bed with her. It was almost as if he did it to tease, knowing that it was only for information from the higher echelons of the Ministry that she endured his attentions. And, it was true, Davies did find Jane's coolness, the subtle cross-questioning that ensued within moments of disengagement, somewhat unnerving. At least his other girlfriends had had the good manners to feign affection now and then. She was too honest for her own good, Jane Goodenough.

'Was there any other reason for today?' he said, after they had made love. 'You sounded rattled on the phone.'

'I needed you.'

Davies smiled at the joke and waited.

'Oliver Sincton kept a diary,' she said.

'Sincton? Was he the man killed in Half Moon Street?'

'You know bloody well he was.'

'Without wishing to be unhelpful—' Davies glanced at the wristwatch he had left on the bedside table '—I have to say that this is your department, not mine. I gave you unofficial authority to use Ministry property for your own personal reasons. An unauthorized murder occurred, placing both of us in a highly vulnerable position.'

'You said the ownership was well concealed.'

'Of course it is. But the surveillance took up time. Once the dust has settled, I want the flat back.'

'Sincton's diaries could be compromising,' Jane said. 'The police have got them.'

'I wouldn't worry too much about the police. The man was some sort of sex freak. Anyway he was American, for God's sake.' Davies ran a well-manicured hand down Jane's arm. 'No chance of double treats this week?' he asked.

'Time presses, I'm afraid,' said Jane, moving her arm. 'Apart from the police, a man called Robin Nicholl has been bothering my father.'

Davies sighed. 'So what?'

'I'd like him to be dissuaded.'

'Dissuaded.'

'Couldn't one of our people—?'

'No, you're pushing it now, Jane. You know I can't let us be exposed in that way.' Davies made to draw the sheet from Jane's body, but she snatched it back to her.

'Why the hell not, Hugh?'

Davies reached for his watch. 'Because it's your problem,' he said. 'I need Half Moon Street back as soon as possible.'

By six-thirty Jane was back at her flat to prepare for a dinner party that evening. She telephoned her father and asked whether she could stay the weekend at Roseclare. She was a bit shaken up by the Sincton business, she explained. Pleasantly surprised, Good-enough agreed.

Socially, Jane was in demand. Amusing but never overtalkative, interesting without being fearfully intense, she was the perfect guest. Most of her friends – her set, you could almost call it – were in their thirties, a stage when some of the chaps had yet to get hitched, so an agreeable single girl (not a husband-snatcher, thank God) was always welcome.

They were unexciting, these people. On occasions even Jane, who rather liked dull company, wearied of them. Not all of them were stupid, but those with more to offer than the ability to bray amiable banalities at one another had somehow lost it along the way, perhaps intentionally. It was as if years spent in single-sex boarding schools followed by dreary, well-paid jobs had extinguished something within them, as if their brains, like their hefty, big-boned bodies, had been set to a programme that they had never quite mastered. Yet Jane felt at home amongst them.

At the dinner party that Thursday night she contrib-uted now and then to the vapid, brittle exchanges (prep schools, property values, a rather amusing new play in the West End, the declining standards of nannies) and she smiled as the dark-suited men boomed inconsequentially across the table, referring to one another by their surnames, as the women asked empty questions, ignoring the answers. It was restful and reassuring, a pleasant contrast both to the murderously efficient meetings of the morning and the malodorous attentions of Davies in the afternoon.

As the conversation eddied around her, Jane found herself thinking of Ollie.

'Penny for them,' trilled a Venetia, who was sitting across the table from her.

'Nothing,' said Jane. 'I'm just listening.'

What Ollie had never understood was that she actually liked these people. They were strong, reliable; unlike him and his flashy friends, they would help if something went wrong. The fact that they had no interest in the futile little world of the media was a positive recommendation. She had grown up with them, seen them change, however slightly.

She had even been out with some of the men, enduring their uneasy courtship rituals. After a few evenings spent in expensive restaurants or at the opera, there might even be a nervous hint at marriage; it was too tentative and self-deprecating to be described as a proposal. With a sweet and modest laugh, Jane had turned her suitors down, but one day, when the time was right for it, she would say yes. There were worse fates, after all, than to be joined in holy matrimony to a husband with a big bottom, a loud voice and predictable opinions. It would be all right. In rare moments of wistful introspection, Jane saw herself married to a great, friendly, well-heeled chap with money, social charm and the libido of a tortoise in winter.

She left the dinner party as early as was polite, with the first wave of parents relieving baby-sitters, and was home by half past eleven.

There she prepared for bed, laying a glass of water on a raffia mat on the bedside table, slipping into a cotton nightdress, cleaning her teeth, setting the alarm. Then, the last part of her nightly routine, she stepped under the duvet and opened a drawer by the bed where, neatly ranged beside a packet of condoms, she kept a small vibrator, some spare batteries and a paperback collection of women's erotic fantasies.

With a whirr, a sigh and the click of her bedside lamp, Jane was soon asleep.

I too had a social engagement that Thursday evening, a less formal event than Jane's and one which, under normal circumstances, I would not mention.

But already, with only one death behind me and a lot more grief to come, I sense something going wrong. As I reconstruct, the distance between the investigator and his investigation is not as great as it should be. Worse, certain questions may have arisen which, in all honesty, can only be answered in personal terms. Why, for example, is this detective inspector so concerned with Robin Nicholl? Is it normal practice for a policeman to slip a key witness, a suspect even, items of evidence?

Perhaps, when I joined the force in the late sixties, part of a generation of bright sparks who were going to break with the knuckle-cracking cynicism of the past, I might have believed that a law and order operative could work in a vacuum, that his private life was an irrelevance. Now I know better.

For a while in those early years, I put up with the amusement that my adherence to correct procedures afforded my less scrupulous colleagues. I refused to cut corners or to make the evidence fit the crime. There are two ways to the top in the Metropolitan Police: the straight and the dirty. I was one of the good guys.

Today I take a more flexible attitude to the law, a development which, without any sense of marital disloyalty, I date back to the night, in February 1978, when I first met Joy.

Her name was Joy Dennis. She was seeing Frank Dimond, the bank robber, at the time. One night I walked into the Water Rat on the King's Road with a view to talking to Dimond about a recent job which we knew (more or less) he had been involved in. She was there. I knew a bit about her reputation but that made no difference. I was in love. Franky was doomed and so, in a way, was I. We married a couple of months after the trial, at which Dimond was sent down for five years.

Joy was always motivated. She never actually spelt out that, in return for marrying a policeman – a serious social handicap in the circles in which she moved – she expected a decent lifestyle, a detached house in an acceptable suburb, proper villa holidays in the sun, and a nice class of dinner party with company directors and estate-agent executives, but she didn't have to. I wasn't stupid. And a police salary, without the fringe benefits, was scandalously low back then.

On the one hand, principle; on the other, love. It was really no contest. Honesty was consigned to the bottom drawer; good faith gathered dust in pending. I lightened up. My career blossomed.

Once you've lost that idealism, that optimism, there's no turning back. Since then, I've changed – not outwardly but deep down in my policeman's soul. Today we live in Purley, with two lovely children, an active social life, members of the local tennis club. Joy has put on a bit of weight but we like it here.

Professionally, I'm to be found about halfway between the creepies and the hard men, playing routine cases with a more or less straight bat, taking advantage of unofficial, off-the-record opportunities as and when they present themselves. Selectively bent, you could say.

We're different, Joy and I. She likes going out – music, films, piano bars. Her general knowledge extends no further than the gossip columns, of whose leading players she is an acknowledged expert. Sadly, I have not measured up as a husband. Joy is one for glamour and excitement; I prefer the quiet life. When you marry, you think your differences will complement one another; after a while, you discover that they merely make you different.

That social engagement. Because it was our wedding anniversary, I had gamely agreed to accompany Joy to her favourite nightspot, a Croydon discothèque named Gordon Bennetts. The final turn of the screw to this night of torture lay in Joy's selection of fellow guests: Gary Starkey, a part-time actor and voice-over artiste, and his girlfriend Roseanne, said to be a model.

It was quite late, about three tequilas after eleven if I remember rightly, before Joy raised the subject of the Sincton case.

'Si's investigating the murder of that kinky American, aren't you, Si?'

Despite the fact that it was midweek, there was a raucous atmosphere at Gordon Bennetts that night. I smiled and nodded, unwilling to compete with the noise.

'Yeah?' Roseanne shouted across to me. 'What kinky American is that then, Simon?'

I shrugged, the careworn detective. 'He was a sort of writer feller. Knew a few celebrities. Died.'

'Go on then.' Roseanne wiggled in her seat, the parody of a little girl about to be told a story, setting the various squares and tassels on her negligible gold dress sparkling in the lights. She leant forward as if a flash of her tanned cleavage would end all resistance.

'Not that much to tell, really. Early days.'

'Probably *sub judice*, darling,' said Gary in the famous mellow tones, but mocking with it.

'Si-aye.' Joy was smiling, but I could sense her disappointment. Tired, grey-skinned, out of place, I had little enough to offer; the least I could do was amuse her friends with a bit of smutty shop-talk, filth from the filth. 'Tell them about the doughnut, Si.'

Yes, perhaps I could fob them off with that. 'He was found—' I hesitated as a drunken cheer from a nearby table drowned all conversation '—with a doughnut on his person.'

Joy giggled.

'On his person?' Gary frowned wittily. 'How d'you mean?'

'On his wedding tackle,' I said briskly.

There were shrieks from both women. 'Wedding tackle,' gasped Roseanne. 'Love it to death!'

'Penis,' I said, more loudly than I had intended.

I am not a natural entertainer, it appears. For the life of me, I just cannot make homicide as amusing as my wife would like it to be. 'You might as well be a sodding accountant,' she told me once.

It was going to be a long night, I could tell. The children were staying with friends, Joy was in full flirtatious mood, the music was deafening. Half an hour later, more or less, I watched as she danced with Gary and wondered whether the fact that his hand rested on one of her buttocks was part of a new dance or had more ominous significance. Roseanne sat across the table from me, nodding in time to the music like someone recovering from electric-shock treatment.

Is there anything sadder than a policeman in love with his wife? All those opportunities for on-duty sexual recreation, those untraceable personal incentives, those interviews which, with a nod and a wink, could be brought to satisfactory wordless conclusion in the bedroom, all those sisters and girlfriends and wives who were prepared to lie down with the law in order to keep their nearest and dearest out of nick, those sunny perks which are no more than what a hard-working policeman deserves? And all I really wanted was to be loved by a veteran bimbo with spreading buttocks and a sun-lamp tan, who led me around the hot spots, discos and tennis clubs of suburbia, led me mercilessly, daring me to be interesting like a TV detective, led me, a man highly respected in the force and feared by the criminal community, by my, well, by my wedding tackle.

Of course, I take my chances, like any other sensible, red-blooded officer would. Domestically under-nourished, I have been known to snack out extra-maritally. Oddly, these passing encounters mean little or nothing to me. It's become a mental thing; the nights I come home, having experienced some unzipped moment during the day, I look at my wife and feel not guilt or regret or sadness – just the same old feeling. Adultery has not done the trick. Love's a sod when it gets you like that.

'Don't you fancy a dance then?' Roseanne asked.

'Not quite my style.'

'Suit yourself. Tell me about these celebrities that bloke knew.'

'Celebrities?'

'The kinky American.'

I mentioned a few names, which seemed to impress. It was probably then that I realized that the Sincton murder, grimy and insignificant as it was, might be worth pursuing. Crime as cabaret: it had come to this.

Joy walked back to the table, her hand tucked easily into the back pocket of Gary's designer jeans. She kissed me on the dome of my head.

'They're thinking of setting up a disco specially for Si,' she said, sitting down and hitching a leg over my knee. 'It's gonna be called Gramps.'

Roseanne laughed. The music thumped. I stared bleakly ahead of me.

An hour later, maybe two, I was driving her home.

'All you had to do was talk about that man,' she said huffily. 'It's a good story.'

'It's not a story. It's true.'

'You know what I mean.'

'I talked to Roseanne about it while you were prancing about with Gary. I told her about the Suzi Ashbourn connection.'

'How does Suzi Ashbourn come into this?'

'Sincton worked with her. I'm going to see her tomorrow. We're old friends.'

'You know Suzi Ashbourn?' My wife was looking at me with surprise.

'It was some time ago.'

'You are something, Simon Potter. After all these boring cases, you've got a really good murder and you won't even talk about it. You'd make Jack the Ripper sound boring.'

'I'm sorry.'

We drove on.

'I just want you to do well,' she said more quietly. 'It seems ages since you were on the news.'

'It's just another sex case. Nobody cares.'

'I care. All those stars. It's . . . interesting.'

'They've got nothing to do with his being killed.'

'You could make something of it.'

I sighed. 'Maybe I could.' Tentatively, I laid a hand on her tanned, shiny thigh, a plaintive, unspoken question. And, bloody hell, she didn't move away.

'As it happens,' I said, the thought occurring to me as I sat there, 'I do have a plan of investigation. Ollie had a diary. I've given it to one of my witnesses. About now, he should find the key to Sincton's flat. I think he could lead me to something interesting.'

'Hey, exciting,' said Joy.

'Funnily enough, he's the husband of Laura Nicholl.'

'Laura Nicholl, Suzi Ashbourn,' she said in a distant voice. 'It could be really great.'

9

There's no recession in my industry; the market's always buoyant. Now, eight days after Oliver Sincton's murder, I was tempted to bank the whole thing. It was hot, the rancid putrescence of the city had burst into urgent, maggoty activity, and I was busy. If it hadn't been for Joy, and a certain niggling curiosity, I might have shelved the investigation and shifted my meagre resources – step forward, DC James Dexter – elsewhere.

In my heart I was still convinced that Ollie had been the victim of the kind of sexual misfit to which he seemed, to judge from his notes, to have become attracted. He had until then been remarkably lucky – the kinkies had been relatively harmless – but, once you find yourself in the market for off-beat pleasure, you never know quite what you're buying. There's no Trades Description Act for bondage or sado-masochism, no ombudsman to adjudicate on cases of deception or confusion in the murky area of recreational pain. It's very much a question of shopping blind.

That Friday morning I looked again at Ollie's seduction file. Even allowing for the chronological shifts in the narrative of which he was so fond, it was clear that, towards the end of his life, he had entered a downward spiral, moving from the normal, good-humoured promiscuity of youth to something sadder, seedier and, of course, more risky. In the end he fucked a loony; by the law of averages, it had to happen.

Those affairs, those absurd blind dates. In Ollie's version, he moved from one encounter to the next, amused and untainted. In fact, there was not one, however quick, demeaning, furtive, funny or pointless, which failed to touch him in some way. Each defined Ollie, made him into what he was on the night someone put a knife through his throat.

He had, it seemed, a system. In the early days there were social dates – researchers, editors, publicists picked up at media parties, taken home, enjoyed, dropped. Social dates provided contacts and gossip: there were times when he felt that he took these girls to bed only for the post-coital revelations about their friends. There were disadvantages: boredom, the occasional shrill rejection, the tiresome insistence on further meetings. Sometimes, at the worst possible moment, they went serious on him, wanting to talk about Us in the early hours of the morning. There was only so much of that sort of thing a man could take.

Then there were fast-stranger dates, incidents of glorious romantic spontaneity. One minute he'd be sitting opposite someone on a train, in a bar, at a restaurant, the next – a glance, a word or two was enough – they were in bed. It used to happen a lot to Ollie; he had that trim, confident manner, those boyish looks, the hint of the exotic and the foreign that made it easy; and he was almost always ready. While other men turned in on themselves, thought about their jobs, read a book, he was on constant date-alert; he could sense a fast stranger at ten paces, like some form of heat-seeking missile. While you or I would hesitate before bravely stumbling into conversation, Ollie would be in there: no gibbered introductions, offers of cups of tea, Mr Nice Guy small talk, but straight to it. 'What am I *doing* here?' they'd laugh later, in bed. 'I don't even *know* you. I'm not *like* this.' And Ollie would smile with pride. He had a particular weakness for girls who were not like this.

Chance meetings were the best. Unexpected, dangerous, they contributed to some of Ollie's most memorable moments.

*　　*　　*

We never close — we're always open for business. Sunday morning, and I'm making with the tape machine round at Martin Coleman's house — our jokes-and-religion Christmas package *Blessed are the Laughtermakers* being way overdue — when we have to break off for the Lord's work. Martin invites me to sit in on one of his Talk-and-Pray Workshops — matins, it used to be called — at his church nearby. 'Of course, the praying's optional,' says the rev quickly. So, in the hope of getting extra material for the book, I tag along.

I'm used to Martin's flock by now. I can recognize them as they gather in their Sunday best for a weekly interface with the Chairman of the Board.

Of course, Coleman's good-hearted waffle is for the birds — it looks like I'll have to write this little fucker myself. I'm working out a Laughtermaker schedule in my mind when I happen to glance across the aisle. Dark, straight hair, apparently alone, praying — call me a sicko but a girl praying really gets to me. She looks ahead of her as Martin moves into his routine, the theme of which is that God is Good, no not just good, but God is the same as Good, the two are interchangeable (bad news for the Big Guy with the flowing beard, but convenient for the rest of us), and, while I'm half-listening to this crap, she looks back at me. Hallelujah, a fast stranger.

At the end of the service, she walks out quickly. Had I misread the situation? Oh please, do me credit. On her pew she has left her service sheet and there, of course, is scrawled a telephone number.

The Lord is Good.

'We're all going round to Richard's house for a glass of wine,' says Martin. 'You're very welcome. Thirst after righteousness and all that.'

I explain that I have a pressing personal appointment and the rev, who's sometimes not as dumb as he looks, dismisses me with a guys-together wink. He has a curiously approving attitude to my private life, I've *found, as if it were simply a different, hands-on version of his own mission of love.*

A telephone call. A mercy dash down the road to a small apartment in Camden Town and, as the rest of Great Britain settles down to roast beef and Yorkshire pudding, I'm in bed with an ardent, born-again fast stranger, crazy as a bedbug, of course – there's much splashing about in the shallows of guilt and self-loathing, with the name of the Lord being often and deafeningly taken in vain. God, Good – yes, I can see it now.

I called Dexter into my office and invited him to take a seat.

'D'you believe all this?' I asked, waving a hand at the printout of Ollie's notes. 'Our friend's rampant promiscuity.'

Dexter smiled. 'It certainly dates him,' he said. 'He seems like a true sixties man. Doing his thing.'

Briefly, I felt the urge to defend Ollie against the sanctimonious disapproval of Dexter's new, sexually responsible generation, but I kept my peace. When there were no more eager telephone calls, when the gorgeous dark locks thinned at the temples, his moment would come.

'Perhaps Jane Goodenough is telling the truth,' I said. 'They met at a gallery, had a bit of a fling, then parted. Only, in Ollie's fictional version, he had to weave a fantasy in which she was Ministry moll by day and singles-bar raver by night.'

'He certainly seems the type to have difficulty with the idea of a woman putting her career before her private life,' said Dexter, moving into his most irritating psychological mode. 'Jane was a looker and all she wanted was to be a successful civil servant. I can see that might have annoyed Ollie.'

'I'm not sure any of it's relevant anyway. I made some enquiries at the Ministry of Defence. Both she and her boss Davies would have been positively vetted on a regular basis. I can't see them getting away with an affair.'

I glanced through the notes once more. 'Did Ollie ever live with anyone?'

'No, and from the look of his Putney house women didn't stay long there either. It was almost as if, by meeting them at his Mayfair place, he was keeping them away from him. He seemed frightened of involvement, always on the move.'

'As he was in his work. Any news from Forensic?'

Forensic, it transpired, had lived up to their reputation as masters of useless information. Imprints on the carpet had apparently revealed that more than one person had visited the flat in Half Moon Street during the twelve hours prior to the murder, one of whom had been wearing high-heels. There were no fingerprints, apart from Ollie's. Oh, and the doughnut on his pecker had come from a bakery in East Acton which supplied shops throughout West London.

'Does the term "pro-active" mean anything to you, James?' I asked, after Dexter had completed his summary.

'Sounds like a dog food.'

'It's a word Jane Goodenough used. It means that, instead of waiting to react to events, we initiate them.'

'Nice one.'

I looked at my assistant, so fresh, so eager for new challenges. 'James,' I said, 'you are going pro-active.'

'Sir?'

'You're going to meet some of Ollie's contacts – the names he marked in the magazines.'

'Meet them?'

'As a punter.'

'What, you mean – ask them a few questions?' Dexter was beginning to look uncomfortable.

'Questions, yes. Personal questions. Like, your place or mine? The sort of questions you probably ask your girlfriends.'

The blush that showed on Dexter's dark features might have been from embarrassment, but I suspect it was a rare moment of anger. 'I don't quite understand,' he said.

'You are, as from now, the station's resident sex machine a-go-go.'

Dexter didn't laugh.

'How many?' he asked.

'As many as it takes,' I said. 'I realize that, for a man of your sensibility, this might be slightly distasteful but it's all part of police work. Some of our most respected officers served their early days in public lavatories standing around in tight jeans waiting to have their bottoms touched by politicians. Someone has to do it.'

'And how far do you want me to go?'

'Something of a grey area, I admit, James. Perhaps I could leave that to your discretion. The first thing you need to do is get in touch with the women who wrote back to Ollie. Pretend you saw their ads. Of course, you'll have to enclose a photograph. I suggest you get that done right now.'

Miserably, he stood to leave. 'Right, sir.'

'And James—'

'Sir?'

I winked at my assistant.

'Don't scowl at the camera.'

There was still time to kill before I was due to see Suzi Ashbourn so, after Dexter had left the office, I went back to my homework.

It appeared from his notes that Ollie had graduated from fast strangers to move into the more dangerous world of the contact date approximately three years ago, presumably on the cusp of a mid-life crisis.

Sometimes I think it was more than mere chance that brought me to this little island. Mother England and me – we're a perfect fit. Leave aside my career, where clearly I'm an essential part of the country's famed service industries, and look at my private life.

There will be those who – grinding their teeth with envy – will argue that my natural pluralism, my ceaseless, heroic quest for romantic change and variety, is a kind of sickness – that I'm homosexual or afraid of women or that my behaviour is all about power, subjugation and fear. And in one sense they're probably right. The road I'm treading leads only to a sad, undignified old age when one day, the veneer worn thin, my anxieties will be there for all to see.

'He slept around,' they'll say as I'm spotted shuffling slack-jawed into a Soho peep-show. 'See what happens to you if you fuck too many women.'

I admit it. I'm a mess. My only excuse is that, as I exorcise this mother-fixation, or latent homosexuality, or obsessive satyriasis or whatever it is, I'm having one hell of a time.

And here's the beauty of it. I have landed in a country that is the world capital of sexual unhappiness. Erotic anguish is everywhere you look – in football crowds, in the House of Commons, on the subway – and Englishmen, those confused and guilty creatures, haven't a clue what to do about it. They marry fierce, bullying women. They grope one another in public lavatories. They pay large amounts of money to be whipped within an inch of their lives but, sorry old chap, nothing does the trick. They're still afraid of this terribly undignified business that they need so much yet which makes them feel so frightfully, frightfully silly.[1]

---

[1] *Scholarly footnote. Overstated? Take a look at the average British sex symbol. She's either a squeaky-voiced airhead with outsize breasts, a freakish child-woman or some faintly rude aunty figure, a former madam who talks dirty on chat shows. They're comic, absurd – by parodying female sexuality, they have taken away its danger. In any other country, sex symbols – film stars, the former mistresses of presidents – may be dumb but at least they're erotic. Not here.*

So where does this leave the Englishwoman? She too is confused and guilty but she has no-one to nag her. Girls rarely appeal to her nor – to the disappointment of millions of traditional male sadists – does punishment. Desperate, she looks for love, frequently turning – uh-oh – to an Englishman.

It's probably true what they say – the English are the worst lovers in the world. Jeez, I could write a book on it. There's Mr Cuddly in his baggy trousers: clumsy, inept and then, after much evasion and rummaging about, disastrously precipitate (the true vice anglais is premature ejaculation).

Mr Cuddly has a fantasy which I've heard several times now. He does it with his clothes on! Yes, even in the privacy of his own bedroom he wants to fumble about with fly-buttons and underclothes, letting the lower man get busy – quickly, furtively – while the rest of him is looking the other way. Talk about sad.

Then, younger and more modern, there's Mr Bonk, energetically applying lessons swotted up in the sex manuals. When a Suzi Ashbourn clone goes tabloid about her Night of Passion with some minor TV star, she'll say, 'He pressed all the right buttons.' And that, in this country, counts as praise! The quintessential Mr Bonk – he'd grown up wanting to be an engine driver, and here he was, pulling levers, pressing buttons, his dull, handsome face frowning with concentration. Now which button?

Foreplay is something of a problem area for the English male. Too much and there are mumbles of boredom; too little and there are squeaks of complaint – it's all damnably tricky for a fellow. As for foreplay in the morning – admittedly a complex and unresolved area of sexual etiquette – neither Mr Cuddly nor Mr Bonk have even begun to master it.

So these are lush pastures indeed for a simple American boy who just loves to love in the old-fashioned way. Not only does he provide a welcome

*release from the agonized writhings of the English
male but, on the subtle scale of guilt that's so
important in this country, he benefits from being just
slightly foreign – doing it with an American rates well
below a fellow countryman, who might just know
mummy and daddy, or a true foreigner, who almost
certainly suffers from some scruffy Mediterranean
disease and expects one to do all sorts of disgusting
dago things with him.*

*Ollie in Limeyland – it's a public service I'm doing
here.*

'Well, excuse me, Casanova,' I muttered as I finished
reading.

Sitting in my office, I could hear the voice of this
expert prober of the romantic Englishwoman, this
maestro of foreplay. And where had the simple
American boy ended up? Dead in Mayfair, trussed up
with a doughnut on his pecker. Not perhaps how a
man who just loved to love in the old-fashioned way
might have expected to finish his days.

It appeared that times changed, and so did Ollie. He
lost the knack of seduction, the ability to conceal the
well-practised move. What had once been charm
gave way to a wry, self-mocking, take-it-or-leave-it
insouciance that somehow invited rejection. At key
moments he would destroy the mood with a loud,
almost brutal laugh. By this time only the very lonely
or very mad would take a chance with a cynical,
cruising, older man. Risk was anyway out of fashion;
somewhere along the line love with a perfect stranger
had lost its allure. There were occasions when Ollie
felt that, just to get to first base, he needed a reference
from a reliable third party and, even then, the stranger
was likely to be not so much fast as scared, edgy.

At first out of curiosity, then out of need, he took to
contact dating. Seedy swop-and-shop magazines, discreet personal ads in the weeklies; he explored the

subject fully, discovered the codes. The mention of a husband, for instance, tended to mean that some sad, paunchy individual would be involved as participant or observer. Photographs were invariably taken ten years ago. The perfect lover – 'Brunette, early twenties, seeks older man for good times' – spelt business girl. Ads which specified sexual hobbies, destroying all hopes of erotic surprise, were embarrassing; real hobbies, particularly theatre-going, good food and walks in the country, were an even worse sign. Various words set alarm bells ringing: 'fun', 'laughter', 're-lationship' were particularly reliable indicators of gloom and intensity. Advertisers who aimed for the leering, come-hither jokiness of a blue video were saggy and disappointing. No-nonsense economy – 'Girl, 29, wants a damn good rogering' – alarmed Ollie.

But, once he knew the subtext, meeting through contact magazines had much to recommend it. A busy man these days, Ollie took a pragmatic attitude. The question was no longer 'Is this the girl of my dreams?' but a more simple 'Is she available?' Convenience and geographical location were now more significant fac-tors than looks, a slightly plump secretary with her own light and comfortable single-bedroom flat in Kensington being preferable to someone younger and more personable who shared a house with several giggling friends in Chingford. Most importantly, they needed to understand the way it worked: no expec-tations beyond the first night, no extreme sexual deviance unless specifically requested, and, above all, no tears.

So Ollie developed an eye for the right contact date. After a while he was rarely obliged to turn sharply on his heel at the door of a wine-bar on his way to the exploratory pre-date date. He learnt the rules. At this, too, he became an expert.

Word spreads fast in our shop. By the time I was due to

95

leave for my meeting with Suzi Ashbourn, it was clear that some of Dexter's less sensitive colleagues had heard of his project. Somehow the idea of our man stepping bravely into the world of lonely, middle-aged sex, sitting in a bar with some hot-eyed Raunchy Rita, was found so unlikely as to be amusing.

This, to speak personally, I put down to jealousy on the part of contemporaries less blessed than Dexter in the hunkiness department (people join the police because they're not happy with the looks they've been given: to their hearts, they're heroes; to their mirrors, they're accountants).

When I emerged from my office, a couple of Dexter's fellow police officers were harassing him at his desk. Nearby I could see a pile of photographs which would doubtless push the temperature in the suburbs up another couple of degrees.

'You lucky bastard,' one of the men was saying.

Dexter pulled the photos to him, shielding them with an arm like a swot in an exam. 'You can fuck off and all,' he said.

Suzi Ashbourn was not exactly on the game. It was just that the connection in her life between sex, about which she was generally indifferent, and money, about which she wasn't, was unhealthily close.

In another, more innocent age she might have been a mistress, set up in a flat in Knightsbridge by a fat, red-faced businessman; indeed, when Suzi first emerged from secretarial college at the age of eighteen, that was the first step in her career. One moment she was in the typing pool of a merchant bank, the next pirouetting about in a recently acquired mink coat in front of the smiling chairman of the board, his eyes moist with affection and anticipation. It was easy peasy, she told her friends, a piece of gâteau. On the other hand (it took her a profitable but slightly yucky six months to discover this), being an old fool's mistress was not a fun way of getting on. In fact, it was seriously dullsville.

During the next few years, having ditched grandad for a recently divorced gossip columnist after which she went freelance, Suzi earnt a modest salary as a dancer in a club, a public-relations assistant for a record company and stringer for a listings magazine. But her real talent lay in exploiting her ceaselessly active personal life. She seduced. Then hours, weeks, years later, she unburdened herself to the press about it. She was a kiss-and-tell virtuoso.

Contrary to general opinion, it takes more than a good pair of legs and the suspension of any sense of decency or morality to make a living this way; it requires a high level of skill and dedication. Sleep with the wrong racing driver, enjoy raunchy romps with a rock star whose next single disappears without trace, get involved in sicko three-in-a-bed scenes with a top football manager who is fired before you have the chance to tell all, and you're finished. The invitations dry up, your confidence goes, you spiral downwards, ending up in a Novotel in Hammersmith with a middle-aged former soap star of financial interest to absolutely no-one, however raunchy, however sicko.

Suzi avoided these pitfalls. She had an instinct for men who would make good copy. She knew how to play it (little-girl-lost for the football manager, wild hedonist for the racing driver, sophisticated woman of the world for the rock star) and, because she looked bad enough to be interesting without ever descending to overt vulgarity, her score rate was high.

Celebrities, Suzi discovered, are not bright; most of them are dazzled by the excitement of it all. Even those who had read her previous confessions in the newspapers failed to see the trap until it was too late. One night was all it took.

Of course, competition was tough – the clubs were full of nineteen year olds on the make – but Suzi had a natural advantage: she had given up love at the age of seventeen and sex, at which she developed a certain brisk competence, was never an urgent imperative in her life. This was tremendously liberating when it came to career seduction.

Yes, we knew Suzi. From her early days in London, she had been a familiar name to my colleagues in the Drugs Squad but, by taking a co-operative line with the law-enforcement officers (let's just say Suzi was copper-friendly and leave it at that), she had managed to keep out of trouble.

My dealings with her had followed one of her more memorable bedroom coups which had been celebrated under the tabloid headline 'BOOKIE NOOKIE! SUZI'S WILD NIGHT WITH ON-THE-RUN CONMAN!' As she assisted me in my inquiries, Suzi and I had become well acquainted – but not as well acquainted as on one evening she had proposed. Suzi wasn't my type.

It was some months now since her breakthrough romance with a member of the royal family so, when I rang the intercom bell outside her flat in Maida Vale, I was reasonably confident that we were not being watched by some scurfy representative of the fourth estate.

After a few sleepy curses, Suzi asked me to give her five minutes. Half an hour later I was in her neat little sitting-room discussing her relationship with Oliver Sincton over a cup of instant coffee.

'You haven't changed a bit,' I lied. Daylight didn't agree with Suzi. She looked all of her thirty-four years (geriatric in her line of work) as she sat in a baggy white T-shirt, puffing occasionally at a cigarette.

'Wish I could say the same for you,' she said with the lightness of touch I remembered so well.

'It's been three years,' I said.

'I can't help you with this Sincton business if that's what you want. We were friends for a couple of months. Then we weren't. End of story.'

I said nothing.

'Hadn't seen him for about three weeks before he died.'

'Were you surprised?'

'It's a tough old world out there.'

'But he didn't seem to have made enemies.'

Suzi shrugged.

'What did he think about your dealings with the palace?'

'Nothing to do with him, was it?' Suzi inhaled deeply on her cigarette.

'Did Ollie tell you he kept a diary?'

'Not that I remember. What sort of diary?'

I reached into my pocket and handed her a few pages. Suzi read them, smiling now and then.

'What a romantic night that was,' she said. 'Served the bastard right for taking me for granted.'

'What I don't understand is why there are no more references to you after that occasion.'

'Search me.'

'Was he going to write a book for you?'

'He talked about it. Ollie talked great book.'

'Seems funny that you split up just after the Mustique business. I would have thought that he'd have been interested in your royal romance.'

Suzi laughed, coughing on her cigarette. 'He wanted to cash in,' she said. 'I told him to sod off.' For a moment she stared into space. Then she added, 'Just don't drag him into this, will you?'

'Him?'

'You know. Mustique.'

'Ah.' The royal him.

'I wouldn't want to embarrass the family.'

'Of course not.'

After I had left Suzi I sat in the car looking again through Ollie's notes. Sincton and Suzi: how well they suited one another.

*   *   *

Now that I know her, I can see that my first meeting with Suzi Ashbourn owed much to chance. She wasn't on the pull that night and, even if she had been, my public profile was too low to grace her boudoir. Suzi's no civilian in these matters: desire, attraction mean nothing to her.

I'm at a club for the launch of an expensive book of sub-pornographic snaps by the New York sophisticate Saul Chabon. The party's an unhappy mix of Saul's friends, who share his enthusiasm for gossip, off-beat sex and recreational drugs, and the duller, more literary connections of his British publisher.

I move quickly into the fast stream, of course.

It's about two in the morning. The corduroy-bags set have tottered off to Hampstead, the sound of dance music and good times echoing in their ears. I'm on late-date alert when I see Suzi – lithe, moving with the music, definitely part of the nightclub army.

Now there's kind of a misunderstanding here. Even when straight (which she isn't), Suzi is incapable of communicating with a man in a nightclub without a fair amount of breathy flirtatiousness. As it happens, her pretty little pantomime of facial foreplay – the provocative twitch of the lip, the occasional widening of the eyes – is for Chabon who, earlier in the evening, may have said to Suzi that he'll 'catch her later'. Suzi, who takes such remarks literally, is still waiting, filling in time with yours truly.

'You know he's gay,' I tell Suzi when eventually I catch on.

'You wish,' goes Suzi but then, as if on cue, the carnival's moved on, Saul having befriended a young male journalist now on his way to discovering a previously untapped capacity for narcotic and sexual excess.

I guess the only reason that she lets me drive her home is because, in her line, it's bad for your reputation to be seen leaving a nightclub in the early hours all on your own. And since I do appear to know a few stars, she invites me into her apartment doubtless to weigh me up in terms of column inches and serialization rights one last time before throwing me out.

Whatever. The poor innocent is in the apartment in full seduction overdrive when Suzi changes tune. It turns out that no-one has taught her the standard kiss-off lines about boyfriends being out of the country or the importance of friendship before sex. Her style is: 'Oh my god, is that the time?'

'Yeah, bedtime, Suzi,' I go, but already I'm getting a bad feeling about the way the evening's panning out.

'You must be joking,' she says, and suddenly, as I sit there patiently on her little couch in her little apart-ment, she's making like the total housewife, fretting about the place, feeding the cat, glancing at a bill, lighting and stubbing out a cigarette. I guess she's still pretty wired from whatever stuff she did in the Ladies back at the club although she's coming down fast.

I know that the sensible thing is to beat it, get the hell out of the place, but, all the same, she did accept a ride home, goddamnit, she did invite me in. There's a protocol here – call me old-fashioned but coffee at three in the morning equals fuck, right? Maybe, I'm thinking in my innocence, maybe she's the shy type. But those legs, that neat, knowing body . . .

'I expect you want to see my portfolio, I'm in the papers quite a lot, you know,' she says in the hard resentful voice that seems to have crept up on her.

This is a small improvement on the feeding-the-cat routine. 'Sure,' I say.

From a bookcase she pulls out a big, leather album. I skim through the cuttings. They're from tabloid newspapers, mostly confessions showing Suzi in various states of plaintive undress.

Reacting to semi-naked glamour shots of someone who's pacing backwards and forwards in front of you

101

isn't easy. It's kind of difficult to know what's expected. I take the plunge.

'You're even more beautiful without your clothes.'

Wrong! There's a triumphant told-you-so look in her eyes as she snaps, 'Thought you were interested in my work. Wouldn't have showed you if I'd known you were just another boggler.'

I lay the book aside and stand up. This crap I do not need.

'Look,' *I say, placing a hand on each of her sharp, angry shoulders.* 'Let's not get hostile. Why don't we just go next door to that bedroom of yours?'

As I lean forward, she whirls away, ducks down to pick up my coffee. 'Just because I asked you in,' *she calls out over her shoulder, scurrying off to the kitchen where she throws the cup and saucer into the sink,* 'it doesn't mean I want to bonk, does it.'

I slump, comically poleaxed, back on to the couch.

'Bonk?' *I've seen this term in the papers where it's just gaining currency but I have never actually heard it used.* 'Did you say "bonk"?'

'Yeah.' *She's still in the kitchen, pouring water from the kettle into — the woman's a monster — a hot-water bottle.* 'Don't they bonk where you come from or what?'

'Bonk,' *I say, like a man who's prepared to talk through the night. By now, I'm seriously pissed at the way things are going.* 'There's something very English about a bonk.'

'Other people do it, so I've heard.'

'Bonk. The sound of a rubber ball hitting a wall. Bonk. As if it's some sweaty stupid game, like tennis. Hey, maybe that's why you guys are so bad at it.'

'Wouldn't you like to know.' *Suzi gives a humourless snort of laughter.*

'Yes, it really is interesting, the erotics of this language of yours.' *I'm virtually talking to myself now. The rude bitch is turning the lights off in the kitchen,*

*humming tunelessly to herself as if I've already gone.
'Like, with English terms of abuse, they're nastier than
where I come from – more anatomical.'*

'Oh yeah.'

*'In the States, if you refer to an asshole or a jerk, in
your mind's eye you see some sort of inadequate
person.'*

'Bloody right,' Suzi mutters.

*'But here, it's arsehole, isn't it. It's wanker. See what
I mean? There, unavoidably before your eyes, is the
precise image – the orifice, the flying hand. And
motherfucker—'*

*'Are you going to sit here talking dirty or am I going
to have to throw you out?'*

*'—yes, motherfucker's a banal, everyday term of
abuse back home. Here it's unusable because everyone's so fucking literal.'*

*'Booring.' She's actually standing at the front door
now, holding it open with the hot-water bottle under
her other arm. 'Time to go home.'*

*'Yeah, I thought you'd be interested,' I say, making
my way out in my own sweet time, unable to resist
patting her ass as I walk by her.*

*'I was totally fascinated,' she calls after me.
'Motherfucker.'*

That, I confess, did make me laugh.

I drove back to the station, thinking of Suzi. Somehow
she seemed an unlikely consort for a member of the
House of Windsor.

That royal exclusive of hers can be briefly described.
Beyond establishing a distant, tentative link between
the slimeball Sincton and Her Gracious Majesty the
Queen, it was of little interest to me. Indeed, by the
time of my visit to Maida Vale, even the most avid
palace-watcher had tired of Suzi Ashbourn and her
Shock Allegations.

The problem, as the tabloid newspapers had quickly

recognized, was not that Suzi's story was all lies, but that it looked uncomfortably like the truth. The royals were there to be tickled, teased and goosed up, but in a respectful, affectionate way. Somehow the idea of a Grade A royal becoming involved with someone like Suzi Ashbourn was too charged with everyday seediness to be deemed safe or desirable.

This was a shock to Suzi who, after that fairytale night when she bedded her prince, believed that only good things, the best things, awaited her. Pictures in the paper, a personal manager to field the absurdly lucrative offers that would come flooding in, the chance to meet Hollywood stars, open supermarkets, enough cash in hand to keep her supplied with the newest and nicest recreational drugs: it was a simple, girlish dream, but it seemed to be within her grasp. How sadly wrong she was.

The alleged relationship had all happened a year previously. The prince in question was taking a holiday in Mustique. His wife, for reasons the newspapers only dared hint at, had returned home early. Implausibly, the prince was attending a party at which Suzi – it was a small island, the community of white, moneyed hedonists was tight-knit – happened to be present. Her escort was, wouldn't you know it, elsewhere. The prince and the bimbo met; later that night, after much ducking and diving to avoid his detectives, she made it to the prince's bedroom. He was, of course, a gentle lover, considerate, slightly shy. Afterwards they discussed the vegetarian way of life. It was all so beautiful that they agreed to do it again. She visited him twice more, Suzi's friend having been conveniently called away on business.

Why had she waited a year to tell her story? Was it all, as the palace press office said, a 'pathetic, publicity-seeking fantasy'? Did Suzi know enough about vegetarianism to keep her end up (later 'discussing vegetarianism' became a euphemism for keeping one's end up)? And what could a previously well-behaved, if rather dull, member of the royal family see in Suzi? For a week or so these questions reverberated through the country. There were unpublished but widely circulated rumours that Suzi had used some kind of sophisticated sexual trickery to ensnare her prince, a topic about which my wife speculated with unnerving expertise. Then, gradually, the fuss died down.

Frankly, I saw nothing of particular relevance in this. So what if the Ashbourn woman, a passing acquaintance of Ollie Sincton, had subsequently bonked, as she insisted, a prince?

Joy, of course, had her own view

10

Late that evening, while writing up my notes back at the station, I received a call from Jane Goodenough.

'D'you have any news of developments in the case?' she asked briskly, as if I were one of her double-barrelled minions at the Ministry.

'Unfortunately, Miss Goodenough, I am not at liberty to divulge details of an ongoing investigation,' I said, electing to play the straight Inspector Plod line.

There was a pause. Jane had been wrong-footed, but only briefly. 'I'm ringing about my father. You've spoken to him, haven't you?'

'If you say so, Miss Goodenough.'

'I do. So why's he being pestered by this man Nicholl?'

'Nicholl?'

'Robin Nicholl. He claimed he was some kind of friend of Oliver Sincton's.'

'Ah yes. That would be the literary executor. He's in charge of Ollie's words.'

'Oh, for Christ's sake, Inspector.' I pictured Jane at her desk in the large office, her perfect legs crossed, staring ahead of her with those cold blue eyes. 'My father has served his country in the army. I work for the Ministry of Defence in Whitehall. If you've got some undercover snoop on your team, we should bloody well be told, don't you think?'

An image of my undercover operative, DC Dexter, heading at this very moment for the mucky end of Lonely Street, flashed through my mind. 'That would rather spoil the point of it, Miss Goodenough,' I said. 'Have you met Mr Nicholl?'

'No. But he's got my father coming up to London

next week on some idiotic pretext. If he's anything to do with you—'

'And Ollie never mentioned Nicholl?'

'Oliver? Not as far as I remember. Look, I had rather hoped we were on the same side in this.' She was more subdued now. 'Have you spoken to the Ashbourn woman?' she asked suddenly.

'Miss Ashbourn has been most helpful. Now please don't hesitate to get in contact with us if you would like to add to your original statement,' I said, tugging gently at Jane's lead before bidding her a good weekend and returning to Ollie.

OK, so we date. Not like, when are you going to move in with me, is this more than just a physical thing for you, not a relationship or anything like that, thank you very much, but a date maybe twice a week, a dinner, a party, a club, a bit of chat followed by a spot of low-pressure action back at her place.

For just a while, I'm uneasy that Jane's figuring to fall in love with me – girls get weird like that when they hit thirty – but I'm underestimating her. She has her rules, personal, professional – and not even meeting Ollie Sincton would change that. Anyway, Englishwomen of her type lose the ability to love before they hit puberty.

But whoa there – what exactly is happening? These evenings, these nights out on the town, they take time. She's attractive, sure, but after that first night it's strictly routine sex; first that, then this, no not that, please, Ollie, you know I don't like that. Good manners quickly return to the bedroom. It's back to Ye Olde Englishe Cuddle. My dear, too too dreary.

And yet I stick around. There's something about Jane which makes me curious. Why the ambition, the singles bars, why the strangers? Call it what you will – a creative artist's impulse, the strange, sixth-sense awareness that she can help me in some way –

whatever the motive, I decide to play her along.

Fool, blind young fool! Too late, I discover that it was she who was playing me. In my innocence, I'm unable to see that I've been transferred from the personal to the professional. That's right, suddenly I'm down there among the red-faced lobby correspondents and prematurely ejaculating MPs.

Jeez, do I feel dumb when I finally figure this out. Eventually, of course, I manage to turn the situation to my advantage but for a while I feel angry, exploited, cheated.

It all becomes obvious when, lamb to the slaughter, I'm introduced to dear, devoted daddy.

There may have been a certain spring in my step as, a couple of hours later, I stepped off the commuter train on to the platform at Purley station. DC James Dexter had been satisfactorily launched, an unguided missile at this very moment cutting its way through the churning waters of female desire. Jane Goodenough appeared to be on the point of losing her legendary poise and distance from events. The curiosity of an old-fashioned literary executor had been twitched into being; heaven only knew what Robin Nicholl would reveal as he blundered through the minefield of his late friend's life.

There was much to discuss with Joy.

'So what will James do?' It was astonishing, miraculous even, that news of the Sincton case was of greater interest to my wife than her weekly Friday-night trip to the local cinema. We sat together by the rock pool in the garden, talking, drinking a bottle of white wine. 'Will he, you know—?'

'James is a very dedicated policeman,' I said.

'Si, you're awful. Honestly.' She laughed. I shrugged modestly.

You start to reveal yourself, when reconstructing. It happened to the starstruck fools who innocently unburdened themselves to Ollie Sincton and his tape recorder, and it's happening here. You try to give a context, to explain motives, and soon you're stripping off, laying bare what really should be left to the imagination.

It was on that Friday night that something strange and wonderful occurred, domestically speaking. Soon after eleven I was about to put the cat out for the night when Joy, sleepy and unsteady from the wine, walked through the kitchen, saying in her smiling voice, 'I'm going up now.'

Most couples develop a code after a while, a marital nod and a wink designed to avoid problems of rejection or misunderstanding, and this was ours. Joy was going up! I hurled the cat through the back door and followed, a song in my heart.

That night it wasn't Joy at her best (those first weeks after we had met, post-Frank Dimond, will stay with me for ever), but it was Joy and that was enough. In younger, braver days I might have insisted she take off her nightdress, look at me occasionally, hold back on the martyred sighs, even move around a bit now and then, but I had discovered that a word out of place and she'd shut up shop altogether, leaving me stranded, wracked, bursting with foolish desire on my side of the bed. These days making love to my wife demanded a high level of self-control and diplomacy. In the battle of the bedroom her policy had been to whittle away year by year what might reasonably be expected on a night of marital conjunction so that by now I was grateful for anything – *anything*.

I said nothing. She said nothing. It was a short-lived, economical, minimalist event. Like two creatures on the sea-bed who drift towards one another, coalesce and move apart, we merged, we mated. Not the ultimate, but nice.

Afterwards my nose was causing me problems. I sniffed restlessly.

'What's the matter, Si?' she asked in a quiet, wifely way.

'Hay fever.' I was wondering if maybe, after all, I should give Nicholl the disk Ollie had marked 'LAURA'.

There was a pause. What was she thinking? That I was crying with relief?

'The pills are on the dresser,' she said.

Some time that weekend, while Brigadier Harry Goodenough was in the garden at Roseclare, his daughter visited Colin Thompson in the small flat at the back of the house.

'Colin?' She looked round the door into a room where Thompson sat on a large, bald armchair in front of the television. 'Sorry to bother you.'

Thompson stood up and turned down the volume.

'I was wondering if we could talk.' Jane perched on the side of the second armchair. 'Do sit.'

Uneasily, Thompson lowered himself back into his chair and sat to attention, closer than he liked to be to Jane Goodenough.

'It's about a problem that the brigadier has,' Jane said.

'Yes, Miss Jane.'

'A problem I rather think you might be able to help him with.'

Thompson listened. His eyes remained fixed on the flickering images of the television set, not out of an interest in what was being shown, but because Miss Jane always had this effect on him. He didn't like it when she came visiting. There was something of her mother in her, something leery and independent. He had no time for leery women. Her taste in men left a bit to be desired, too.

11

Never mind the tourist muggers, joyriders and race rioters who were gleefully dismantling our beloved city in the August sun; that Monday morning my superior officer Detective Superintendent Norman Biddle had more urgent matters to consider.

Norman was seeing stars.

'What I'm asking you, Simon, is – taking a global broadbrush view – will the Sincton murder play on *Crime Time*?'

Wearily I watched him as he paced backwards and forwards in front of my desk, the shifty, dark eyes, set in that big, honest-copper face, sparkling with antici-pation. A rivulet of sweat made its way slowly down my back.

'Take a seat, Norman,' I said. 'You're giving me a headache.'

Biddle sat in my guest chair, but his large frame continued to writhe as if another little dance around the office was imminent.

'Sincton's not that interesting,' I said. 'Middle-aged man with a dodgy personal life: it's hardly classic crime. He's not even English.'

'American. That's good. International. Then there are all his celebrity friends.'

It was thanks to policemen like Norman Biddle that the television programme *Crime Time* had become such an important part of the nation's Sunday-night viewing. A leading member of the force's presentation brigade – plausible idiots who make it their business to transform the image of the police – Biddle was less interested in catching villains (I doubt if he's ever fingered a corrupt collar, apart from his own) than in being seen to keep his beloved general public safe from crime.

Over the past few years he had regularly appeared on discussion programmes, contributed firm but fair appraisals of law and order issues for middle-brow newspapers and generally made himself available when microphones or reporters' pads were in evidence.

So when the idea for a television programme which could bring to police work all the glitter and crassness of a game show found its way from a production company in Camden to New Scotland Yard, Biddle was one of its keenest supporters. *Crime Time* was born.

At first the programme – in which unsolved crimes were racily enacted, witnesses interviewed and then viewers invited to phone in with evidence – was popular only with weirdos and cranks, but sanctimonious disapproval was becoming all the rage and soon everyone joined in, boggling with horror at the activities of other people before grassing up the neighbours. Because *Crime Time* exploited the great British virtues of prurience and a sense of moral superiority, it quickly established itself in the ratings. Few crimes were solved but the image of the police improved.

Biddle was our shop's link with the *Crime Time* studio. Every week we were required to report to him on work in progress, assessing each investigation with a view to winning us a coveted spot on next month's programme. By now the superintendent had developed a sure instinct for cases that would 'play' – set the phones ringing, the viewing figures soaring. Sex figured largely, of course, then abduction, robbery with violence, fraud, then back to sex: its very repetitiveness was reassuring.

Under normal circumstances I tended to give my

112

work a low TV profile (the sight of Biddle moving into showbiz mode does nothing for my digestive system), but Joy was eager for a blast of marital celebrity and, besides, I had become curious about Sincton. So, when submitting my report, I had played down the case's seedy banality but carefully included a few eye-catching names. He was in my office within seconds.

'Russ Targett, the Reverend Martin Coleman, Laura Nicholl, Suzi Ashbourn,' Biddle read from the pages in front of him. 'They're good. They're bankable.'

'The famous names are by the way,' I said casually. 'This is just a sleazy sex thing, Norman.'

'Yes, of course,' said Biddle, his big, clumsy features twitching with excitement. *Just* a sleazy sex thing? The man *lived* for sleazy sex things. 'Would you be prepared to appear on the programme?' he asked.

'If it would help the case.'

'And there's no-one else involved in the investigation?'

I hesitated. The prospect of James Dexter, whose vacant good looks made him a media natural, appearing in sitting-rooms throughout the land did not appeal. 'I have someone working undercover, but no way am I going to risk exposing him,' I said.

'Where's that in the report?'

'It's low-profile, Norman,' I said. 'I didn't think it was relevant.'

'What's his line?' Biddle was no fool. There was an angle here and he knew it. 'Maybe we could use actors.'

'His line?' How could I put it without Biddle spontaneously combusting? Actually, Norman, I've got him going to bed with a lot of lonely single women in the Greater London area. 'He's following up certain contacts on a one-to-one basis,' I said.

'Sounds good. Let's film him against a bright light and—'

'I think the Ashbourn woman would be a better bet,' I interrupted. 'The royal connection might be a problem, but she's quite media-friendly at present, isn't she.'

'Suzi Ashbourn.' Biddle put the fingertips of two pudgy hands together. 'You think she'd co-operate? I read that she had an exclusive contract with one of the tabloids.'

'Our Suzi has never knowingly turned her back on a camera in her life. And the newspaper's hardly likely to ignore the chance of another little wrinkle to the story. I could talk to her.'

Biddle was hooked. 'You know her?'

'We've had dealings.'

'Hmm. Media-friendly, might be something we could go with,' he said, glancing at his watch. 'I'll run it past the producer and get right back to you.'

After he had left I pulled a folder from the top drawer of my desk and read through my case notes. Outside the office Dexter sat crouched before his word-processor, his hands poised above the keyboard like a man stalking a small animal. Whatever horrors he had witnessed when making an exploratory visit to the Bunch of Grapes over the weekend were taxing his powers of expression.

Vaguely I wondered whether our literary executor had found the key that I had left inside the dust cover of the second of Ollie Sincton's disks. Surely, with that, even Robin would be able to find his way into Ollie's former love-nest in Half Moon Street.

He slammed down the receiver as if he wanted to destroy it, muttering 'Fucking prat not fucking picking up' as he pushed past a startled French family who were waiting to use the telephone.

He didn't like public transport and he didn't like London and he certainly didn't like travelling by public transport in London, not at all. Scurfy, smelly riff-raff, foreign, jostling, fat women squeezing up against you, grimy kids treading on your toes, people staring at you as if being smart with a decent haircut made you different, young skimpy-dressed bints flashing tit and arse like it was natural, nig-nogs – nothing but nig-nogs – all with angry, flick-knife eyes. And late. And dirty. And dear. Fucking hell, did he hate London transport.

He took Hyde Park at a brisk march, a yomp. It was good to be operational once more, body on red alert, mind a bright, thin laser beam of undeflectable intention. There was a certain look to his eyes, his breathing was more marked than it might have been in his prime, but you didn't have to be 100 per cent hard to survive these days. Three-quarters hard, half hard and you were fucking Superman in these soft times. Old twats with dogs avoided him as he walked, eyes front, across the park, briefing himself, grunting with every stride. Yobs on the grass with bulging trousers, virtually at it with their tarts, looked up and smiled like he was funny. Mingle, they taught you. Merge. Become one with the landscape. That was all very well in the handbooks, on the parade-ground, on an exercise – but mingle, merge, here? Become one with *this* landscape? You've got to be fucking joking.

In the Hyde Park underpass an old bastard sitting on the stone floor, playing 'Danny Boy' on the harmonica, held out a hand. 'Fuck off,' said the man.

So the prat was already there. Never mind, he could wait. He crossed the road and stood beside a stall selling pictures of black women, bollock-naked mostly. If the lads could see him now. He smiled and stood easy.

'Marvellous man.' Brigadier Harry Goodenough took a freshly ironed handkerchief from his pocket, unfolded it and, with a frown of concentration, wiped the knife in front of him, then the fork, then the wine glass. 'I had a lot of time for Oliver.' He smiled, returning the handkerchief to his trouser pocket.

Robin glanced down at the gleaming Cavalry Club cutlery. He said, rather quickly to cover his surprise at this fastidiousness, 'Yes, he was remarkable.'

'You were a friend, were you?'

'I met him at Cambridge,' said Robin.

'Good show.' There was a pause, during which Goodenough looked around the room, nodding at an acquaintance at a nearby table. With his carefully combed grey hair, his dandyish clothes and manicured hands, he seemed to Robin an unlikely soldier.

'He changed a lot over the years,' Robin continued.

'Can't say I remember him mentioning you, but then our relationship was mainly professional.'

Robin tried to ignore the reproachful little twist that Goodenough had appeared to give the word 'professional', as if he had already sensed that professionalism was one of the many attributes that Sincton had possessed and Robin lacked.

'It was very kind of you to see me, sir,' he said. 'I've been asked by a magazine to write a tribute to Ollie. I thought you might like to contribute.'

'Magazine, eh?'

'Yes.' With a coolness of which Ollie would have been proud, Robin told the lie wide-eyed, without a blush.

'Good kit,' said the brigadier.

'I would have been happy to visit you or to give you lunch,' Robin said.

Goodenough held up a hand. 'My pleasure.' He took a menu from a waiter who had been hovering behind him for some time. 'Now let's order.'

Over lunch Robin was given a brisk summary of Goodenough's dealings with the American.

'It was never my idea to write my memoirs,' Goodenough said at one point. 'The musings of an old soldier—' he flicked a crumb from the tablecloth '—

116

who cares? But Oliver was insistent. Schooldays, army, war, my little job as a royal equerry; anyway, he thought it might be of interest.'

'Had you started work when he died?'

'I'd spent an afternoon chatting into his machine about my childhood, if you can call that work. Funny the things that come back to you when you begin jawing.'

'But by then, presumably, he and your daughter were no longer together.'

'No, they had split up.' Goodenough seemed about to enlarge on this, but checked himself. 'I thought that would be the end of it, but Oliver rang a couple of months ago. Started chatting about the book as if nothing had happened. So I invited him down for lunch during the week. Jane disapproved, of course. Have you seen her yet?'

'No,' said Robin. 'I've had difficulty making an appointment.'

Goodenough disposed of his food at speed, possibly a habit learnt under fire. By the time Robin had caught up with him, he was uneasily aware that he had failed to make a positive impression.

'Coffee?' Goodenough asked, but in such a pained, watch-tapping way that only a brave or insensitive fool would have accepted.

'A cappuccino, please,' said Robin.

Goodenough scowled. 'What I liked about Oliver was his sense of purpose,' he said. 'He had go.'

'Erm, yes.' Robin was unsure quite how to respond. 'Yes, he had bags of all that sort of thing.'

'I like a man with go.'

Moments later, his coffee half finished, Robin followed Goodenough through the dining-room, down the stairs to the front door where, with a brief handshake and a glacial smile, the brigadier bade him farewell. The Cavalry Club expelled Robin into the street like a body rejecting alien tissue.

The lunch had not gone well, Robin thought as he made his way slowly towards Hyde Park Corner. No new information had been acquired, he had exposed more of his own plans than he had intended, and there had been something about the brigadier which suggested that a further meeting would not be welcome. He was jostled by a group of young Australians outside the Hard Rock Café; one of them, he noticed, was wearing a T-shirt reading 'OPINIONS ARE LIKE ARSEHOLES — EVERYONE'S GOT ONE!' Sweating in the dark suit he had worn for the lunch, he felt uncomfortable, a pale outsider in this sweltering, unfamiliar London.

He descended the steps into the underpass. Ahead of him he saw an old man playing the harmonica, and he reached into his pocket for change. Obscurely anxious not to linger in front of the man, risking conversation and stares from passers-by, he threw a pound into the hat without checking his stride. The coin bounced out and rolled a few feet away. Robin hesitated; his gesture suddenly appeared haughty and contemptuous. On the other hand, to turn and pick up the coin with a mumbled apology would look unduly craven. It was strange how these days even small acts of generosity conspired to make him feel guilty. He kept walking.

The time when travelling underground had been tolerable to Robin had long since passed. He worried about the people who lived down there — beggars, hustlers, loons of one kind or another, looking for action. The commuters seemed to take the growing subterranean anarchy for granted, but it frightened him.

He bought a ticket from one machine and put it in another which rejected it with an angry alarm tone. A uniformed man, his cap on the back of his head, wandered over and, without looking at Robin, said, 'Other way up.'

'Sorry?'

'Ticket.' With stagy sarcasm, the guard pointed to it. 'You. Turnee ticket over. Comprende?'

'No need to be rude,' said Robin. The automatic barrier let him through.

An escalator took him deeper into the ground. He was in no hurry, unlike the person behind him, the click-clack of whose boots echoed in the tunnel. Robin sighed, sinking his hands into his trouser pockets. Rush, rush, how he hated the underground. He was just slowing to let the owner of the boots past when someone hit him hard on the back of the neck.

'Wha—'

Still conscious, Robin fell heavily to his knees. A hand grabbed his hair and held his head forward as if he were about to be decapitated.

'Don't fucking look at me, right,' said a voice above him.

'No,' Robin whispered as his head was pushed towards the stone ground.

The man started walking slowly down the passageway, leading Robin, who shuffled foolishly on his knees, by the hair. It was school, he was being bullied again, tears of pain and humiliation filled his eyes. '*Don't* look, shitface.' There was another vicious jerk to the crown of his head. 'Listen.'

'Yes.'

'Mind your own fucking business, right.'

'*What?*'

'Mind—' Robin was dragged to his feet and, with his head bent back, found himself staring at the ceiling. 'Your own—' He was being pulled from side to side, stumbling, crashing against first one wall then the other. 'Fucking—' Distantly, he heard sounds of protest as, walls flashing by, the dance continued. How did his hair remain connected to his scalp as he turned and turned? Why didn't it give? 'Business.'

Robin tried to sob his agreement, but it was too late. He saw the fat knee jerking upwards towards his face.

The hand pushed him forward and he lost consciousness.

When Laura rang me that afternoon to report Robin's mishap, I confess that my first reaction was to consign the incident to the bulging, dusty police file marked 'LIFE, That's'. So our man had been mugged underground. Frankly, he was the sort of person whose very existence attracts the violent and undesirable; it was his role in life.

'Apparently, the man was wearing heavy boots. He seemed quite strong and swore a lot,' Laura said. 'He told Robin to mind his own business.'

'Was Mr Nicholl staring at him or something?'

Laura hesitated. 'He doesn't think so. He's a bit woozy, Inspector.'

I mean, really. This town is full of people who would take a negative attitude towards an amiable time-waster like Robin Nicholl.

'An officer will be right over, Mrs Nicholl,' I told Laura. After all, Dexter could do with a break from the rigours of heartbreak patrol.

In the meantime I would pay a visit to Half Moon Street with the one disk that was the perfect cure for a headache.

Robin turned painfully in his bed. It felt as if some rather important connection between hair and scalp had been severed, that a sudden move would leave him bald and bloody, his mop lying on the pillow like a dead animal in the road. His nose was a bad joke, misshapen and vast enough to impinge on his vision in both eyes as if he had been the victim of some vengeful transplant surgeon. Now and then the delayed shock of his treatment at the hands of the loon caused fits of tears and shakes which left him damp, runny-nosed and trembling.

The police didn't believe him. Taking down his

statement, the tired, good-looking constable had shown all the interest of a traffic warden writing out a ticket. Laura fussed over him, only losing her good humour when Robin tried to talk about Goodenough, Jane and Ollie.

'Please go back to work,' she said, laying a cool hand on his. 'Alan Gyles is worried about the company. This Ollie business, it's making you unhappy. You're different.'

'He wanted me to be his literary executor.'

'He's a bad influence, even now.'

Robin smiled. 'He was always a bad influence, wasn't he?'

'You're sick, Robin. I was hoping this would make you see sense.'

He was unable to sleep for any length of time, but drifted in and out of consciousness, his mind full of feverish memories of himself when young, with that heroic villain, that enigma, that little pile of malicious dust, Ollie Sincton.

Why had he liked Ollie? Why had anyone liked Ollie?

Two days after Robin had been attacked, Laura brought him breakfast in bed. The swelling around his nose had subsided but, with two neat black eyes, he looked like a Disney owl.

'Good news at last,' said Laura, sitting at the end of the bed. 'I've just heard from Claire Nash. She's got a major project lined up.'

'Congratulations.'

'Not me, you. She wants to represent you.'

Robin frowned, then winced. 'Me? Are you behind this?'

'It's the first I've heard about it.' Laura stood up, catching her reflection in the mirror. 'I said you'd go in on Friday.'

'Like this?'

She walked to her dressing table, opened a drawer and returned to the bed with a pair of dark glasses which she carefully lowered on to her husband's nose. She stepped back and smiled.

'Perfect,' she said.

12

In Media Village the silences of Claire Nash were legendary. While others gushed and hustled, she remained quiet. With her expensive clothes and dark, fine-boned good looks, she might have been mistaken for an accomplished society hostess or the wife of a successful diplomat, but Nash hated parties, was too busy for gossip and had long ago outgrown matrimony.

The deceptively passive style with which she conducted her business had evolved by accident. She had come to London in 1971, Mademoiselle Claire Jullien, a fragile nineteen year old from Angers engaged to an English timber merchant several years her senior called Frederick Nash. Shortly after her marriage, Claire had found work in the foreign rights department of Morley Browne, a dusty, tweed-and-pipe literary agency, now defunct.

Something awful happened between Mr and Mrs Nash, some dire bedroom tragedy. After six months, Frederick Nash left to take up employment in Canada; his wife remained in London. When the divorce was finalized, she surprised her colleagues at Morley Browne by informing them that she had no intention of returning to France, that she would pursue her career in London. Indeed, she would retain her new English name.

Marriage and agency work changed Claire Nash. As if determined to lose all trace of the charm and frivolity associated with the country of her birth, she forced herself to buy English clothes and adopted a severe upper-middle-class accent in which only a slight difficulty with the letter 'r' betrayed her. When someone, in a mood of misplaced gallantry, addressed her in French, she would reply, without a smile, in English.

Nash's unhappy experience of matrimony had persuaded her that more satisfaction was to be gained from making money than from any kind of intimacy. Her private life was put on hold until she was in her mid-thirties when, by now an influential agent with her own business, she became mildly besotted with a young actress from the Royal Shakespeare Company. Since then, her sexuality had ceased to be a secret, the more daring literary gossips referring to her as part of a high-powered sapphic network known as 'the Muffia'.

During her early years as an agent, Nash had taken to rationing her words, enunciating carefully. A quick learner, she discovered that what had initially been a strategy of self-defence was an offensive weapon of considerable potency. In a profession where words were cheap, unless written by a client, silence was stylish, strong. Over time, Nash's English accent had become more icily genteel, her technique of dumb negotiation more honed and lethal.

Yet no producer could afford to refuse the invitation to a working lunch in that airy, desk-free office of hers. After the driest of sherries, some smoked salmon would be served by one of her startlingly attractive assistants (Matthew, Saskia, Bryon). Then, having allowed a minute or two for social chat, Nash would establish, in her clear, good-natured tones, the 'parameters of discussion', smiling, frowning, as calm as a monk, before allowing silence to do its deadly work.

The strength of these silences was that they were entirely neutral. Having made her case, she would sit back impassively, waiting for the opposition to crumble, never showing anger or impatience. You might, if you were aware of these things, sense a whisper of disappointment in the wings, but she was much too well mannered to hint that her time was very, very precious, that every second of this never-ending void could be better and more profitably employed. It was the subtlest, cruellest form of negotiation: people would do anything to break that moment – present wild, instantly regretted bids, crack absurd jokes, offer incentives – *anything* to get the words flowing again.

The worst mistake an adversary could make on these occasions was to descend to flattery or even flirtation. Sooner or later, the man who, for reasons of habit, embarrassment or genuine lust, introduced a note of intimacy into a business conversation with Nash would pay for it. She didn't like that sort of thing, not at all. It insulted her.

Nash worked at her craft, adding different gradations of colour to her silences: ice-cold blue; bleak and weary grey; ominous, threatening red. When delivered at the right time, with those unwavering eyes, it rarely failed. She was never obliged to spell out her message: 'Keep talking' or 'Much, much too low' or 'We both know what I want, don't we' or, most frequent of all, 'More, please.' The silence did it all.

At a moment of supreme inner strength, fortified perhaps by a couple of powerful mood-changing pills, Robin might just have resisted the force of a Claire Nash silence. He could have struggled to his feet, prowled the minimalist office, broken the spell by chattering about the rather unusual view over Soho. But he was bruised and uncertain when, wearing Laura's dark glasses, he went to see her.

Hardly had the sherry hit the bottom of the glass before Nash explained that she needed to talk project.

'It's about Laura, I suppose?' Robin asked, wondering what kind of bizarre career move Nash had dreamt up for her client that could involve him.

'Laura?' Nash frowned. 'I'm talking to you as a person not a husband. As an expert.'

'Expert?'

Nash weighed her words carefully. 'As a merchandiser,' she said. 'You have many admirers in the business . . . Which is why you're on a shortlist for a project which could make you, well, a household name, bringing you some really quite significant rewards.'

'A shortlist of how many?'

'One.'

Robin hated opportunity, particularly when offered with compliments. Opportunity led to challenge, followed inevitably by disappointment. There was something in his personality which resolutely refused to rise to the occasion. 'I'm not that experienced,' he said. 'I happen to have been involved in something which was reasonably successful but, as to working to a brief, I'm really not sure.' The summary of his many and varied professional failings took some time before Robin spluttered inarticulately to a halt. No-one could fail to be unimpressed.

Claire Nash, in a kind of intense reverie, looked at him for what seemed to be a couple of hours, and then smiled.

'You're so fucking English, Robin,' she said almost affectionately. 'You just adore to run yourself down. You have, believe me, a very special artistic talent.' She was talking so quietly that Robin found himself sitting on the edge of his chair in an effort to hear what she was saying. 'You should use it.'

'Maybe,' he said, laughing foolishly.

Nash reached out to press an intercom on the low table before her. 'The Robin Nicholl file, please,' she murmured. Moments later Saskia entered and gave a file to her employer, offering Robin the full VIPs-only smile as she left the office.

'Saskia will be looking after you,' said Nash. She pulled a single sheet of paper from the file. 'Here's the deal,' she said. 'You'll like it.' She paused before proceeding in precise, economical sentences to outline a proposal based on a series of children's programmes to be introduced on the West Coast for the international market. It was high profile, a good idea, seductively straightforward. Robin would be required to design books, toys and articles of clothing. His work would be the basis of the series.

Nash paused, as if awed by the sweet moneyed simplicity of it all. 'You cannot turn this down, Robin,' she said finally.

'But why me?' Robin asked.

'The Coast feels you're under-used. I agree.'

'It's incredible.'

'I've looked through the proposal on your behalf and I can see only two drawbacks. One, you have to accept me as your agent—'

Robin laughed politely, but Nash gave a shrug of her narrow shoulders, suggesting that not everyone wished to be represented by the best agent in London.

'The other is the schedule's . . . rather tight. It would be full-time work for nine months. As from next week.'

'Ah. That might be a problem.'

'I understood from Laura that you had no immediate commitments.'

'Not professional commitments, no.'

'The chance of a lifetime, Robin. The chance . . .'

It was now that Claire Nash deployed a major silence – an ice-blue, mid-sentence lung-crusher of a silence. Robin writhed. He muttered questions which died in his throat. He sighed. He embarked on a foolish monologue which quickly petered out. He thrashed about in that still pool while Nash watched him pitilessly as he drowned. Days passed, weeks. Dry-mouthed but dripping with sweat, Robin managed to say, 'I'll talk to Laura.'

'Do that. I'll stay in the office until I hear from you this afternoon. Congratulations.' She held out a hand. 'I think you just got rich.'

'I'll call you,' said Robin, shaking Nash's hand with a half-bow and backing towards the door.

In the blazing heat Robin walked from Nash's office down Piccadilly into the territory that had once been Ollie Sincton's, a key for the flat in Half Moon Street in his pocket. It was odd how unobservant the modern policeman could be, he reflected.

'Sir?' The doorman looked up at Robin from a desk in the lobby.

'I have to work on the late Mr Sincton's papers,' he said.

'Would you have any documentation?'

'Only—' Robin reached into the top pocket of his jacket in which, by chance, was a twenty-pound note '—this,' he said with a new confidence. He had survived a lunch with Claire Nash; getting into Ollie's flat was nothing.

'Fine, sir,' said the doorman without any particular gratitude.

Apart from a thin layer of dust over the furniture and surfaces, the flat seemed the same as when he had last been there shortly after Ollie's death. There was an unpleasant smell in the kitchen which Robin traced to a cheese dish on the top of the fridge.

He sat at the desk in the sitting-room and opened a drawer. Inside he found one of Ollie's packets of cigarettes and, although they were stale and Robin hadn't smoked for years, he lit up now, putting his feet on the desk.

Ollie, Robin remembered, had liked Mayfair.

Home at last. From the moment I moved into Jane's dinky flat in Half Moon Street, I knew this was where I was meant to be. It was all so simple: shit, Jane, I just can't seem to work on your daddy's memoirs in Putney where half a dozen neighbours are simultaneously extending their houses upwards and sideways.

And Jane, through some nobby contact I really don't want to know too much about, came up with Half Moon Street, a week-by-week arrangement, low rent, which suits my needs just fine. I might even do some work here.

English history, the great heritage – you can keep it. What I like about Mayfair is the way its past – the bad old world of style and class, the square mile of money, clubland, the Ritz, privileged dorks drifting about in evening clothes – has been entirely erased by the present. No part of London could be less English than Mayfair – the cash, the people, the atmosphere are bland and international. Its cottage industries are gambling, hustling in art, hotels, spying (I'm told MI5 favours the area for its safe houses) and, of course, whoring, only one of which is a naturally English occupation. It's like a great vacuum at the centre of the city.

Home.

Robin stretched his arms and yawned. He looked forward to telling Laura about the Coast's interest in his work, although explaining why he would be turning the project down would perhaps be not quite so easy. Casually, he opened another drawer in the desk. The plastic casing of a computer disk knocked against the wood. Frowning, Robin took it out. Printed on the cover in Ollie's neat handwriting was the word 'LAURA'.

A small confession. When I had put James Dexter on full-time crumpet duty, it had not been with any great sense of optimism. As far as I was concerned, it was a useful apprenticeship for the lad: see your first body, face your first riot, survive your first grope in a singles bar; it's all part of a policeman's education.

But Dexter took his quest very seriously. He had worked his way through Sincton's magazines, sending off a brief autobiography and snapshot to those names Ollie had marked. The letters may have been touchingly sub-literate (women looking for 'good conversation' were unlikely to find much encouragement) but the photograph was irresistible. Out of sixteen submissions, Dexter received thirteen takers, only one of whom failed to show at the Bunch of Grapes where he had chosen to make his halting, uneasy pitch.

Twelve hot dates! Sometimes (I fear that quite often our man would make his excuses and leave before matters progressed beyond the conversational), he saw three in an evening. No wonder that, a week after Operation Casanova had been set in train, he looked drawn and tetchy as he laid a four-page progress report on my desk.

'Excellent, James,' I said. 'How many are there still to see?'

'Five more replies came in this morning.'

'A policeman's work is never done.'

'It doesn't feel like police work.'

'One of them may be the murderer. It's useful what you're doing.'

The telephone on my desk rang which Dexter took as a cue to leave. I picked up.

'Simon, Norman, *Crime Time*.' Biddle's voice had reached the upper registers, a sure sign of impending excitement. 'Jonathan's going for it. We need you at the pre-prod case conf next week.'

'The what?'

'Jonathan's coming in next Wednesday, eleven a.m. – can you do? And your undercover man, we'll need him there.'

'That's fine, Norman.'

'Keep this under your hat, Simon, but I think we could be talking Crime of the Month with this one.'

'Golly,' I said. 'Shame that we brought our suspect in this morning.'

'*What?* What the fuck are you talking about?'

I laughed. 'Only kidding, Norman. I'll see you on Wednesday.'

Crime of the Month. Joy would be pleased at least. Sighing, I reached for Dexter's report and turned to the list of his girlfriends to date.

BARBARA SMITH (suspect false name). Short blond hair, late thirties, big girl. Says not interested in one-night stands. Showed no reaction when I mentioned the Sincton case.

LINDSAY BAKER. Dark, small, forties, married. Mentioned husband Tony a lot (suspect he may be involved sexually). No reaction to Sincton story. Invited me back on first date (declined). Insisted 'no rough stuff'.

JO CULLEN. Quite young (late twenties). Reddish hair. Has child looked after by her mother. Seemed shocked by Sincton story. Said only available on Tuesday nights when mother goes to bingo.

PAULA MATTHEWS. Late thirties, unmarried. Part-time barmaid. Talks a lot, particularly about writing stories for magazines. May have drink problem. Did not react when I mentioned Sincton.

INGE CARLSSON. Danish, blonde, forties, quite big, divorced (maybe twice). Works in computers and seems intelligent. When I mentioned Sincton case, she asked if I liked bondage. Follow up with police interview?

And so on. What a charade, I thought to myself. Poor Barbara, Inge and the rest of them. All they had wanted

131

was a spot of tactile reassurance. Yet here they were, their most intimate needs recorded and scrutinized because, in this incorrigibly wicked world, nothing was simple any more: one moment you were after a Tuesday-night tumble while Mum's down at bingo, the next you were part of a murder investigation; one person's bondage was another's knife in the throat.

I walked out of the office. Dexter was sorting through the latest batch of love-mail on his desk.

'Doesn't seem to be an obvious psychopath here,' I said.

'No.' He looked up at me. 'They're really very ordinary, you know.'

'I can see. This Inge – could her bondage have got out of hand?'

'Doubt it. She seemed the sanest of the lot. It's just her hobby. Do you want me to interview her?'

A vision of my colleague under the lash of a hefty Dane flashed before me. 'I don't think that's necessary. What was all this about a writer?'

'Paula? Bit scatty, bit sad. Not Ollie's type at all, I would have thought. The only surprising thing about her was that, in his notes, he referred to her as a teacher, didn't say anything about her writing.'

'Odd.' I'd have to look into that. 'By the way, keep next Wednesday morning free. It seems we're going to be on *Crime Time*.'

To his considerable credit, Dexter was clearly un-excited by the prospect of fame.

'That's all we bloody need,' he said, reaching for the next handwritten letter on his desk.

Staring out at her small paving-stone garden, Laura dialled her agent's home number.

'What did you say to him?' It was almost a wail of despair. 'What have you done, Claire?'

There was a pause.

'Robin? We had a very useful meeting, after which

he said he would go away and think about it.'

'You didn't tell him anything about us?'

'Don't be absurd. What is all this, Laura?'

'He appears to have moved out. A suitcase has gone, some clothes. He just scrawled a note – "Can't explain right now. I'll be in touch."'

'Sounds like he's having one of his decisive turns.'

'Don't.' Laura hated the way Claire spoke of her husband. 'It's not like him to do this. He's just taken the Custard Beast and gone.'

'Dare I ask what the Custard Beast is?'

'It's his car, a yellow Morris. He called it—'

Claire was laughing. 'I'm sorry,' she said. 'I can't help it.'

'Oh, you wouldn't understand.'

Laura slammed down the receiver and, for the first time since one of her novels had been savaged by a critic in the *Sunday Times*, she wept.

Part Two

13

It was four days since Robin Nicholl had left home and already he was on what Alan Gyles liked to call a 'learning curve'. He knew the truth about Ollie Sincton's greatest triumph and the part his wife had played in it. He knew that, while he was ill-equipped after his hasty departure (too many ties, not enough socks, no address book and last year's diary), his initial worry that Laura would close their joint account and starve him of funds had been unfounded. And, although there was much of which he remained ignorant, he knew that London – even hot, mad, tropical London – was not as frightening as he had once thought.

Yet sometimes, as he looked down from the window in Ollie's flat to the street, humming and seething with life below him, he felt alien, like a missionary in a foreign land. This was no longer an English summer; it was a Delhi summer, high season in Riyadh. And what the hell was happening out there? If he closed his eyes he could imagine dark-skinned street traders, limbless beggars howling from the gutter, knife gangs, fat and raucous whores, mangy donkeys, camels belaboured by angry men with silver teeth.

But no, this was England. There were traders, of course – drugs mostly, but now and then hot watches or fake smells in fake bottles – and beggars, huddled in doorways, wrapped in blankets despite the heat, and, God knows, enough whores to service an army. The only animals to be seen were killer dogs, red-eyed and broad-shouldered, proudly paraded in massive leather and chain restraining gear by beefy men who wore T-shirts bearing cheerfully abusive messages: 'LOOKING

FOR LOVE BUT SEX WILL DO'; 'SAME SHIT — DIFFERENT DAY'; 'GET LOST, DICKHEAD!' Or, most sinister of all, the shirts consisted of a plain Union Jack, on which no words were necessary.

London was fighting back. This bedlam was home grown. Visitors expecting to find a nation in charming, decrepit decay were startled by its vibrant energy, its career muggers and motivated dossers, its upwardly mobile call-girls. Maybe that was why Ollie had liked it so much here in the deafening, cosmopolitan epicentre of the new England. It was a party, wild and out of control, careering dangerously towards the dawn.

Londoners had yet to learn the protocol of corruption. They didn't know where to stop. High spirits were expressed with murder, good humour with rape. One afternoon Robin had heard the sound of beery cheers and laughter. He looked down to see twenty or thirty youths, some white, some black, making their way up the street, hugging strangers, dancing from one alarmed tourist to the next. It was only when he caught the flash of a blade that Robin realized they were taking valuables as they went, hoovering up anything worth selling. The next day three smartly dressed young men had approached two teenage Asians and, after a few moments' conversation, punched them to the ground. A middle-aged tourist who protested was thrown against the wall. Seconds later, two dark vans and a police car drew up disgorging a number of uniformed officers who, after the Asians and the tourist had been taken away, congratulated their colleagues, the smartly dressed young men.

Casual sex was often involuntary. The local paper told the story of a Swedish au pair girl who asked directions to Piccadilly Circus from three lads sitting outside a pub in Bayswater. They took her the scenic route, through a wasteland of squats and derelict buildings to an evil-smelling flat in some forgotten part of North Kensington. Tearful and distraught – no sense of humour, these Scandinavians – she was found in a graveyard in Golders Green by a whey-faced, middle-aged man who, having offered to help, apologetically pushed her to the ground behind a large stone coffin and joined the party. He grumbled a lot, she told the police later, as if it had somehow been her fault.

Every day Robin would spend hours visiting the places Ollie had once known: the Bunch of Grapes, the Groucho, media watering-holes in Covent Garden. As he strode through the streets of London, unshaven, muttering to himself, still wearing Laura's dark glasses, people stared. Yet their eyes were not guarded, evasive or embarrassed but curious, interested – in the case of the girl who offered him a drink at the Grapes, very interested. What they saw was no longer the shambling, feckless husband Robin had once been, a mid-life trauma on the move, but someone alive, in a hurry, maybe dangerous. If he happened to take off the glasses to reveal yellowing bruises around his eyes, he was regarded with even more respect. A bit of a scrapper perhaps, but a true Londoner.

He became attuned to the quickening pace of human relationships. Just as the dusty pavements were littered with evidence of hastily snatched hamburgers, paper bags full of greasy chips consumed on the march, so it was with men and women. Fast food, fast sex, everyone was grabbing what they wanted. As soon as your back was turned, they were upon one another, quickly, furtively, as if going for some kind of bizarre sexual record. It seemed, Robin thought, utterly without pleasure; at least when other civilizations entered a downward spiral of terminal decadence, there were a few good times on the way. Not now. Flirtation was out, foreplay an occasional indulgence. Next, next, next.

Or maybe he was imagining all this: the noise

outside, the violence, the edgy, rampant misbehaviour of the English in decline.

That afternoon when Robin had visited Claire Nash's office, he had found the agent in conversation with her receptionist. There was something about the angle of her body, the way the employee looked up at her, that suggested a subtext of surprising intimacy. It couldn't be, could it? Did Claire like women or had Robin been infected, inflamed by Ollie's version? Then, when Saskia walked into the room, she had glanced at him, the VIP look, allowing her heavy blond hair to fall forward so that, unseen by Nash, she was peeking at him, playful, hopeful. Take the offer, the message appeared to be; become a purveyor of bicoastal packages, do it for me, for us. Saskia with Robin? No, really, if that was on, anything was permissible. What was it? Ambition? Curiosity? Boredom? The need to conform? What exactly was wrong with men of her own age? Where had all the boys gone?

Once, at one of Laura's parties, he had found himself talking to a beautiful, languid, unshaven youth with dark, curling hair. Their conversation was impeded by a number of women, fluttering about the man in a helpless state of desire. He deflected them wearily like a colonialist brushing away flies. No, he didn't have a girlfriend, he had said; he couldn't be bothered with all that any more. Now it occurred to Robin that, if you were under twenty-five, there were many more amusing and useful things than sex: fashion, words, success.

Thirty: that was when people began to misbehave. And by the time they reached tubby, stringy, desperate middle age, all fear of disapproval, scandal, heartbreak or danger had disappeared. It was strange.

Robin slept badly, suffering, for the first time in his life, from feverishly disjointed dreams in which, everywhere he turned, the world was in hot-breathed conspiracy against him. One night it would be Jane with a balding, self-conscious stranger who, on closer inspection, proved to be none other than the detective in charge, yours truly, DI Potter. Then he would be in a city street, nervously aware that something was amiss. The row of shops he was walking past seemed to be banks, each one with a hooded cash machine outside. He bent down to look into the small, letter-box screen of one of them. It showed, in silent, explicit detail, a blue movie, the star of which, he realized with horror and shame, was Laura – naked, leaning back over her desk, writhing under the eager form of Ollie Sincton. There was a queue of people behind Robin, and he was aware of them becoming restless, but was unable to tear himself away. One detail in particular would haunt him later. Laura was lying on the keyboard of a word-processor; as Sincton thrust at her, words and sentences were filling the screen. He awoke, calling her name.

Considering how distressed she had appeared to be when reporting Robin's disappearance, Laura was surprisingly unhelpful when I paid an unscheduled visit to the family home and asked whether I could see her husband's office.

'Do you have a warrant, Inspector?' she asked.

I smiled. Although she was pale and had lost weight, Laura looked good. 'I could get one if it made you happier, Mrs Nicholl,' I said.

'No.' She sighed. 'I'll show you.'

As she took me to the top of the house, she put on a fine show of embarrassment. 'I don't often venture up here,' she said. 'You'll see why.'

She opened the door with a humorous flourish. 'The world of Robin Nicholl,' she said.

Immediately, I could see the problem. There had been an air of decorous, slightly bohemian disorder to the rest of the house but here confusion was fully off the leash.

'Oh dear,' I said.

If it's true that style is the man, then Robin was in trouble; this was not the work station of a person at ease with himself. Frankly, I've seen flats done over by a gang of teenage vandals on a crack binge left in a better state.

Sensibly, Laura stayed at the door as I entered, treading something into the carpet as I went. I glanced around, taking it all in: the dust, the papers on the floor, the dead flowers, the coffee cups organic with mould, the overflowing waste-paper basket, the chipped Max Beanbag mug, the – no, please – pair of mildewy underpants over a radiator, odd scatterings which Forensic would, I fear, reveal to be toe-cuttings and – enough. You get the picture.

'And you have no idea where he is?' I asked.

'God knows. He left a message on the answering machine yesterday. He sounded quite cheerful.'

I looked at her and for a moment I wanted to step across the room strewn with her husband's trash and put an arm around her shoulder, she looked so abandoned. It was no place for Laura Nicholl, purveyor of glitter to the masses; she deserved better than this. After all, on the general scale of things, a spot of cheating is of no great significance when you've given as much pleasure to so many ordinary people as Laura had.

'Perhaps,' I said, as I picked my way through the debris back to the door, 'you could ask Mr Nicholl to contact me if he rings again.'

'Yes, I will, of course.'

As she showed me out, I asked her casually whether she was working on a new novel.

'Not right now. There's going to be a bit of a gap.'

'Ah. My wife will be disappointed.'

'Research takes time.'

'Of course.' It would.

Sad to say, Sincton had been right about Laura.

14

Robin lay in his dark room, half-lit by neon from the street outside, his eyes wide open, his breathing fast and shallow. He felt tense and engaged, as if at any moment something wild and sinister could happen, something dangerous where he was at the centre, he was the danger. Haggard and red-eyed, he paced the floor, now and then standing in front of the window. He had read all he needed to know about Ollie and Laura; yet still he returned to the word-processor.

In a career notable for the almost dull recurrence of brilliant, marketable ideas, this is the ultimate. It's a killer of a project. Laura's fine, apart from a certain squeamishness – justified in my view – about keeping Robin in the dark. Claire Nash is fine. And, of course, I'm absolutely fine.

Eight years ago Laura had been a journalist, a second lieutenant in the human-interest army, first over the battlements when it came to plucky kids with terminal illnesses, or arthritic Northern grannies who wrote bestsellers, or the loyal wives of errant cabinet ministers. Her editor, a trim, hard-faced woman, had once predicted great things for her, but Laura's writing lacked 'the tear-duct factor'. She held back from the outrageously maudlin, frequently including jokes and puns in her pieces which suggested a worldliness quite out of keeping with the girl next door. Too bright for bleeding-heart journalism, yet uninterested in the big political and economic issues: it was an unpromising position. She had also failed, almost uniquely among her generation, to establish a part-time relationship of mutual benefit with a senior editor of either sex. As a result, she was slightly mistrusted: to be clever, to look as good as she did and yet to be cheerfully faithful to her crumpled loser of a husband, who was trying to run a restaurant at the time, showed a lack of seriousness.

Yet Laura was ambitious. Oliver Sincton had noticed that when, late one night, he called to see Robin at work. After the last drinker had been ejected and Robin was washing up glasses in the kitchen, Ollie had sat at the bar talking to Laura, casually describing to her his killer of a project.

As he had expected, Laura nibbled at the bait. The next day she telephoned him, suggesting they do lunch. The rest was easy.

Laura's hot to trot. A bright girl, she sees the crushing unanswerable logic of a proposal which can't fail.

Theoretical backdrop: right now, book publishers are experiencing one of their occasional boom periods. They need product. They're crazy for tales of glamour, money and perverse sex. That, and the kind of celebrity trash I turn out in my spare time.

There's no shortage of raunch – it's the suppliers who are the problem. Jowly Hollywood screenwriters, dumpy middle-aged romancers turned bad, spivvy journalists with a fictional bent throng agents' offices with beautifully presented proposals for boardroom-to-bedroom sagas replete with brand names, sophisticated cocktails and every type of orgasm imaginable.

No problem, I can do that. But who wants to read a silk-sheets saga by Oliver D. Sincton?

If only I were Olivia Sincton, sultry model with an eventful romantic past, draped around the cover in a state of undress, lips slightly parted as if to say 'Do it to me, dear reader', appearing on chat shows to deflect teasingly the prurient questions of an interviewer. Now that would be something. The author as sexpot, as highly desired role model. Curl up in bed with Olivia's book and it will almost be like curling up with Olivia herself. She's part of the fantasy.

Catch my drift? Laura did. In the television age, the writer – the real writer, that is, the one that pulls in serious money – has a double role: to make with the words and to provide the on-air fantasy, to write and to promote. And here's the problem. Sexy little Olivia Sincton is far too busy living her life – her in-depth research – to put down all those words in more or less the correct order. And who would buy a used fantasy from tired old Oliver?

'Joint authorship?' asks Laura, sharp as a whip.

'Too messy. Blurs the image.'

'You mean—?'

I nod. 'We cheat.'

She laughs at the glorious simplicity of it all. 'Fifty per cent?'

'I'm comfortable with that.'

So we get to work.

Robin could hear Ollie's voice. Staring into the darkness, he saw him, laughing and happy, at work with Laura. These days he lived on three or four hours' sleep a night. Like Suzi Ashbourn at the moment when her coke and speed cocktail was on the turn before the sickening downward plummet, like me on the trail of Frank Dimond, the vision of Joy before my eyes, Robin was in a state of heightened consciousness, tense and volatile. He had the picture now: Ollie, Laura, Nash. He saw it all with icy clarity.

Was Claire Nash taken in at first? Probably not. Laura Nicholl's proposal had arrived with the flotsam and jetsam that any successful agent attracts. Nash's assistant of the time, a vague Eurasian with green eyes by the name of Raksha, read the sample chapters one evening, reporting the next day that the pages were fine, competent, but basically one of those so-what projects, you know? Nash nodded, yes, next. Pity, said Raksha, putting them aside, because she looks nice. The agent glanced at the photograph of Laura attached to the letter. Is there a number? Nash asked. Raksha, slightly annoyed (not only was her literary judgement impugned but she had spent a couple of afternoons herself with Claire since landing this job), left the paperless office as the agent reached for her telephone.

'Laura Nicholl?' she said. 'Claire Nash. Just read your chapters for *Ruby Midnight*. I think we might have something here. Could we meet?'

Like Ollie, Nash knew that the age of the book personality had arrived. The text mattered, of course, but it was the total package that was important. A sexy concept, sure, if possible with a title that snared the brain, but a sexy author too. Articulate, accessible, eager to learn the art of discreet vulgarity that these days passed for charm. 'Promotable' was a key word in Nash's vocabulary.

She riffled through the so-what chapters on which Ollie had worked so hard, and was impressed. The writing was crisply sardonic, witty but with a soft centre. 'Reader, look at these people' was its subtext. 'So rich, so beautiful, so successful, so sexually inventive – and yet so unhappy. Deep down they're as fucked up as you or me. All their achievements, about which I'll be telling you in lip-smacking detail, have merely brought them misery.' Yes, it actually made the punter – beached, pink and peeling on holiday, propped up at home beside a snoring, over-weight husband – feel superior, made her thank the Lord for her ordinariness. The action moved with commendable economy from film studio to boudoir. In those first sixty pages there was only one sex scene, a pleasingly perverse seven-page epic involving a decadent film producer, his bisexual wife and a briefly virginal starlet. It contained combinations which made even Claire Nash raise an eyebrow. She read it twice, then glanced again at the photograph of Laura, so laughing and knowing. Yes, it worked. Author, concept, tone. As a total package, it positively sang.

Agent and fledgling author lunched at a restaurant in Soho. They hit it off. Apart from one tricky moment when Laura forgot the name of one of her characters, she was perfect: worldly yet good-humoured, warmly businesslike. A strong project, an author who offered professional, maybe even personal, advantage; Claire felt good about it.

Robin, naturally, was no trouble at all. A few hours later Laura found him at the restaurant and told him that London's top literary agent was going to sell the novel she had been working on at the office. Publishers would be invited to compete in a sudden-death auction.

'That's fantastic.' Robin actually blushed with pride. 'What exactly is a sudden-death auction?'

'One bid and that's it. You gamble on publishers throwing themselves at you in one wild moment of impulsive generosity. It's a good time for it, apparently; they're all feeling terribly rich but insecure. They want new talent. Claire, my agent, is a tremendous believer in sudden death.'

'When does it happen?' Robin asked, his head in the fridge as he searched for a bottle of champagne.

'Claire wants a couple of changes. Then there's the photo session and off we go.'

'Photo session?'

'Author pic.' Laura had the good grace to look abashed. 'Publishers need the total package.'

'The total package.' Robin shook his head in admiration. How he had underestimated that wife of his, working away, springing her success on him. He

147

popped the champagne. 'My wife, the novelist,' he said proudly.

Ollie was pleased too.

The publishers cream. Claire sets up a photo session with a fat, bald man who produces a heartbreakingly glamorous photograph of Laura at her desk, legs cutely crossed with schoolgirl concentration, lips nibbling thoughtfully at a pen. Claire sends it to a selection of publishers, majoring on romantically inclined males with unhappy marriages. They fall like skittles. They ache for sudden death at Laura's feet. It's shockingly easy.

Claire has added one neat little twist to the normal auction procedure. Laura Nicholl is a major author of the future, she tells the publishers. While she's eager to make a killing – the precise phrase is 'We'll be looking for serious commitment' – she also needs to be confident that, when she takes that important decision, she will be among friends: an editor who can work with her (soft chortle from O. Sincton), an art director who will avoid vulgarity of presentation (splutter of barely restrained laughter from O. Sincton) and a marketing team whose media plan will be subtle and dignified (O. Sincton now rolling around the floor clutching his sides). For this reason, Laura would very much like to visit publishers interested in her work. These casual, get-to-know-you sessions would be taken into consideration come Sudden-Death Day.

Of course, neither Claire nor her new author nor her author's mentor, winging it behind the scenes, has the slightest interest in the publishers. The point of her visits is not some obscure bonding process – we know that all the editors will be sincere and charming, the art directors will be inarticulate and brilliant, the marketing team will behave as if failing to acquire her book would cause them all to commit suicide, some

pin-striped bastard will descend from the top floor to
assure her that she will be treasured at the highest,
most fiscal level. No, we just want the chance to
parade that essential part of the package, the author
herself.

And of course they love her, even the women. Their
bids rocket when they discover at first hand the
sensuous charm, the shapely wit, the sheer bloody
promotability of the product before them. It's a
masterstroke.

£50,000. £70,000. £85,000. £105,000. These are the
blind bids which my words, Claire's murderous Gallic
cunning and Laura's allure pull in. In the end, we
squeeze Alec Frewen, a balding, beer-gutted former
hippy working within a firm owned by a cold-eyed Old
Etonian – both of whom, naturally, have extra-
editorial designs on Laura – up to £110,000, the
sudden-death rules being bent for their, and our,
benefit. Claire, Laura and the love-struck publishers
celebrate their blind bid – no bid has ever been blinder
– over an expensive lunch.

Later Laura and I dine out at a modest but accept-
able Indian restaurant in Holland Park and consider
Ruby's UST. Then she goes home to Robin to give him
an edited version of our brilliant coup.

Ollie was convinced that the formula for bestselling
glamour fiction should include not only wealth,
beauty, deals and death but what he called a Unique
Sexual Trick, an erotic gimmick that would be the
subject of conversation at Tupperware parties
throughout the country.

With characteristic thoroughness, he had spent a
month making notes in the Special Books section of
the British Library, combing works of arcane sexual
lore, from H. Cutner's *Short History of Sex Worship*
(1940) to L.F. Rasmussen's *Curiosities of Erotic Life in
the Orient* (1956), before settling on an exotic practice,

said to be popular in Tahiti, involving the intimate and thoroughly inhumane deployment of young frogs in the act of love. As Ollie anticipated, the ponds of Britain were invaded by a host of sexually adventurous women after the publication of *Ruby Midnight*, causing outraged comment from the RSPCA and the Council for the Protection of Rural England. The book's success was assured.

It was frog-insertion that Ollie was discussing in the Raj Tandoori House the evening that Laura became a professional author. They talked about other Unique Sexual Tricks to be included in future Sincton/Nicholl productions, and laughed late into the night about the vanity of human desire.

Robin had been working at the time. Now he was working again.

15

Detective Constable James Dexter and I sat in the absurdly spacious office of Detective Superintendent Norman Biddle that Wednesday morning, awaiting our first pre-prod case conf. It was eleven o'clock and neither Biddle nor *Crime Time*'s producer Jonathan Miles-Thomas had appeared.

'Ten minutes we give it, James,' I said. 'Then it's back to the real world.'

Dexter ran a hand through his dark hair. He looked shattered. 'Bloody television,' he said.

At eight minutes past eleven Biddle burst into the office, exuding breathless self-importance.

'Simon, Dexter, sorry.' He threw himself into his leather executive chair. 'Bit of a shit-storm upstairs, I'm afraid. We're going to have to tighten this thing up before we bring Jonathan on board. Frankly we have a problem.'

Dexter and I waited in silence as Biddle paused dramatically.

'There's been a copycat murder based on last month's *Crime Time*. Some crazed teenager is claiming that the programme gave him the MO.'

'That'll help the ratings.'

'True,' said Biddle, a stranger to irony, 'but to be honest it's the kind of sequel we can do without. That's why I really want to push the Sincton case. It's sexy, without presenting major role-model problems.'

'Norman, there have been one or two developments since we last spoke,' I said.

He looked up sharply. 'You haven't arrested anyone, have you?'

'No. We think Suzi Ashbourn could tell us a bit more and Dexter here has come up with one or two possible leads with his undercover.'

'Good good.' Biddle fixed me with a candid smile. 'Now it's the undercover stuff I wanted to talk about. My problem is that, while I see your case as being well worth the airtime, Jonathan's not a policeman like you and me. He's a television man. You've read about the Oxfordshire rapist.'

'Of course.'

'He's talking seriously about giving it the Crime of the Month spot instead of Sincton.'

'Oh damn,' I said.

'And he struck again yesterday.'

'Bad timing from our point of view.' I tried to keep a straight face. 'Some people will do anything to get on television.'

'Quite. If we lose out to this bloody rapist, we could be off *Crime Time* altogether.'

Clearly I failed to react with the correct degree of shocked disappointment. 'The way I see it,' Biddle said, 'we have to re-submit, counter this new rape with some developments in our case, sharpen it up in presentational terms. Give it a bit of . . . grit.'

'Grit?' I had to laugh. 'The man was handcuffed to a bed and stabbed in the neck. Isn't that gritty enough?'

'Sure sure, but what about the investigation? From your report – forgive me, Simon – it looks as if you've just been wandering about asking a few questions.' He held up both hands. 'I know that's what police work tends to be but, forgive me, in televisual terms, it's slightly dull.'

'All right,' I said. 'James here has been meeting women the dead man may have slept with. Hanging out in a singles bar, acting like a punter.'

'Now we're talking,' said Biddle.

I turned to Dexter. 'James, perhaps you could tell the

superintendent about how you've been conducting your line of enquiries.'

Haltingly, looking my way occasionally, Dexter provided Biddle with his grit. Singles bars, relation-free sex, punishment freaks; this was more like it. Norman all but did a little dance on the spot.

'Would you be prepared to talk about this to camera?' he asked.

'There's the small problem of James's cover,' I interrupted.

'Yes, of course.' Biddle seemed irritated that the piffling demands of crime detection should stand in the way of some truly great television. 'Perhaps Special Effects could work on something.'

'Actors?'

'No.' Biddle appraised Dexter. 'I think it's best to use the real thing wherever possible.'

'What about the women?'

'Sincton's girls, his contacts. We need one of them to be interviewed – tell us more about the man, the whole contact scene.'

'Sir.' Dexter sat forward in his chair. 'I don't think—'

'Leave that with me, Norman,' I said.

In one sense, this account is like *Crime Time*; there's no room in it for the everyday banalities of police work: the dreary trudge from one unhelpful witness to the next, the taking of statements, hour after mind-numbing hour spent in the interview room. Likewise, my own domestic life. That noisy night out with Gary and his bleached blonde friend was hardly typical – nor, heaven knows, was the moment of tender conjugal reconciliation I have so movingly and unwisely described. A true record of the fortnight following the death of Oliver Sincton would, for example, take you to my garden where in a torn work-shirt I would be pruning the roses while nearby on the lawn, my wife, with her still acceptable figure, lies working on her tan. Or to a local park where I'd be watching my boys Mark (nine) and Dominic (seven) skateboarding. Shopping mornings, homework, fish-fingers in the kitchen, TV nights.

This is the edited version, shaped to make sense of it all, re-invented.

I had seen three of the women Dexter had chatted up in the Bunch of Grapes without learning anything particularly new. All of them admitted, under questioning, that they had met Sincton; all of them, I suspected, had been to bed with him. Yet Dexter was right. They were essentially ordinary; the idea that any of them had plunged a knife into the American's neck or decorated his intimate person with a doughnut was absurd.

That afternoon I was due to travel to East Sheen to interview Paula, who wrote stories or taught children or was a barmaid or simply told lies good enough to take in Oliver Sincton.

Paula was ideal for *Crime Time*, and she might even be helpful to the investigation itself. I needed a plausible witness to the private life of Oliver Sincton. Not a social date, or a fast stranger, both of which belonged to history, but a contact, someone who advertised for it.

Normal, that was what I wanted. Driving through East Sheen, quiet in the afternoon sun, with its gardens and estate cars with baby seats in the back, I thought of Joy, what she would have made of Ollie's legendary seduction technique.

Part-timers never understand. They have no concept of the time, the planning, the work, not to mention the risk – husbands, boyfriends, my other girlfriends – involved in serious promiscuity. Sometimes I think it needs a small company, complete with Personnel, Sales and Administration, to handle the affairs of Ollie Sincton. And all for what? Change, a private journey into the heart of darkness.

I see myself as an adventurer, evading the banal and domestic, forever pushing back the frontiers of admittedly tacky experience to move into territories unknown. In another age I might have been an explorer, a conqueror of mountains and forests. Now, although my quest is closer to home, the unexpected is still there. Maybe one day the heroic exploits of people like me, fighting the forces of boredom, will receive the public recognition they deserve. We'll be mobbed by reporters as we go to work on the Paula of the moment. Mr Sincton, why do you do it? And I'll pause, my eyes scanning a distant horizon, as if considering the question for the first time. Why? Why am I about to fuck Paula? Because she's there, I guess.

Not that she's exactly the Everest of seduction. I'm not particularly proud of Paula, as it happens, and she's quite possibly not proud of me.

Three years ago, a year ago, I might have had the nerve to call it off. When I see her the first time, sitting there at the bar, it hits me – Christ, she's no date – she's a grown-up, a person. What on earth is she doing advertising like that? What's she looking for?

So, standing at the door, it's not too late to get the hell out of it – but I'd feel bad leaving Paula there, a middle-aged woman alone in a bar. And so what if some of the adjectives in her advertisement could have used a few qualifiers – almost attractive, formerly brunette, for a start? And maybe she had shaved a few years off the top of her age. Neither of us was working in ideals any more. Paula was marginal and these days marginal was just fine.

We chat, we laugh, sound each other out, observe the proprieties of the blind date and, despite the spreading bum, the air of suburban ennui, I find myself warming to Paula. I like her sense of humour. It's going to be OK.

Paula's flat was in a house at the end of a quiet street.

For a few minutes I sat in my car a few yards away from her front door, wondering whether Gary visited our house while the boys and I were out. After all, if the Sinctons of this world (I saw them as lone scavengers, who didn't kill but infected beyond cure) could reach a back street of East Sheen, why not Purley? Perhaps Robin was right. Everyone – the nannies, the meter maids, the lady in the library – everyone was at it.

She appears on her doorstep in a T-shirt and jeans, her hair uncombed. She might have been opening the door to the milkman – perhaps she already has. At least I've put on a clean shirt and brought a bottle of champagne.

'I've come to service the boiler.'

She gives an abrupt laugh. 'That's nice,' she says, showing me through a hall to her ground-floor flat. I notice that she seems less relaxed than she had been at the bar, almost resentful that, by taking up her offer, I've put her in this position.

She leads me into the kitchen and pours me a glass of wine from a bottle that has already been opened. Relaxed conversation, a welcoming glass of sherry in the sitting-room, is rarely an option on these occasions, I find: kitchen, bedroom, out is the way it goes.

'One of the advantages of this kind of arrangement is that there's no need for small talk,' she says in a chillingly matter-of-fact tone as she raises her glass.

'I quite like small talk.'

'We both know what we want.'

'Sure.'

She sips her wine and smiles. 'So we're a talker, are we?' There's a note of mockery here which makes me nervous. Putting down her glass, she steps forward. When it comes, hers is a shameless, panic-inducing kiss (they seem to get wider with age, kisses – one day

I'll go missing in action, consumed into the darkness by a ravenous, middle-aged mouth).

'Let's go to bed,' I say, surfacing.

In the bedroom, I'm relieved to see that she has made the bed with clean sheets. Paula draws the curtains and pulls the T-shirt over her head. I unbutton my shirt.

Take away affection, shared experience, laughter, a past or a future from this kind of affair, leaving only good old need, and the result is not wonderful. We lie in bed together, touching one another tentatively before our bodies – both of which are in pretty good shape, thank god – take over. Suddenly she's tugging at me painfully, like a madwoman weeding the garden. Paula knows what she wants, that's for sure. 'Coming doesn't matter,' they used to say; now there's nothing else. At one point, kind of aware that I may be performing in an insultingly professional manner, I summon up a small groan of pleasure; misunderstanding, she gives me a look of surprise and disapproval – you haven't, have you, not already? But all's well, Paula enjoys her tense little climax, thereafter taking only a distant, slightly bored interest in proceedings. 'Bloody hell,' she mutters at one stage, 'I'm exhausted.' I manage to stop myself apologizing.

Afterwards she seems eager to talk and tells me more than I want to know about her teaching career. I listen politely before, my heart singing, I slip on my clothes and beat it, leaving Paula in her suburban anonymity.

Of course Paula was shocked. In East Sheen, where the closest to a police presence is the local plod advising school kiddies to have a care when crossing the road, you don't expect a plain-clothes inspector investigating a murder to appear on your doorstep one Wednesday afternoon.

'A murder, oh my God, how awful. Come in, Inspector. In this road, was it?'

I was shocked too. Ollie had been right. This was no crumpet; it was a serious person. There were flecks of grey in her brown hair. She had the worry lines of the anxious and middle-aged. The idea of Paula Matthews being active on the contact circuit seemed ludicrous.

She showed me into the sitting-room where, over a cup of tea, I told her some of what I knew and what she would be required to do.

'What about the neighbours, my job?'

'Your face won't be shown on the programme,' I said. 'Your voice will be disguised.'

'He wasn't what you would expect,' Paula said quietly. 'Not sleazy. Nice. Amusing. When we met in the bar, I liked him. He said he was a writer.'

'Like you.'

She laughed unhappily. 'Slightly more successful.'

From Dexter's report, I had expected her to talk about the stories she wrote, but she seemed more interested in discussing Ollie.

'He said it was the first time he had used a contact magazine, but then it was my first time too. It always is. When you're playing this game, you have to stick to the rules, keep up the pretences.' She walked to the window and stared outside.

'Did he tell you anything about himself?'

'Only that he wrote with famous people. He mentioned a few names.'

'Like?'

'Russ Targett. Martin Coleman. People like that.'

In the corner I noticed a small desk on which there was a typewriter and some notebooks.

'Have you had anything published?' I asked.

'Not yet.'

'What else did he tell you?'

'Not much, thank God, a few lies. The last thing you want on these occasions is the truth.' She gave me an

158

odd look. 'Actually, once he was away from the bright lights, he was a bit pathetic – just mid-life crisis trying to improve his average before it's too late.' She laughed. 'He was very concerned that I had a good time. All right? he'd ask now and then. All right? Like the owner of a restaurant hovering over your table. Everything all right with your meal, madam?'

I glanced at Paula. There was something crazed about this reminiscence.

'He was the sort of man,' she continued, almost as if she were talking to herself, 'who'd be keeping an eye on the statistics – how many times a night and all that.'

I smiled. 'And what about you?'

'I have only one statistic that matters. Thirty-eight.'

'I find that hard to believe,' I murmured. There was silence for a moment.

'I do it for myself,' she said, reading my thoughts. 'It's not that unusual. Some people shop, or seduce their friends' husbands. I have the odd fling.'

'Will you do the programme, Paula?' I asked.

'I'll be anonymous, right?'

'You have my word.'

'Good.' She nodded. 'All right, Inspector, you're on.'

I drove straight home that evening. So this was where promiscuity led – down the Sincton road. Sitting in the traffic, just another bored commuter on his way back from work, I thanked God for marriage, for the kids, for the occasional comfort of safely contained affairs, for Joy.

Doubtless, if our roles were reversed and it were Oliver Sincton raking over my life as presented on small computer disks and corroborated by evidence from friends, he would see it as a series of retreats and compromises: from idealist to time-server, from obsessive hot-blooded lover to pale, dead-eyed husband.

He honestly believed he was moving forward, with his silly deals, his desperate, frantic seductions.

16

Gaunt, unshaven, his skin white as cocaine, Robin looked every inch the Claire Nash client as that Thursday he sat in the lobby of Nash Associates, one foot tapping to a fast and angry rhythm in his head.

'Claire's secretary appears to have no appointment for you.' The receptionist smiled nervously. Somehow she felt that she should recognize this man in his distinguished dark glasses. 'She's checking to see whether Claire has a window in her diary later.'

'Now,' said Robin.

'Of course.' It was true that Claire was keen on open access for clients but her suggestion that they should just call by was for some reason only taken up by celebrated directors and producers. The receptionist made another call. 'Claire's doing her correspondence with Saskia right now, Mr Nicholl,' she said. 'She'll be five minutes.'

'Good.'

Robin studied the film posters and personality shots of Nash's clients which were displayed on the walls. Were they all phoney? Behind those handsome, smiling faces was there always a ghost at work, an Ollie Sincton, unphotographed and unsung, just as there had been with the famous novelist and total package Laura Nicholl?

'Mr Nicholl?' Saskia, who seemed to have left her VIP smile at home this morning, stood before Robin, holding a folder of letters. 'Claire will see you now.' She showed him into Nash's office.

'So . . . The return of the prodigal.'

The agent was seated in an executive chair in front of

the window, through which the morning sun shone brightly. When Robin sat in a slightly lower chair, he was unable to see anything but a dazzling silhouette. It was like being interviewed by the Angel Gabriel.

'We need to talk,' he said.

'Of course.' Claire Nash had many better things to do this morning than to fritter away time in an unscheduled meeting with this loser but, over the past few days, the man's wife, who did matter, had been having problems. In fact, if Claire hadn't enjoyed going to bed with Laura quite a lot, she would have resigned as her agent. This hassle she did not need. 'Laura's worried about you,' she said.

'Good.'

'Now,' Nash smiled coldly. 'I expect you've been thinking about the LA deal. I'm afraid . . .' Because there was nothing to negotiate, it was a momentary silence '. . . that the project has gone elsewhere.'

'Who's it gone to?' Robin asked. 'Anyone we know?'

'The name escapes me. Someone rather young and brilliant, I fear.'

'Of course. I'm not here to talk about deals.'

'No?'

'I need some information before I talk to my wife – or rather confirmation of what I already know.'

'Information?'

'About my wife and—' he chose his words with care '—your little games.'

Nash leant back in her chair so that the full force of the sun shone in Robin's eyes. 'Games,' she said.

'I know everything. Just give me your version.'

'Not a game, Robin.' Nash spoke more quietly now, shifting easily into sincere mode. 'It's really quite serious.'

'Did the thought not occur to you that I should be involved in some way?'

'Involved.' Claire Nash pondered. It came as no

161

particular surprise that Laura had confessed all to her husband, although it was a bloody nuisance, and a warning that Robin was on his way would have been helpful; she liked to be briefed, prepared, on these occasions. 'We rather thought that it had absolutely fuck all to do with you,' she said.

'What?' Robin laughed angrily. The idea that his wife could build her writing career on a coolly planned deception without confiding in her own husband was ludicrous.

'You see, Robin, what we're talking about here is not some pointless fling . . .'

Fling? Robin frowned. He was used to Nash deploying the language of the bedroom when discussing her business scenarios – publishers were frequently hot to get into bed with Laura but sometimes couldn't get it up, came too soon or were simply jerking off – but he was damned if he could unscramble this one. 'Fling?'

'What we're talking about is, well . . .' The silence that followed, stretching over several seconds, was one of Nash's favourites, a brief to medium pause, punctuated at last by the one word or phrase, carefully enunciated, that the other person least expected (it might be 'charm' or 'masturbation' or 'sudden death') '. . . love,' she said.

'Love?'

'Yes. I was absolutely convinced that when she broke the news you'd take it in your stride. You're so good at taking things in your stride, Robin.'

'Did you say—?' Robin shielded his eyes in an attempt to see whether Claire Nash was smiling.

'Yes, surely you remember love, don't you? *Amo amas amat.* I love . . .' She stood up, pulled the blind and sat down again. '. . . Laura.'

'*Love?*'

It was a word used widely and often in Laura's world – love the concept, love the package, love the deal – but somehow, in this context, *I love Laura*, it reclaimed some of its traditional potency.

'The point is she doesn't write her own books,' Robin said weakly.

'Her books?' Nash looked surprised. 'Oh no, of course not. I thought you knew.'

'Ollie Sincton wrote them.'

'The actual line-by-line, words-on-the-page work was his but there was considerable input from Laura.'

'Surely the line-by-line, words-on-the-page work—' *Laura and Nash*, he simply couldn't grasp it. 'I mean, that's the book, isn't it?'

'In many ways the writing is the easy part. Laura's non-written contribution in terms of concept, promotion, image-development was enormous.'

Love. Claire loved Laura. Maybe Laura loved Claire. Robin shook his head as if to rid himself of the thought. 'Do the publishers know?' he asked.

'The publishers don't want to know. They get a wonderful product. In fact, nobody wants to know – even the punters would prefer to keep the fantasy alive.'

'The husband wanted to know.'

'Now . . .' Nash glanced at her watch '. . . the other matter. As I'm sure Laura has explained, it's not that she doesn't like you, or men, it's really nothing personal.' There was something about the way Robin was looking at her which made Nash pause. 'She *has* told you, hasn't she?'

'I haven't spoken to my wife for a week.'

'Right.' It was one of Nash's strengths as an agent that she never allowed herself the luxury of regret, even when she made the occasional negotiating error. At this moment she was slightly annoyed that an interface which might have been handled more tidily had, through no fault of her own, become more complex than was necessary. Nash hated mess. 'I'm very sorry, Robin,' she said, standing up and walking towards the door.

Robin remained seated. *'Love?'*

'Correct.'

'Love,' said Robin to the receptionist as he made his way through the lobby.

' 'Bye,' said the receptionist.

There are several ways to put a man's lights out for good and all. Sleights of hand, a squeeze here, a push there, and it's Exit Shitface, his life-support systems well and truly fucked. Most of the previous night Colin Thompson had tried to remember precisely where the pressure points were. He had stood in front of his bathroom mirror at Roseclare, applying pudgy fingers to different parts of his head without feeling queasy for even a moment. In the end he had resolved to forget advanced technique and go back to more traditional methods: jumping up and down on the enemy's windpipe in your heaviest boots until the usual signs of life – breathing, screaming for mercy and that – had ceased and desisted.

That morning Thompson took an early reveille and dressed in normal civvy gear – normal, that is, apart from the shit-stompers, freshly shined and lethal, on his feet. Then he caught a train to London. It was good to have orders again. Ignoring the uneasy stares of the pale, shagged-out, shit-brained commuters, he arrived at Paddington at nine-fifteen and made his way towards Mayfair.

His task was simple. Our tall friend, Miss Jane had said, appears not to have understood the message you gave him. He is not minding his own business. Don't ask me for details, Colin, she had said, but he has access to information which is not in Brigadier Harry's interest.

Right, Miss Jane.

Go and see him at this address, Colin. It's us or him. Just discourage him in some way.

Fair enough. The good soldier is an instrument of

war; he asks no questions. Discourage the fucker. Discourage him in the name of everything that was fine and honourable, discourage him so that any future discouragement would be surplus to requirements.

And soon really, she said. Tomorrow if possible.

Right, Miss Jane. Say no more.

I don't know what the brigadier would do without you, Miss Jane had said. You're a good man, Colin.

And, for that brief moment, he had forgotten she was minge.

Why did they all fucking stare in this town? As the hobnails on Thompson's boots hit the pavement – hard, with parade-ground precision – people's eyes widened like he was some kind of freak show on the move. All right, so the shit-stompers didn't go with the dark suit which seemed to have shrunk since he last wore it, or the shirt and tie which were like a noose round his neck, but, apart from the footwear, this was how it was in London, wasn't it? His eyes swivelled left to right, back to left. No, it was not.

People were dressed for the beach, scruffy, randy bastards. And all their shirts had words written all over them, words bloody everywhere. Thompson, who wasn't noticing much, did notice that. And sometimes – this was fucking strange – the words meant absolutely sod all. They were there for decoration, for design, no-one read them, just like no-one listened any more, there were too many words to take in. If Thompson had been walking down the street wearing a T-shirt announcing 'I AM A HARD BASTARD ON MY WAY TO KICK THE LAST LIVING BREATH OUT OF A FRIZZY-HAIRED PRAT CALLED NICHOLL', he would have attracted less attention than he did in this perfectly normal civvy suit.

You're a good man, Colin, she had said, and she was fucking right and all.

That was it. That was what worried him. Thompson turned the corner into Half Moon Street and quickened his stride. It was a basic rule of his life never to trust minge. They were unpredictable, sly. Mrs Goodenough, for instance: one day she was at the head of the table for the brigadier's dinner parties, the next she had hopped it over the Channel with some long-haired pillock she had only met twice. Or Miss Jane, taking up with all sorts of foreign rubbish. It hardly gave you confidence in the judgement of minge. And the way they looked, down here in London, showing off as if they were in charge. It had gone badly wrong somewhere along the line.

Was this a trick, a mingy double-cross? He had never really liked Miss Jane. He saw the way she looked at her father, wrapped him round that elegant little finger of hers. Basically, she was one of them: the prat, the yappy American, Jane – they had merged in Thompson's mind to become one entity, alien and hostile.

Yet she was giving him an order, one that made sense. Maybe she was a bint, maybe he'd never been given orders by a pair of legs like that, but she was right. The prat had to go.

There was an old geezer in the lobby. Thompson hesitated briefly, then marched past the block of flats. Miss Jane hadn't said nothing about a doorman, but then perhaps she had expected him to wait until the prat was outside, maybe her idea of discouragement involved loitering on street corners, peeping around newspapers, hiding behind dustbins. Do me a fucking favour. Thompson grimaced as he reached the end of the road, wheeled around like a guardsman and headed back towards the flats.

The logistics of actually getting to the prat in the first place had never occurred to him. His mind had been on other things – nut him first, then knee, chop, stomp, or maybe *open* with the chop, smash his head against the wall, and then—

On a doorstep to his left he saw a pile of envelopes

which resentfully – he didn't want to talk or think, not now – he picked up.

The old man was in his shirtsleeves at a desk, reading a newspaper. As he looked up, Thompson said, 'Mail, right.'

The man took a drag on his cigarette. 'Leave it on the desk, mate,' he said.

'Eh?' Thompson didn't want extra, unscheduled bother but no way was he stopping now. 'I'll deliver it.'

The doorman peered at the envelopes in Thompson's hand. 'Oh, collecting, are you?'

'Collecting, yes.'

'Save the Children.'

'Too right.'

'You won't have much luck with these tight bastards. Here you go.' The man held out a fifty-pence piece. Frowning, Thompson took it and, walking to the lift, put the coin in his trouser pocket.

On the fifth floor he stepped out, muttering, 'Save the fucking children, right.' The corridor was empty and he found the prat's door without too much difficulty.

Something was wrong. The front door was slightly ajar. It was moving. The prat was behind it. Taking one step back, Thompson ran at the door, applying his right shit-stomper to it with considerable force. There was a cry of surprise and pain and the door flew wide open, hurling whoever was behind it against the wall. Save the fucking children, right. Thompson saw a flash of neck as he entered, he aimed, he gathered strength, he raised his right leg.

He was hit on the side of the head. *What?* The prat had a friend? Whoever he was, the second one was no fighter. It was a tap, a tease, a wind-up. As Thompson straightened, the man put an arm around his neck, bad idea. Thompson bowed briskly, bringing the man's head against the wall with a crack. 'Steady feller,' the

167

man was screaming, like he was some kind of horsebreaker, 'I can expl—' Thompson ran across the room and tried the old ducking trick again, hurling both of them against a shelf on the other wall. Books slewed over the floor. Couldn't shift the fucker. 'Right,' gasped Thompson, heaving the man towards the computer thing in front of the large window, 'out you—' His foot caught a small, shiny plastic book, which cracked under his boot, and he pitched forward like someone diving for the line in a piggyback race on parents' day. There was a crash, and two and a half seconds later to the sounds of a busy Mayfair street were added the untidy *thwock* of flesh hitting concrete and the scream of a woman.

A man talking on the telephone in his Mercedes, double-parked outside, accelerated away quickly.

Released from the offices of Nash Associates, Robin sat in a café behind Piccadilly Circus, a cup of coffee growing cold in front of him. Across the empty room two youths, one with dark, greasy hair, the other with no more than a vicious stubble on his head, bickered with a younger boy.

'Everton are wankers,' the child was saying conversationally. 'They're a load of poofs.' 'Bollocks,' said the youth with the greasy hair, but with a hint of pride in his voice. 'Fucking girl poofs, they are,' the child called out.

Robin stared into his coffee, anxious not to attract their attention. An hour ago the idea of his wife building her career on a fraud had still seemed unthinkable. Now that deception was nothing. My wife, Claire Nash's girlfriend; Robin laughed at the absurdity of it.

Yet why the hell not? He thought of the pushing and pulling, the huffing and puffing when that vulgar, unanswerable male conversation-killer rose up, demanding satisfaction. Can't we just talk, Laura used to say, and no, they couldn't. It was either chat or bed, sex or companionship; one excluded the other. Robin found it easy to imagine Laura with Claire, laughing and loving. What a relief it must have been.

There was a telephone in the corner from which Robin rang his wife.

'Robin.' She gave the laugh of surprise that he knew so well. 'Where are you? I've been so worried.'

'I've just been talking to your agent.'

'I know. She's just rung me. I'm sorry.'

'Tell me about it.'

'Don't try the tough-guy act, Robin,' Laura said. 'It doesn't suit you.'

'I meant, tell me about it.'

Across the café the little boy was dancing around the table, shadow-boxing with Stubble Head. 'Gonna give you a flat nose now,' he was shouting. The Italian proprietor was remonstrating with the boys.

'Where are you? It sounds like a zoo.'

'It is.'

'Come home, Robin. I can explain everything. I miss you.'

'Claire says she loves you.'

'That's words. We were just . . . playing.'

It was odd, Robin thought, that something so important could be reduced to the same tired questions. How long has this been going on? Was she the first? Is it serious? What now? 'I don't understand,' he said, as the clamour of voices behind him grew louder.

Laura said something – it might have been 'She made me feel like a woman' – which Robin was unable to hear because the Italian had just put a fat hand behind the older youth's head and cracked it hard on the side of the table. There was a scuffle during which the proprietor bellowed, 'Calla police, calla police.'

'I think I had better go,' said Robin, hanging up. As he dialled 999, the boys disappeared on to the Soho streets, one bleeding, one laughing, one singing out 'Fucking dago shit bastard' in a piping treble voice.

Robin made his way down Piccadilly, turned right, and found that Half Moon Street had been cordoned off. There were three uniformed policemen outside the front door and, looking up, he saw, without particular surprise, that the large window to Ollie's flat had been shattered. The pavement below was stained with blood.

Muttering to himself, he walked to the car-park behind a pub in Victoria where, nearly a week ago, he had left his car. Somewhere deep in his subconscious he might have been aware that the Custard Beast had been vandalized with white paint, but he stepped in without examining the damage.

He drove west, held up frequently in traffic queues beside cars each of which seemed to have its own coded message: 'LITTLE MONSTER ON BOARD', 'A DOG IS FOR LIFE NOT JUST FOR CHRISTMAS', 'TRAINEE HELICOPTER PILOT – MIND MY CHOPPER'. Under the harsh sun Robin's car, its bright yellow decorated with white graffiti, looked jokey and youthful, like a gaily coloured mobile meringue. Scrawled on the side of the Custard Beast were the words 'I'M A WANKER'.

17

I've never had much time for the theory of detective work which sees investigation as a fluid, unpredictable thing, changing direction with the terrain like a stream making its way down a hillside. A log here, an unexpected gully there, and off we go, twisting and turning before ending up, inevitably, where we would have arrived without the diversions.

Forget it. Life is short. You can spend days considering zany alternatives, tracking down witnesses who may or may not be relevant. As far as I'm concerned, a detective should resist an easy fascination with the tangential, otherwise known as 'having an open mind'.

Keep your options under control. Limit the *dramatis personae* to manageable proportions. That has always been my approach and it has rarely let me down.

So, while a less self-disciplined detective inspector working on the Sincton case would by now be darting about, diving up blind alleys in urgent pursuit of the irrelevant, I had fixed my eyes firmly upon my destination. Nothing would deflect me: not the list of angry lovers whom Ollie had apparently left in his wake, not the media lightweights he had provided with words and respectability, not the connection with Suzi Ashbourn and her Shock Allegations, not Laura's guilty secrets, nor her eccentric husband's obsessions.

For me, all this was no more than background colour. Ollie Sincton had been unfortunate enough to cross the path of a doughnut-toting pervert who had killed him. That was where I had started and that was where I now stood. Our chances of finding the perpetrator remained slim but, so long as the file showed a creditable effort on the part of Her Majesty's Constabulary, there were greater tragedies in life than an unsolved solus murder and the continued freedom of a fun-lover whose moment of over-enthusiasm had resulted in there being one less amoral, smooth-talking bastard cruising the singles bars of London.

Of course, if the killer developed a taste for tying up strangers and stabbing them through the throat, different standards would pertain, a new approach to the investigation might well be required, but right now there was no sign of what Norman Biddle would call 'a sequel'.

There were, on the other hand, unavoidable complications. Two bodies cooling in the Mayfair sun beside a screaming prostitute tugging at a lead (her poodle, primped in the wrong place at the wrong time, provided a third corpse) cannot easily be ignored.

Then there was *Crime Time*. It was clear that the fatalistic perverts-will-be-perverts line was unacceptable for nationwide television. We had a show to put on. The investigation needed to be shaped, dramatized for public consumption.

When they called me to Half Moon Street that Thursday afternoon, a couple of hours before Robin returned from his meeting with Claire Nash, I found myself slipping into a Biddle mind-set. How were these new deaths going to play? Were they part of the main story or just a sub-plot? Could we edit the chronology a bit and present them as an exciting late flash? Or would it be tidier to cut the whole thing on the grounds that a double death in Ollie's block of flats so soon after his murder was just one of those strange coincidences? And time was against us; the programme was due to go out four days from now, before which we had to knock the filmed reconstructions on the head.

I looked at the chalk marks and blood stains on the pavement. To my experienced eye they proved beyond doubt that two male bodies had hit concrete at a speed inconsistent with continued health and happiness.

Upstairs, Scene of the Crime were fussing about, well on their way to discovering what I had already guessed: that this was the hideout of Robin Nicholl. It was, I confess, a surprise to learn that no less than four sets of fingerprints had been found at the flat.

'Four?' I asked.

Detective Sergeant Burton pointed to the door.

'Someone was changing the lock,' he said. 'According to the doorman, two men had been sent by the owner of the flat. Someone disturbed them. One ended up on the pavement. The other scarpered.'

'The someone presumably being the occupier.'

'No. The doorman says he hasn't seen the occupier all day. It was a man who claimed to be collecting for Save the Children.'

'So the fourth set of dabs would be the person who lived here.'

'The doorman's given us a description.'

'Tall, late thirties, scruffy bastard,' I said.

Burton referred to his notes and frowned. 'Could be,' he said.

The flat, I could see, bore the unmistakable mark of Robin's recent presence: clothes strewn about the sitting-room, scrawled notes near the word-processor, a coffee cup, its contents blue with mould.

I glanced at the jottings on the desk.

'Want copies of those, do you?' the detective sergeant asked.

'Yes,' I sighed. 'When you've finished with them.'

On the floor was what appeared to be a book but which, thanks to the mighty boot of Colin Thompson, was shown to be a well-made plastic case. I crouched down beside it.

'Anything on this?' I asked.

'Nothing,' said the officer dusting the place for prints. 'Help yourself.'

I picked up the container, a dark blue volume

173

entitled *Other Men's Flowers.* Carefully, I opened it. 'The hollow man's hollow book,' I murmured. Inside was a computer disk, on which was written the word 'ROY'.

It was while the disk was being examined that the telephone rang. With a dainty finger and thumb, I lifted the receiver.

'Detective Inspector Potter?' said the voice from the other end. 'Hugh Davies, Ministry of Defence. We need to talk.'

Robin drove through Fulham on to a motorway clogged with cars heading out of town. Perhaps all would become clear in the country, away from the dust and smell and violence, where this unrelenting heat meant no more than a decent harvest and thronging pub gardens. Then, as the traffic thinned out, he dawdled. He was tired, but he wasn't ready to leave the city yet.

He was discovering parts of outer London he had never known existed. Bedfont, Cranford, Heston. On the bright, open streets Asian families went about their business, enjoying the sun. He pulled into a garage and filled the car with petrol.

'You're needing a respray, mate,' said the young Sikh behind the cash desk. 'We can do it here, very reasonable.'

'I'm looking for somewhere to stay.'

'B and B, is it?'

The man reached for a dusty telephone beside him, dialled a number and spoke urgently in a foreign tongue to someone. 'Just one?' he asked, holding a finger up. Robin nodded. 'My friends have B and B,' the Sikh said, after hanging up. 'Third right along this street is High Street. My friends are a few yards on the right, the Fame Hotel. They have a room for you. Cheers, mate.'

The Fame Hotel turned out to be a small semi-detached house on a busy road. At a desk in the hall an Asian woman with dark, weary eyes gave Robin a form to fill in. She too seemed surprised that he was alone.

'If you want guests, you tell us, all right.'

'I won't have guests.'

'So many couples now. They arrive late and just, you know, scarper in the night. Always hurry-hurry. We have to take payment in advance.' As Robin wrote out a cheque, the woman shook her head as if she knew that, in spite of what he had said, he would soon be needing a double room. 'So many couples.'

His was a small, dark room with a view of a wall some five yards from the window. When he sat down on the single bed, Robin was startled by the crackle of a rubber sheet beneath him.

The only people who slept alone at the Fame Hotel, it seemed, were the old and incontinent.

There was something reptilian about Mr Hugh Davies. His skin had an unattractive office pallor to it. As he sat behind a large desk at the Ministry of Defence, I thought of his appearance in Ollie's notes. Our American friend had been right about one thing: the man's breath smelt like an abattoir.

'Thank you for responding so quickly, Detective Inspector,' he said, choosing to ignore the fact that I had arrived a full forty-five minutes after our agreed time. 'This is a matter of some delicacy. I thought an off-the-record briefing might be of assistance.'

'Off the record?'

'There are certain aspects of this situation which touch on national—' he looked at me sternly as if nothing in my line of work could ever transcend the pifflingly provincial '—national security.'

'We're just looking into a murder,' I said. 'There were a couple more deaths this morning which may or may not be connected. I rather doubt if there's anything here to upset the international balance of power.'

When Davies smiled he revealed a row of uneven teeth with the complexion of Gorgonzola. 'I can see that I'm going to have to take you into my confidence,' he said. 'The flat where your man Sincton was found belongs to us, the Ministry. After he died one of his friends appears to have gained access to a key and has been living there. This morning I sent a couple of chaps from my works department to change the lock. They were disturbed – and one of them was killed. Drink?'

I accepted a glass of Ministry Scotch, the Whitehall equivalent of a peace pipe. Now we were chaps drinking whisky together, unravelling the tricky little problem of a dead foreigner with a view to distancing ourselves, and our people, from the untidiness.

'And what was Oliver Sincton doing in an MoD flat?' I asked, without relaxing for one moment into my chair. I've never had much time for chaps. Give me the honest villainy of a Franky Dimond any day.

Davies winced. 'Bit of a cock-up by one of my own people, actually,' he said. 'I've taken entire responsibility.'

'Go on.'

'As you know, the Ministry has a number of dwellings in London used for visitors, friends from abroad, the occasional interview. In this instance, one of my staff took it upon herself to give the key to this Sincton man. She claimed that he was of interest from the security angle. Unfortunately I believed her.'

'Jane Goodenough.'

Davies nodded. 'Always used to be so reliable, daughter of a brigadier. Bit ambitious but sound, I thought. I blame myself. The flat of course is wired. My men tuned in for a week at which point it became clear that our friend was using the flat as a sort of one-man dating agency. That, we discovered, was his relationship with the Goodenough girl. Strictly below the belt. We pulled the plug, of course, told the girl to get him out. He was due to move the day after he died.' Davies reached into the left-hand drawer of his desk and took out a reel-to-reel tape. 'For what it's worth, here's what we recorded. I doubt you'll get much from it.'

'Unfortunate that you pulled the plug when you did.'

'From your point of view, yes. Of course—' he gave an insincere little shrug '—you couldn't have used it in court anyway.'

'No? I wasn't aware that the Ministry of Defence was above the law.'

'We're not going to have our activities bruited about because some randy little American gets himself killed in one of out flats. Half Moon Street is in the name of a perfectly respectable landowner by the name of Lord Dartington. Perhaps you know him.'

'Can't say I do. If I need the tape in court, I have every intention of using it.'

Davies stood and stared bleakly out of the window, his hands deep in his pockets. I believed what Ollie had written about the man's affair with Jane; there was something weak and sensuous about his mouth. 'Inspector, these things can be kept out of the public eye, whether you like it or not,' he said. 'My people talk to your people; it's all very relaxed.' He turned and spread his hands, like a conjuror who has just completed a trick. 'National security. Damned important.'

For a moment I thought about it. Biddle, or even the Deputy Commissioner, scurrying down to White's or Boodle's, summoned by an effete and sinister Whitehall mandarin. What was the problem? Inconvenient, you say? Unsafe? Leave it to me, old boy, that was the way it went.

'What's going to happen to Jane Goodenough?' I asked.

'Shifted her sideways to Agriculture and Fisheries,' said Davies. 'In her own interest. Indiscretion is a bit less of a liability there. She's spitting, of course.' He sighed, repeating what was obviously something of a catchphrase, 'I blame myself.'

We talked on for half an hour or so. Davies grew more confident and less apologetic as time went by. Having taken me into his confidence, he expected me to adopt the responsible, patriotic attitude and exclude the Ministry from my investigations. When I pointed out that I had a duty to solve a murder, Davies dropped more heavyweight names and implied that, if a chap's honour meant nothing to me, my superiors were likely to take a more co-operative line. Maybe – he gave a humourless little laugh – I would, like Jane, find myself being diverted to a department where I could make less trouble. The police equivalent of Ag and Fish: it was an uncomfortable thought.

On my way out I glanced into the office that had been Jane Goodenough's. Hudson-Black, her assistant, was at the desk where I had last seen him. Jane, he told me, had been given a few days' leave before taking up her new post. There was something cold and dismissive about his tone, as if human error had put his former boss beyond the pale. She was, after all, just a woman.

Laura Nicholl sat at her desk, an unmarked lined pad in front of her. Words failed her.

Until now the act of creation had, for Laura, been largely a question of committee work. Since graduating from journalism to fiction, she had rarely written alone. With Ollie, she would provide the original concept, some character sketches, perhaps one or two opening lines; then, later, she would go through the manuscript, re-writing, adding that special Laura Nicholl quality, a knowing mix of humour and sex that her readers had come to love.

The middle bit, the task of putting flesh on the bones

178

she had provided, was Ollie's job, and she had always considered it the easy part. It was the initial idea and the finishing touches, both of which were her responsibility, that made her novels different, or so she had always thought.

She tried to bring style to her work. The column which she wrote, with the help of an able young journalist called David McKinley, enraged fellow writers for the same reasons as it pleased her readers. It was predictable, espousing the right, old-fashioned values, distrustful of experts, full of common sense and self-deprecating jokes. The gloss which Laura gave to McKinley's draft presented the familiar and third-hand as if it had just occurred to her while she pruned the roses or prepared a dinner party for her famous friends.

None of this success was gained without effort. In his eager early days Ollie, for example, specialized in steamily tumescent prose. Male prurience is different from female prurience, she used to explain; there's too much action, it's so solemn, all this pushing and pulling. Relax, Ollie, think female. Sometimes, as she delegated, instructed and corrected, Laura felt more like a managing director or a teacher than a writer. In moments of exasperation with her collaborators – not to mention a nagging sense of shame that she had never confided in her husband about her work methods – she was almost tempted to write the damned words herself.

That, she realized now, was self-delusion.

She sat in her secret office, the location of which only Nash, Ollie and McKinley had ever known, and stared at the pad before her. She had her concept, but now was obliged to write the story on her own. Laura Nicholl was going straight at last.

If only the words and ideas would come as easily as they did during editorial meetings. She sighed.

Nope. Nothing.

18

I telephoned Joy from a call-box in Whitehall to tell her I would be late home again as I had a date with Suzi Ashbourn. She understood entirely.

'Yes, you're right, love,' she said. 'You need to see her again.'

I muttered something male and distracted, and hung up.

Somehow it irritated me that this unpleasant little murder had, thanks to the benediction of public exposure, acquired status and glamour. In normal times, for example, the only 'love' or 'darling' in Joy's life would be the Gary of the moment.

Another thing. Whereas, a matter of weeks ago, she would turn from me when I came to bed, moving to the very edge of the mattress like a bird on a cliff-face, now it was different. Often, when I awoke in the morning, it would be me whose face was to the wall and Joy whose arm was around my waist, as if she were trying to detain me from leaving for somewhere.

I made my way past dead-eyed, sweating commuters towards Piccadilly and the Ritz. When I had rung Suzi earlier in the day, she had insisted, with the true paranoia that attends regular substance abuse, that we should meet on neutral territory. Not the Maida Vale flat, not the station, but the Ritz tea-room.

'*Tea*-room?'

'I'm an alcohol-free zone these days.'

Of course. For people like Suzi self-denial was now all the rage.

Despite the hour, there were a few tourists in the

high-domed room enjoying English tea and cucumber sandwiches. Suzi, naturally, was late.

Sitting there, drinking tea at eight o'clock in the evening, the only Englishman in the place, I found myself slipping into the part of the modern police detective, a quiet intellectual, sardonic, a lover of Vivaldi with a slightly tragic private life. Now, over a pot of Earl Grey, I was unravelling my case by sheer force of logic. For a moment I felt nostalgic for a good old-fashioned crime, one uncluttered by publicity-crazed civilians – a City fraud perhaps, or a refreshingly honest contract killing.

'Hullo, good evening and welcome.'

I looked up to see Suzi Ashbourn standing in front of me, hand on hip. She was wearing a garish cardigan that was falling from her shoulders, revealing one of those tops with plunging armpits which allow the observant or double-jointed the occasional glimpse of breast.

'Glad you could make it,' I said.

Suzi sat down opposite me and, with a nervous shrug, rid herself of the cardigan. 'Tea for two,' she said. 'What fun.'

She didn't look her best. Despite the sunlamp tan, her face was pale, with dark shadows under the eyes. Her nostrils were red and inflamed. Somehow I doubted that she was suffering from a summer cold.

'I think I'm being followed, Simon, I really do,' she was saying. 'Someone's been hanging round outside the flat, that's why I needed to see you here.' She glanced over her shoulder and wiped her nose with the back of her hand like a truant schoolgirl.

'Followed?' I poured her a cup of tea.

'Sodding journalists,' she said. 'My newspaper knows I'm appearing on *Crime Time*. They say it breaks our contract.'

'Helping the police solve a murder?'

'I've got a public-exposure clause,' she said, a hint of pride in her voice. 'They seem to think that I'll give

181

away some big secret when I appear on television. Scoop them, the silly bastards.'

'This isn't a celebrity show,' I said. 'You won't be discussing your life story, merely your relationship with Oliver Sincton.'

'Shame about that.'

She had become used to disappointment, Suzi. Innocently, she had imagined that the story of her royal romance, a sad tender thing really, would elevate her in the gossip-column hierarchy, that she would become more than a body, a name in a caption, be recognized as a person in her own right with interesting views and a troubled but noteworthy private life. Instead, she had become, briefly, a smutty pub joke. She hadn't even been invited on to a decent chat show to discuss things that mattered to her – the environment, the fight against fur, the quest for a lasting relationship.

I took a folded photocopy of Suzi's royal exclusive from the inside pocket of my jacket. 'Tell me about Ollie, you and your prince,' I said.

She glanced down at the article. Besides the inevitable shots of Suzi falling out of her clothes, there were photographs of her prince, frowning as if in anticipation of the story she would tell. 'Of course,' she said, 'my writer wanted to play up the physical side.'

'Sex.'

'What else?' She sniffed again. 'For instance, I told him that we were just two lonely people from different worlds, and it ended up like this.'

I looked at the headline. It read, 'TWO LONELY PEOPLE FROM DIFFERENT WORLDS – AND ONE THING ON THEIR MIND!'

'He cut a lot of our conversation,' Suzi said. 'They just have to drag sex into everything, these people.'

'Just like Ollie Sincton.'

'What's that creep got to do with it?'

'Don't piss me about, Suzi,' I said gently. 'I've read the disk.'

182

I guess it makes me unique on this little island that I am not in love with the royal family. Let me put it this way: I have no particular objection to a bunch of privileged turkeys gobbling and waddling from Scotland to Gstaad, back to Knightsbridge and on to Mustique so long as they don't expect me to stand by and applaud. In fact, given half a chance, I'd shift the lot of them into the private sector. After all, this craze for privatization is big right now among the locals – as if making something private makes it more truly British. Why not knock the whole goofy dynasty down to the highest bidder and bring a healthy whiff of competition into this bastion of privilege? 'The Christmas Message from Her Majesty the Queen is this year brought to you by Mitsubishi, the Multinational that Cares.' Why not give them promotional tags, like the goddamned nags they love to ride – The Princess Pepsi Royal, Prince Sony Philip, the Duke of Crown Paints Kent? Makes sense to me.

Don't be ridiculous, Ollie, Jane would say. You wouldn't understand.

But I do. Over here, Mr and Mrs Windsor with their dull and ugly brood are the drug prescribed to this lovable, hilarious nation as it spirals ever downward into obscurity. No-one can do royal work – the polo matches, the shoots, the parades, variety performances, the endless holidays to recover from the rigours of shaking hands and smiling – quite as brilliantly as the Windsors. It's the ultimate celebrity show without which no news bulletin is complete. Take away their Royal Goofinesses and the country would just give up the ghost, disappear, glug glug, into the grey waters of the North Sea.

All this seems – excuse me for viewing the situation in crude career terms – too good an opportunity to waste. Like me, the royals are part of the fame game; they're product, I'm the means of production. Of course, like all product, they depend on packaging, the occasional introduction of new material.

Enter Suzi Ashbourn.

Call me a sleazebag if you like, but I have this astonishing instinct for bringing together the right two pieces in life's sexual jigsaw. Yes, Suzi and one of the princes. It was perfect.

In fact, it was such beautiful and interesting casting that, with a degree of self-abnegation that was almost Buddhist, I shifted effortlessly from personal into professional mode: sex with long-legged Suzi could come later. Right now, there was money to be made.

'Yes.' She looked as guilty as a first-former in the head teacher's study. 'He was involved at the start.'

'He set the whole thing up. Were you lovers?'

'No way. Not then.'

'But he took you to Mustique, where you both stayed in the holiday home of Mr Russ Targett.'

'In separate rooms.'

'I'm not interested in where you slept, Suzi.'

'I needed a break,' she said. 'I had been working really hard, so when Oliver got in touch with me and said there was this house—'

'What you should understand, Suzi,' I said, 'is that I really don't care about what happened between you and a member of the royal family. Or didn't happen.' The way she reacted suggested that I was on the right track.

'I didn't like Sincton,' she said. 'But it was a free holiday – the chance to meet really interesting people I'd read about in the papers.'

'And go to bed with them, wired for sound.'

Suzi looked away. 'I wasn't keen on that,' she mumbled, 'but Ollie insisted. How did you know I was wired?'

'Guesswork.'

Briefly, I felt sorry for Suzi as she sat there, edgy and

confused. It wasn't her fault that she had been born with the kind of blank, thought-free looks that some men are unable to resist. It wasn't her fault that, thanks to her God-given assets and the efforts of a scheming American, she had found herself in a royal bed. It wasn't her fault that, by going public on her big moment, she had become not the romantic heroine, the Cinderella that she had planned, but a joke celebrity. Nothing was really her fault.

'It was true what I wrote in the papers,' she was saying. 'When we met it was as if everyone else at that party had just faded into the background. I forgot about the wires and about Sincton listening in. We were just so close when we started talking. What happened later was like such a natural thing, you know?'

'I know.' And, in spite of myself, I thought of Joy. How would she have reacted if a prince, or even a minor duke, had looked into her eyes and said, to quote Suzi's version, 'This is all absolutely fascinating. Why don't we talk about it later, somewhere a bit quieter?' Would she have stepped back, hand across her chest, 'Excuse me, sire, I happen to be married to Detective Inspector Simon Potter'? I fear not.

'And Sincton was tuned in all the time?' I asked.

Suzi started to laugh – an unattractive cackle which cut through the murmur of conversation at the Ritz. When she had recovered her composure, she said, 'Not when it mattered, he wasn't.'

Jesus wept. You establish the scenario. You find a suitable star. You coach her, setting aside normal desires in your quest for artistic excellence. You take her halfway around the world to your chosen location. You find, to your delight and astonishment, that she has remembered her lines and that her unwitting (and witless) co-star plays his part beautifully. They make it to the bedroom with surprising ease – given that

185

*between them they have fewer brain cells than he has
private detectives. You have the perfect English scene
– beauty, class, sex, royalty. You have the technology.
And what happens?*

She disconnects the fucking mike.

'I put a pillow on it.' Suzi was laughing again and I
confess that the vision of our friend, on boggle duty in
the next-door house, furiously tapping his earphones,
was one of this case's more enjoyable cameos.

'So he had to depend on you for details?'

'I wouldn't tell him a thing. I was proud of what I
did. The royal family should be protected from people
like Sincton.'

'What about your secret meetings later that week?'

'I told him where to stick his wire.'

'What was he going to do with this material when
you got home?'

'We were going to write a book. My life – ending up
with the prince. Next thing I knew, Sincton was dead.'

'You hadn't started work.'

'I rang the palace, but I couldn't get past the private
secretary.'

'Were you Sincton's lover in the end?'

Suzi seemed annoyed, as if she had been reminded
of something she had just managed to forget. 'We had a
last night together on the island, after the royal party
had gone home. I felt happy. You know how it is.'

'I know. What was he like, the prince?' I asked,
raising a hand for the bill.

Suzi hugged herself, a well-practised, dreamy look
in her eyes. 'He was very, very gentle.'

'Of course.' I smiled. 'He would be.'

186

19

During the twenty-four hours since, with a camp flourish, Biddle had revealed that the coveted Crime of the Month spot was ours, the Sincton case had become the focus of attention down at the station. Suddenly it was Ollie-this, Ollie-that wherever you turned, as if posthumous celebrity had brought him back to life.

That Saturday morning, the day before *Crime Time* went out, members of a camera crew arrived for what the producer Jonathan Miles-Thomas, a small bearded character who pranced about like a bad Shakespearean actor, described as 'atmo-shots'. Several scenes, I was told, would show the quietly thoughtful Detective Inspector Potter at work in his office, riffling through reports, answering the telephone or discussing the next step in his intrepid investigation with his valiant if sombre sidekick DC Dexter. For an hour or so the technicians illuminated the whole of the floor with lights so that soon the spottiest, callowest constable of our division was to be seen walking tall, strutting to his desk in shirtsleeves, chewing nonchalantly, stabbing at the buttons on the telephone with studied weariness.

By now I was no longer DI Dull but something of a local hero. Tough-talking canteen cowboys who used to ignore me now treated me as if we were old buddies. What was all this about Ollie being MI6? Any sign of the Nicholl fellow, was there? What was the SP on the Half Moon Street skydivers? The men were hungry for pub talk, titbits of gossip they could take home and share with their mates.

Biddle was at the centre of all this, lumbering about

the place like a bear on amphetamines, talking in a new mid-Atlantic accent which hovered uneasily between gumshoe drawl and Basildon English, like the first efforts of a radio disc jockey.

'We're going live with shots of you at your work station, Simon,' he told me in my office while I was trying to get some work done between atmo-shots. 'Voice-over from Andy the presenter. Then it's you direct to camera – the full poop on what happened to Ollie. A few head-to-heads with people who knew our man when he was alive – Martin Coleman, Laura Nicholl – to give us like a snapshot of the man as he was.'

'Head-to-heads?'

'Jonathan's handled that. Laura and Martin were interviewed last night.'

'Excellent,' I sighed.

'Then—' Biddle clasped his hands in front of him '—then we segue from you discussing the case with James Dexter into a reconstruction of the night Ollie died – very grainy, like *Taxi Driver*, you know? Hidden camerawork while James does undercover work.'

'Who's playing the girl?'

'The girl's playing the girl. We're going for one hundred per cent authenticity, so it'll just be his contact date for the night. Maybe we'll have to blank out her face. We close—' Biddle hurried on, rightly anticipating an objection from me '—with you inter-viewing Paula – back to camera, voice disguised – talking about Ollie's secret life.'

'She only met him twice.'

'Didn't they all?' He waved away the detail. 'We're hoping the recon and interview will be fairly raunchy so that pre-prog the announcer can do a general those-of-a-nervous-disposition warning. Apparently that puts a million or so on the viewing figures. How d'you want to play the Robin Nicholl card?'

'I'll say that we need to see him to eliminate him from our inquiries.'

'With a subtext, right? Like, we know he's our man.'

'What?'

'We've got to have a pay-off line that shows we're on to something. Reassures the punters at home that we're on top of the case.'

'But we're not. Nicholl's not our man.'

'He's gone AWOL, hasn't he? What more do you want?' He gave me a showbiz wink, a habit he had caught from Miles-Thomas, and turned to leave.

'What about Suzi?' I asked. 'When's her head-to-head?'

'Ah.' Biddle touched his brow as if suddenly remembering something. 'Minor change of schedule there,' he said, dropping his voice. 'We've decided to deep-six Suzi.'

'Deep what?'

'She's canned, put into turnaround. We're going to go without her, Simon.'

'I thought she was important.'

'Nah, silly tart.' Biddle pointed to the ceiling with a comically self-important pout. 'Word from upstairs.'

'You're joking.'

'Something about the privacy of the royal family,' Biddle said dismissively. 'The Deputy Commissioner rang me at home. Norm, he said, Norm, is this Ashbourn woman absolutely essential to our investigations? Cut a long story short, I had to agree to drop her from the programme.'

'Suzi will be upset. It was her last chance for stardom.'

Biddle smiled. 'That's showbiz.'

After the superintendent had bustled out of my office, I found that Suzi's enforced defection from The Norman Biddle Show began to niggle me. In police work, as in any other career, experience teaches you to read the signals, to sense obstacles and problems well before they are put in your path. Although the removal of Suzi Ashbourn from the televised interviews was, on the face of it, irrelevant to my inquiries, the involvement from the Deputy Commissioner was ominous.

What was it to do with him? Who was leaning on him? A keener, more innocent detective inspector would have picked up the telephone, referred up. I knew better.

That morning I looked again at Ollie's royal disk. Apart from the few fragrant, tantalizing memories of Mustique, there was little of interest. If Suzi had been telling the truth about her autobiography, Sincton would not have started work by the time of his death. I would probably need to see Suzi once more.

DC Dexter drifted in late, hardly bothering to acknowledge me as I sat at his word-processor. He was behaving oddly these days, as if the combination of hot times in Singles City and the prospect of celebrity had dimmed his enthusiasm for the Sincton case. He was quiet, rarely interrupting my work with his touchingly naïve questions. Although he continued to file reports on his evenings' work, an uncharacteristically surly tone could be detected in them. It would be an overstatement to describe this behaviour as 'mysterious', as Dexter steadfastly resisted the enigmatic, but it was intriguing.

'Everything all right, James?' I asked as he stared gloomily over my shoulder at the screen.

'Fine, sir.' He seemed to pull himself together. 'Anything new on the disks?'

'No.' I switched the machine off.

'Actually, sir,' he said this quickly, 'I'm unhappy about the TV programme.'

'Unhappy, James?'

'It's not that I'm nervous of appearing,' he said. 'I just think . . . I just think it's wrong.'

'Go on.' For Dexter – for any officer – this was a startlingly original line of thought. Matters of ethics and morality are rarely discussed in a busy police station. 'In what way, wrong?' I asked.

'I don't think we should use real people, sir.'

'You mean the girls – Paula and the rest.'

He hung his head bashfully. 'It seems unnecessary. Like it's entertainment or something. They're nice people – a bit sad, some of them, but nice.'

I played a hunch. 'There's nothing more to this, is there, James? Nothing more personal?'

He looked up, a hint of colour in his dark cheeks, a smile which refused to be kept at bay. Oh my God, Dexter in love – that was all I needed.

It was chance, and a rare moment of determination and nerve, which brought Robin Nicholl together with Jane Goodenough.

Within hours of clearing her desk at the Ministry of Defence, Jane had sensed what was on the way. At first she resisted – cleaning the flat, buying clothes, flicking through the appointments pages of magazines, angrily ministering to herself with the motorized comforter from the bedside drawer – but the Grapes would not be denied. One night, she told herself, one hot, heavy, utterly disgusting night. Then she would start again.

Robin was aware of none of this. He simply knew that sometimes Jane Goodenough picked up strangers at a wine-bar in Knightsbridge, and that he needed to see her.

The more he thought about Ollie's death and its aftermath, the more important Jane seemed. She had been Ollie's girlfriend, or as near a girlfriend as he would permit himself. She had stage-managed, according to Ollie, a dubious literary enterprise with her father, whose employee, Robin suspected, was the oaf who had mugged him in the underground. She had refused to meet him after the murder and would be unlikely to recognize him.

There was only one way. He had to be her stranger for the night.

For two days Robin had prepared himself in the

Fame Hotel. Remembering that the Grapes had a sort of stale gentility, that even its most defeated customers had a freshly laundered, tonight's-the-night look, he bought some new clothes and, that Saturday night, set off for Knightsbridge in the Custard Beast.

Ollie had been right. The days when the Grapes was used as a contact point for the sexually restive had long gone. Once or twice, a practised eye might note a casual encounter – a drink, a shared laugh, lowered voices – which may have led to something, but then, as often as one couple would leave together, another would drift apart with an easy smile, as if sex was the last thing on their minds. Maybe it had once been a singles bar but these days punters were looking for no more than noise, smoke and shared alcohol; what united them was not lust but boredom, the need for company, however dull and defeated that company might be.

Robin made his way to a corner table past the oyster-eyed losers sitting at the bar, hiding away from their wives and their futures.

It was nine-thirty when Jane walked briskly into the Bunch of Grapes, a folded copy of *The Times* under her arm. She was wearing a black skirt and a white silk shirt, the top button of which was undone, revealing a pale throat. Few would guess that she was here, not for an informal meeting with a business partner, or even a pre-dinner drink with a stockbroker friend, but for simple, unscheduled, old-fashioned promiscuity. She ordered a glass of white wine, smoothed her newspaper on the table and started to read.

Robin watched, looking for signs that would give him encouragement. Her long legs were crossed – but then so were his. There was nothing tarty about the way she sat there, leaning forward over her paper, her fine, straight hair hiding her face. Occasionally she glanced at her watch as if she were expecting someone. Robin felt his courage draining away.

He had always found this the most difficult part of any relationship. Stages Two to Ten were relatively easy, but Stage One – How do you do, hullo, my name's Robin Nicholl – tripped him every time. Utterly convinced that no woman was interested in him, he had perfected a technique of self-rejection – a dithering, slightly insulting diffidence that only the most determined could ignore. Hullo, drink, sorry I see you're busy, God how embarrassing, nice to – and he was diving across the room away from her, relieved that he had spared her the trouble and himself the humiliation of being frozen out. All his women (a small, select band) had been won by skipping the preliminaries and moving straight to Stage Two.

He knew what was going to happen. Jane would stay for an hour or so. Then, just as he was bracing his legs for the long, terrifying walk across the Grapes to where she sat, another stranger would move in, or she would go home. Robin gritted his teeth; no wonder he remained, almost uniquely among his friends, an adultery virgin; no wonder his wife preferred women.

After five minutes, Jane looked up from the newspaper and, in the half-light of the bar, Robin saw that there was dark red lipstick on her thin lips; her eyes darted about the room, resting briefly on Robin. The moment had come. He took his glass over to her table.

'May I?' he said, nodding in the direction of the empty chair beside her.

Jane glanced at him, then at the chair. 'Help yourself,' she said coldly.

He sat down. Jane was no longer reading the paper but staring impassively ahead of her. No small talk, he told himself, remembering Ollie's technique. Swallowing hard, clenching his fists under the table, he leant forward and said quietly, 'I want you.'

He waited for the peal of laughter, the stares from nearby tables, perhaps the splash of wine in his face. But Jane turned and, with an odd, humourless

193

expression about the mouth, said, 'Don't they say please where you come from?'

Robin resisted the temptation to smile or, worse, to joke. 'Well?' he asked.

'Let's go,' she sighed, as if she were making some great concession. 'My place.'

They took a taxi to Islington, spending the journey in moody silence. So this is how it works, thought Robin. All that small talk, those meals, hours spent expressing an interest in their careers, their past, their future, when a few ill-tempered monosyllables would have done the trick.

'Are you married?' she asked.

'Yes.'

For the first time since they had met, Jane smiled. 'Good,' she said.

The taxi-driver, who was watching them in the rear-view mirror, caught Robin's eye and winked. Robin looked out of the window. Then, worried that he might be overplaying the coolness, he appraised Jane's legs.

They were good legs. The one question that he had avoided asking himself now occurred to him with some force. Would he or wouldn't he? Sex with Jane was not a primary motive but there was nothing to prevent it being a fringe benefit. He thought of Laura; perhaps, after all, he should exercise the cuckold's time-honoured right of reply. And Jane was undeniably desirable. He swallowed, closing his eyes at the idea of making love to Jane. Hell's bells, why not?

Jane's flat was much as Ollie had described it: tidy, characterless, 'bachelor girl'. She offered him a glass of wine, which he accepted. As she was opening a bottle in the kitchen, he wandered into the bedroom where there was a large bed, its duvet neatly turned back. He glanced about the room: almost certainly, it would be in here.

'Make yourself at home, why don't you?' she said, standing at the door with two glasses in her hand.

'I will.' Robin was obscurely glad that Jane showed no sign of wanting conversation or warmth. A charmless, beautiful woman: it would make his task easier.

He took his glass from her, with some difficulty checking the thanks which were second nature to him. How should a pick-up artist with sadistic tendencies drink a glass of wine? With a careless swig and a rasped 'Don't you have anything stronger?' Gulp it back like a man whose every appetite was out of control? In the end he opted for a long sip, staring at her over the rim of the glass like a gimlet-eyed Nazi. 'Take off your clothes,' he said.

Jane shrugged, put her glass on the bedside table, unbuttoned her shirt and draped it over the back of a chair. So easy. There was that to be said for the Ollie approach, although Robin was concerned to find that he felt not desire but anxiety, as if his normal process of evasive, flirtatious conversation were an essential form of foreplay. He drained his glass, stepped forward and kissed Jane fiercely.

Her reaction was alarming. With a sort of hiss, she fell back on to the bed, tearing at his jacket, cursing him as she did so. 'I said,' Robin gasped, 'take off your clothes.' He fumbled with a zip on the side of her skirt, stood up and, rather more roughly than he intended, pulled it over her legs. 'Bastard,' she said, dragging him down on top of her, yet struggling at the same time. 'Bastard, *bastard*. Leave me alone, you bastard!'

'Sorry?'

At this, the very worst of moments, the old Robin resurfaced. His way of love was tentative and accepting; to mate like snarling cats was quite alien to his nature. 'Did I . . . was I . . . ?' He sat up, frowning. 'Is something wrong?'

Jane closed her eyes and smiled crazily. 'Bastard,' she repeated.

'I'm so sorry, was I hurting you?'

She sighed. 'Bastard,' she said, as if she were talking

to a simpleton. 'As in "Take me, you bastard".'

Robin laughed nervously. He couldn't help it. For years he had fantasized about girls crying, 'Take me!' Now, at last, one had. And it was ludicrous.

'Can we get on with it?' Jane said impatiently.

Robin reached into his pocket. There was no going back. He pulled out an old school cricket tie. 'I'm going to tie you up now,' he said.

'You're going to what?'

'I have to tie you up.'

'Ah,' Jane said, as if the erotic charge had been destroyed. 'Right.' She stood up; even in her sensible, expensive underwear, there was something unnervingly authoritarian about her.

Jane stretched behind her back, unhitched her bra, then took off her stockings with the brisk concentrated air of an athlete before a race.

'Bloody hell,' Robin whispered, his palms damp. He stared at her, longing to reach out and touch but paralysed with embarrassment.

She looked at him and, without a smile, said, 'Well?'

'Give me your wrists,' he said.

It would be a good illustration for the school magazine, Robin thought as, five minutes later, he stood by the bed. The cricket tie, the House tie, the school prefects' tie and the Old Boys' tie held Jane securely. 'Our picture shows Nicholl (Dalton's House, 1962–7) putting College ties to good use,' the caption would read. 'A close inspection of the knots confirms that the afternoons at the Sailing Club were not entirely wasted!' Briefly, as he considered Jane's slim, spread-eagled, pale body, Robin regretted that he was not spending the night in a more traditional way, but then he was reminded of Laura.

'I have to find something,' he said.

'You what?' Jane tugged at her bonds.

'Sorry. It was a bit of a trick, actually.'

Ignoring the infuriated questions from the bed, he

went through the drawers in Jane's bedroom: letters, bills. He was about to abandon his search when Jane said. 'Untie me and I'll show you what you're looking for.'

'And what am I looking for?'

'Money?'

'No.'

She sighed. 'So you're the police. You want the tape.'

This sounded more promising. 'Where is it?' Robin asked.

'Untie me.'

'After.'

'It's in the kitchen. Top shelf beside the fridge. There's a box.'

'Don't try anything, OK.'

'Very funny.'

She was telling the truth. In a box on the top shelf was an unmarked black cassette.

'Do the police always collect their evidence this way?' Jane asked as he returned to the bedroom.

'I'm not the police,' he said. 'It would be unwise to call them about this.'

He took one last look at Jane before, with a little sob of desire, he dashed out of the flat and down the stairs.

You look back; you have regrets. Even the successful cases bring their share of failure. False trails, wasted time, unacceptable casualties.

I should have listened to my wife. When Suzi Ashbourn was written out of the script for *Crime Time*, it was Joy who was convinced that there was more to it than a misplaced sense of propriety.

'It's just a tacky murder case,' I said, sitting in the kitchen on Saturday night. 'The palace shouldn't be involved. It would be guilt by association.'

'They're people, aren't they?' said my wife, the royalist. 'There's something funny going on.'

So, reluctantly, I went to the telephone in the hall

and dialled Suzi at home. There was no reply. I rang her minders at the newspaper. They had finished with her; the Ashbourn story, in their unhappy phrase, was a stiff. They had her mother's number. When I contacted her mother, she told me she hadn't seen Suzi for days.

I left it there. *Crime Time* was tomorrow evening. During the day I was due to interview Paula on camera. Suzi would just have to wait. Joy looked disappointed.

'The show must go on,' I said.

Damn. Robin slammed the steering-wheel of his car with the palm of both hands. There was a limit to his virtue. Like other men, he could be a victim of heady sexual nostalgia: the worst, most appalling moments, of which there had been a few before he met Laura, would foment in his mind until, over time, they developed a mysterious erotic appeal. Already, as he drove through the streets of London, his version of Jane was wilder, warmer, less angry than the original. The panic and embarrassment of the evening were forgotten, replaced by a powerful, dangerous charge. Robin shifted uncomfortably in his seat. Take me.

He must have been mad. The car slowed as Robin considered the situation. He could have had them both, the tape and Jane, yet he had tied her up, pretending to himself that her writhing body meant nothing to him. She was, of course, still tied up; it would take a while for her to master those knots. Maybe, Robin thought, he could go back, pick up where he had left off. Would he untie her? No, sod it, he couldn't wait and nor could she. Without a word, he would step forward, run a speculative hand over her tense, lean body as he unbuttoned his shirt, heeled off his shoes and—

Hell's teeth, he couldn't. He imagined the look in Jane's eyes. Bent *and* slow *and* indecisive, they said. Get *on* with it. Cursing, he accelerated.

It was two in the morning when Robin returned to the family house, taking the stairs two at a time. Breathing heavily, he walked into the bedroom where Laura, awoken by the noise, was standing bare-footed in her dressing-gown, surprised, frightened and, now that she saw who it was, relieved.

'Robin,' she smiled. 'It's you.'

The cheat, the fraud, the dyke wife.

'Let's go to bed,' said Robin.

Laura frowned as, undoing her dressing-gown, she edged back into bed. She had been about to ask him whether he was drunk but, as he advanced on her, his body catching the street light shining through a gap in the curtains, it was clear that this was no moment for conversation. He drew back the sheet and fell on her with a groan that may have been desire or anger or satisfaction at being home.

Something very strange had happened to her husband. He was harsh, masterful – almost manly. At first Laura faked it with the small symphony of noises traditionally associated with coital ecstasy, but then tact gave way to something more genuine. 'Robin,' she said, at once happy and reproving.

He was hissing something as he made love to her. 'Does your agent do this? Does she?'

'No.' Laura found herself crying as she responded. 'She doesn't.' It was a good marital reunion.

At last peace was restored to the bedroom. 'Welcome home,' Laura whispered.

'Why Nash, for God's sake?' he asked. 'Just tell me.'

'I don't know. She took control.'

'You mean she made it easy. Like Ollie.'

'It was a mistake. I'm sorry, Robin.'

Laura moved closer to him, wondering vaguely whether losing Claire as a lover meant she would be looking for a new agent. She hoped not.

'We need to talk,' Robin said, staring into the darkness.

20

Suzi put on her own spectacular: fame at last.

That Sunday morning, while preparations were being finalized for our broadcast, she took herself down by taxi to Windsor where her prince was scheduled to make a regal appearance, presenting prizes at some equestrian event. Horses, clowns, parachutists and, as a grand finale, the Royal Horse Artillery, a parade of costumed wallies who would canter about the show-ring on horses pulling shiny cannons, causing spectators to gasp at their ability to master a figure of eight without ending up in a tangle of gunmetal and horse-meat. At the climax of proceedings, they would customarily draw up before the guest of honour, dismount, line up their cannons and blast a loyal twenty-one-gun salute.

Timing had never been Suzi's strong suit. At first, as she tottered into the ring on her high-heels, there was laughter. The sun was high in the sky. It was a golden day with the promise of autumn in the air, clowns were mixing with the crowds, and this funny little figure, with its hilariously misapplied make-up, its absurdly brief nightclub dress, was an inspired comic counterpoint to the military regalia. Children screamed their appreciation as Suzi advanced towards the line of guns, the mums smiled, slightly embarrassed at the accuracy of the parody, the dads nudged one another knowingly as they eyed her lovely, wobbly legs (heaven knows what exotic dope cocktail Suzi had treated herself to during the night). The laughter increased when one of the prince's detectives attempted to head her off but, as she kicked off her shoes and dummied past him, he slipped and fell in some horse-shit, allowing her to run with really quite surprising speed towards her prince.

A soldier, even a ceremonial toy soldier, does not change his mind. Kneeling beside his cannon, a charge in his hand, the people cheering, poised to express explosive loyalty to the Crown, he is not about to be distracted by some lunatic bimbo staggering towards him. Bang . . . Bang . . . And (it was the third gun that caught her, flinging her backwards some twenty yards across the ring) BANG. What an exit. Bang. The dunderheads reached seven before they realized that killing Suzi was not part of the royal cavalcade.

The event made the lunchtime news, although a filmed record was excluded on grounds of taste, a decision which would have deeply disappointed Suzi.

'Crime does not conform to working hours. It respects no schedule. *Crime Time*, the live television show that brings the grim reality of our violent society to you as it happens, cannot therefore control its content. There may be material in the next fifty minutes which some viewers may find surprising or shocking. We cannot apologize. Because that is the way of modern crime . . .'

The opening words of *Crime Time*, spoken with urgent solemnity by its smooth-faced presenter Andy Craig against the backdrop of a busy police station, were part of the programme's regular set-up; they were never more apt than on the night of Ollie Sincton's last show.

The idea behind the programme was simple. It was to be a report from the front line: fast, compelling, authentic, involving the viewer in police work in all its dizzy spontaneity. The formula – take the surprise of a Saturday-night candid-camera show, add the excite-ment of cops and robbers, topped up with dangerous reality – was irresistible. On occasions it was anti-climactic, or it veered interestingly out of control. Everyone watched it.

It had been claimed that *Crime Time* was not as live and freewheeling as was advertised, an allegation I know to my cost to be entirely false. There were times that morning when Norman Biddle and I begged the producer to pad it out with some pre-recorded scenes ('Can't we just fake the fucker?' Biddle wailed at one point) but, the greater our problems, the more Jonathan Miles-Thomas liked it. The word 'integrity' was muttered like some sort of incantation; too late we realized that part of the attraction of *Crime Time* was that it made policemen look like plods. When TV men talk about integrity, check your back pocket.

Before our section of the programme, Andy was to give an update on past cases ('With *your* help, we brought this man to justice, the Assistant Chief Constable paid tribute to the efforts of *you*, the viewers . . .'). Then he would turn to the officer in charge of the Crime of the Month investigation.

'Detective Inspector Potter, now this was a particularly vicious crime, wasn't it?'

Thirty minutes we had to fill. Talking heads, as Biddle put it, hopping around dementedly behind the cameras, had to be kept to an absolute min.

Andy Crain would step back to leave it to the professionals and, at that moment as I looked sincerely into the camera, I would know how the Crime of the Month was supposed to play: background details read from the autoprompt, followed by filmed interviews with Laura and the Reverend Coleman. More shots of me, working with Sincton's notes, the voice of an actor reading a couple of the less repulsive paragraphs, which would set the scene for the filmed reconstruction in the Bunch of Grapes, starring James Dexter. Then back live to the station, where I would interview Paula, a dramatic figure murkily backlit for anonymity, before the final touch of viewer involvement. 'We need information,' I would tell the viewers. 'Information about Sincton's flat, the people he met at the Bunch of Grapes and, of course, the missing witness, Robin Nicholl. Can *you* help?'

Late that morning I was summoned to Biddle's office to see Dexter's contribution. As a concession to James's sensibilities, and after warnings from a tiresomely unadventurous lawyer, we had agreed not to film our man in Singles Street at work with an unwitting stranger. Instead we had convinced Dexter that he should act out the scene in the Bunch of Grapes with his new beloved Jo Cullen, the bingo waif. Both of them, after all, knew what happened when a couple met for the first time in a pick-up bar.

This, it was now clear, had been a bad decision. They smiled. They sighed. They finished one another's sentences. As an insight into the hard, dangerous world of promiscuous sex, it was resolutely unconvincing.

'I don't believe this,' said Biddle as, with appalled fascination, we viewed the rushes with Miles-Thomas and a couple of his assistants. 'They've only done a fucking *Jules et Jim* on us.'

'We can't use it,' said Miles-Thomas. 'We can get a couple of minutes out of it, but we're left with three to fill.'

'How about extending Crime Time Update at the beginning of the programme?' suggested one of the assistants.

'Not enough material.' Miles-Thomas darted an irritated look in the direction of Biddle. 'We've had to stretch it already.'

'Could you give me an hour on this, Jonathan?' I asked. 'I may be able to fill out the interview with Paula.'

'Fascinating,' Biddle muttered.

Without waiting for a reply, I left his office and made my way downstairs.

'Bad news, James,' I told Dexter as I passed his desk. 'They're cutting your scene with Jo Cullen. We've got to find three minutes.'

He followed me into the office. 'Cut? What was wrong with it?'

'You didn't seem like strangers.'

Dexter shrugged. 'We happen to be compatible,' he said. 'We were like that as soon as we met. We just clicked.'

I had to laugh. A few minutes in front of the cameras and it all goes out of the window: training, discipline, the last few brain cells. This was no longer a police station; it was the film set for an Ealing comedy.

'I'm very happy for you both,' I said.

Somehow, during the night and the morning after, Robin's right leg had found its way around Laura, whose back was turned to him. His face was in her hair, his left arm was under her shoulder, his right hand rested happily between her breasts. As he awoke early in the afternoon, Robin felt a deep contentment. Home: the warmth, the smell of his wife, her little protests as he tried to release the arm, which was still asleep or maybe dead, from under her.

'Mmm,' he said, moving even closer.

If only there weren't some memory niggling at him, like a burglar alarm in a neighbouring street. His wife's adventures? No, that was past. Something to do with Ollie? Ah. He remembered.

'Last night I tied a woman up,' he said. 'To her bed.'

'Never mind.' Laura rolled over. 'You're home now.'

'Picked her up in a bar. Took her home and tied her up.'

'Robin,' Laura laughed. 'Why?'

'It was Jane Goodenough. I thought she must have something that would tell me who killed Ollie.'

'Oh my God,' Laura groaned. 'The nightmare returns. So who did kill that little prick?'

'I tied her up and started searching the flat. She said something about a tape. "Of course," I said. "That's what I want."'

'Do you mean you've got a tape that will tell you who killed Sincton?'

'So it seems.'

'Give it to the police, Robin.'

Robin sat up, like a man waking from a dream. 'I left a knife there,' he said. 'I ought to check that Jane's all right.'

He leapt out of bed and began picking up his clothes from the floor.

Laura watched him. 'Don't go. Or let me come with you.'

'Action,' said Robin. 'Yes, action's the thing.'

As I studied Ollie's notes, looking for ways to extend my interview with Paula, I put a call through to Joy and told her about Dexter's lost three minutes.

'But Paula's dull,' she said. 'And strange. It's not the sex that I find weird. It's the writing it down.'

'Yes. Ollie and Paula had that in common at least.'

Reluctantly, I bade her goodbye and returned to Ollie.

Here's the thing. These days I find myself envying my married friends for just one reason. With their endless variety on the old infidelity theme, they're in touch with true sin. There's the danger, the hidden life, the shared secrets – the sense, however dim and vestigial, of the forbidden.

But for the healthy, independent lover of indoor games, it's more difficult. Where do you find all that? There's a limit to the avenues you can explore with a new date. As simple, youthful need subsides, other priorities become important. You want danger – a degree of refinement rarely to be found in the traditional nooks and crannies. And you can't even cheat.

Where to go? Invite a few friends round for some carefully organized daisy-chain? Urgh. The noise, my dear, the people. Homosexuality? Oh please. Hanging around in lavatories waiting for rough gratification with a soft-eyed truckdriver. Nope, can't do it.

And I've never understood the upper-class Englishman's affection for hitting women. Frightfully boring of me, I'm sure, but inflicting pain has never appealed – something of a surprise to my more sophisticated girlfriends, who have come to accept that a bit of rough goes with the territory. You mean, we just like, do it, no ropes, nothing? God, Ollie, you're so weird.

The other night I wandered into a sex shop off the Tottenham Court Road. Browsing among the outsize dildos and high-tech jerk-off machines, I found a rather intriguing black leather mask and some designer handcuffs. Sure, I bought them. You never know, do you?

Beside the desk there was a cardboard box in which I kept items taken from Ollie's flat: the disks, his Filofax, some papers. I looked once again at one of the spiral-bound notebooks containing, neatly written in a female hand, notes from a novel of sexual adventure. In Sincton's writing on the front was the word 'Laura'.

Until now I had always assumed that the work was Laura Nicholl's. After all, the handwriting was similar to hers.

It's not the sex that I find weird. It's the writing it down.

I made a call. Then, telling Dexter to reassure Biddle and his crew that I would be back by early evening, I drove across London.

That afternoon I discovered what happened to Oliver Sincton on his last night on earth.

21

He should have been safe from the restlessness. Normally it bothered him in the afternoon or evening, not late at night when alcohol had deadened the sting of need. He had dined at the Groucho Club with Jane who had been at her worst, complaining that he was exploiting her father. Fast strangers and relationships, he had thought to himself as her angry words broke over his head; they don't belong together.

Infuriated, Jane had walked out at ten-thirty, claiming she had to be up early in the morning.

It had been about eleven o'clock when Laura had entered the bar of the Groucho, her husband Robin tagging along behind her like an emasculated Irish wolfhound. Ollie mixed well with the Nicholls when they were apart – he played the different parts required, old friend for him, co-conspirator for her, with his normal ease – but now he was caught between roles. With an effusiveness that, even by his standards, was unconvincing, he greeted them, asked them about their evening, then, just as he was going, threw an arm around Robin's shoulders and whispered something in his ear with the slurred gravity of the seriously drunk.

Of course, he wasn't drunk; Ollie was always under control. It was also unlike him to leave so quickly. Held in this absurd grip, Robin had reacted to Sincton's words with a self-parodying facial tic, chin jerking back into the neck while eyebrows took wing towards his hairline. Meant to express astonishment, it conveyed gauche embarrassment. Ollie squeezed his shoulder. 'All right, Robbie,' he said.

Robbie? That was a new one.

207

'What did he want?' Laura asked, after Ollie had weaved his way out of the club.

Robin shrugged. 'Drunken waffle,' he said. 'Something about my being his literary executor.'

As he emerged from the Groucho, Ollie was aware of a figure standing in the shadows across the narrow street – small, hunched, wearing a cheap, light mackintosh, carrying some sort of shopping bag. He hesitated for a moment, sensitive as ever to sexual availability, but it was more curiosity than serious interest that attracted his eye. What was she, some sort of grimy street-dweller, a teenager on the run? She seemed too apologetic and down-trodden to be a whore; her hair was lank, straggly. She didn't smile. No, no thanks, deary. He hurried on. He needed a drink.

After a block or so, he noticed that the woman was walking in the same direction, but on the other side of the street, like an incompetent detective. When he slowed, so did she. He stopped to look in a shop window; she stepped back into a doorway.

He could have ignored her – she was no threat to him – but of course he didn't. He made his way up Shaftesbury Avenue and headed towards Regent Street. It was quieter here and, as if she could sense his indecision, the woman had moved closer. He turned into a side road, then doubled back, to confirm that she was following him. He crossed at an intersection and, as the woman waited on her side of the street, he approached her.

'What do you want?' he asked.

The woman, her hands in the pockets of her coat, gazed down the street and said nothing.

'You're following me,' said Ollie.

She smiled up at him, the changing colours of the traffic lights illuminating her features. Jesus. He shuddered. Some seductress. Make-up had been carelessly applied on the sallow, pinched face, her dark hair, thick and matted, was parted severely in the middle of her head; she had a witchy, Hallowe'en look. Her legs were thin and Ollie sensed a stale, acrid smell coming from her. Now was the time to leave, but he didn't. She was like a nightmare version of all those dates, nights out, strangers, an image of his own slack, decaying sexuality. Getting picked up by a psycho in the West End: it had come to this.

She continued to smile, a charmless sight.

'I live near here,' said Ollie, surrendering.

They walked in silence. The woman – she could have been anywhere between thirty and fifty – stared ahead of her. There seemed something familiar about her face, but Ollie quickly dismissed the notion. She was a stranger, thank God. But what did she want? Did she do this every night? And with whom? Christ, what a thought. As they left Soho and headed down Piccadilly, she linked her gloved hand through his arm. Ollie's date for the night.

By the time they reached Half Moon Street, he had forgotten the events of earlier that evening. Only this mattered: an entirely new adventure, attended by the feelings of dread and anticipation to which over the years he had become addicted. He went into the sitting-room, turned on some lights; then, seeing her standing there, luminously pale in the middle of the room, he thought again. Lights were a bad idea. With a smile of seduction that was more like a grimace, he switched off all but one.

'Whisky?' he asked.

'Yes.'

He went to a cabinet and poured them both a glass. 'Here's to us,' he said uneasily. She gulped her drink down.

'Where do you sleep?' she asked.

He gestured vaguely in the direction of the bedroom. Removing her coat and throwing it on to the sofa where she had left her canvas shopping bag, she walked through the hall. Ollie took the opportunity to open the bag – not searching for anything weird or psychotic but simply out of curiosity. There was a spare shirt, some sweets, a paper bag containing two doughnuts, and a notebook which, if he had the chance, he would try to read later. He was a great reader of other people's notes and letters. He followed her.

Because he liked a touch of last-minute modesty when it was too late to count, Ollie had hoped to find her undressed, in bed, the sheet girlishly tucked under her chin, but the woman was casually looking through his cupboard where he had left his magazines and, he realized with some embarrassment, the velvet-lined handcuffs which, in an honest spirit of enquiry, he had acquired at the sex shop.

'What do you want?' he asked.

She turned slowly. The handcuffs hung loosely from her hand.

'Those?'

She nodded. 'Those.' She stepped towards him and, once again, he caught a whiff of the street with something else, distantly familiar.

'Have we met?' he said, as she unbuttoned his shirt and slipped it back off his shoulders. Frowning slightly, she clicked a handcuff on to his left wrist.

'You first,' she said.

'Are you a writer? Have you been in television?'

'A writer?' For a moment she looked at him as if she were about to make a confession. Then she seemed to think better of it. 'Not me,' she said, unfastening his belt.

'How do I know that I can trust you?' he whispered.

And, for the first time, she laughed.

'You don't,' she said.

He couldn't wait to get this all down on disk.

Paula Matthews sat at her kitchen table. Before her, like a dead rodent, lay a black wig.

'My only regret is that he showed no fear. He thought it was a joke.'

'He didn't recognize you?' I asked.

'I might have known that he'd have no memory for faces. He was pissed as well.' Paula put her hand under the wig like a glove puppeteer and made it dance across the table. She appeared to be remarkably unmoved by my discovery. 'He didn't seem self-obsessed when I first met him. He was a good listener; that was what I liked about him. When he told me what he did for a living, I felt we had something in common. So I suppose I told him too much. The years of writing stories, the evening classes, the rejections. He seemed to understand all that. Yet he knew everyone; all the publishers and literary agents who wouldn't give my novels a sniff, Ollie was lunching with every day.'

'Did he offer to look at your work?'

Paula laughed. 'It was my idea. As he was getting ready to leave, I asked whether he'd like to read a novel I had just finished. He made a good show of being reluctant – it was in notebooks and hadn't been typed up yet – but in the end he agreed and took it away. He promised to phone.'

'You didn't have a copy.'

'Of course not. And I didn't have his address or number. I trusted him. Weeks passed, months. I was in despair. I couldn't turn to anyone because I had met him in such embarrassing circumstances. I stopped writing. Instead of going to evening classes, I met more men. It became a substitute. I told myself that losing my book was a punishment for the way I had behaved. I might have forgotten it all if one day I hadn't bought *Truth or Dare* by Laura Nicholl.'

'Her fourth novel.'

'My book.'

Paula stood and reached up to the top shelf of a dresser, taking down a paperback copy of *Truth or*

Dare, stained and thumbed, its pages falling out. 'If you don't believe me,' she said.

I read the first page of Laura's novel, then Paula's neatly written notebook. There was a certain similarity of tone, but Ollie's version was slicker and more confident than Paula's halting effort.

'See?' she asked.

I shook my head. 'Not really.'

She took the book from me. 'He made a few changes, of course, but it's my idea.' She turned to a page on which a paragraph was heavily underlined. 'Word for word,' she said. 'Stolen.'

'All right,' I said, convinced now that the woman was demented. 'So he borrowed a few words. Was that a reason to kill him?'

'Stole. There are thirty-three scenes that are identical. He had taken my life and re-invented it – destroyed it. For Laura fucking Nicholl.'

Watching Paula as she flicked through the book, her face blotchy with anger, I tried to imagine her rather than Laura on the chat shows, at the parties, signing copies at Harrods. It didn't work; her face didn't fit. The market, people like my wife, would be disappointed. *Truth or Dare* written by Oliver Sincton with extensive borrowing from Paula Matthews: it was hardly a classy pedigree. Once I had thought that it took two professionals to concoct the perfect Laura Nicholl package – a writer and a frontperson – but now I saw that it took three. For all his ease with words, Ollie couldn't tell a story. So he had to borrow. I wondered where the stories for the other Laura Nicholl novels had come from, and how much Laura knew of her accomplice's fictional technique.

'That was a reason to kill him ten times over,' Paula said quietly. 'But, I've told you, I didn't.'

'No-one's going to believe you.'

'You've given me my notebooks back now. I can prove it.'

'Not that. No-one gives a damn about whether you or Laura Nicholl wrote *Truth or Dare*. It's what happened at the flat that matters.'

'All I wanted was to humiliate him once – to hurt him through his precious sexual pride. Right down to the doughnut.'

'Then you walked away.'

'Left him there, tugging and clucking and begging me, all the time with this thing on him. Under other circumstances, it would have been funny.'

'What time was this?'

'Half past one, two. I shut the door, took a taxi home.'

'No.' I shook my head. 'If this comes out, I'll have to charge you with murder.'

She looked alarmed. 'You don't believe me?'

'We need a result.'

'What about the truth? What about who really killed him?'

Yeah yeah. I stood up. At the time I believed Paula, but, even if she had been the person who put a knife through Ollie's throat, I wasn't going to take her in. She was too close to home. I pushed the notebooks across the table. 'Burn them,' I said.

'My book? You're not serious.'

I shrugged. 'The life or the work. You have to choose. You'll have plenty of time to write your masterpiece in Holloway.'

'What about later?' she asked quietly.

'Later?'

'The show.'

I smiled.

Fuck the show.

22

I returned from East Sheen to find the place on full alert. If civil war had broken out in Berkeley Square, it could not have caused more panic than the imminent prospect of the station going live on television without one of its frontmen. Biddle was pacing up and down my office, production assistants were running about self-importantly, while Jonathan Miles-Thomas, seated at my desk when I breezed in, had a sullen, troubled look about his worldly features.

'Where the hell have you been?' squawked Norman Biddle.

'Police work,' I said. 'You know how it is, Superintendent.'

'We're on air in under two hours' time and you wander off to conduct some ridiculous interview.'

I smiled. 'Crime does not conform to working hours. It respects no schedule,' I said.

Miles-Thomas, draped over my chair in a self-conscious attitude of despair, asked quietly, 'Is there something you would like to share with us, Inspector?'

'Paula Matthews won't be able to make the show tonight,' I said. 'She's had second thoughts.' I had their full attention now. Outside the office telephones rang, ignored. 'She's decided not to become involved.'

'But it's nationwide television,' said Biddle faintly.

'What exactly does she want?' Miles-Thomas asked. 'Money? Her own show? A dinner date with Russ Targett?'

'It's not that.'

'I'll talk to her.' He reached for the telephone on my desk.

'She's not there,' I said. At my suggestion, Paula was staying with her mother for the next couple of days. 'She's made up her mind.'

'You're behind this.' Biddle narrowed his dark little eyes. 'You've always resented my involvement with *Crime Time*.'

'Can't you . . . make her talk?' asked Miles-Thomas. For the first time, the producer seemed seriously worried. 'That's what policemen are supposed to be good at doing.'

'She's giving me a statement tomorrow. She just doesn't want to be on television.'

'And what do you expect us to put on instead?' Biddle's voice was now reaching the higher registers. 'Tom and fucking Jerry?'

I shrugged, glancing down at my desk on which had been placed various messages, mostly to do with other cases. Among them was a note from Dexter which read: '4.17 p.m. Laura Nicholl rang, wanting to speak to you. Told me that Robin turned up late last night, claiming he had left Jane Goodenough tied up. Nicholl may have returned to the flat. Called the number several times, no answer. Worth a visit?'

I pushed my way past Biddle and out of the office.

Dexter looked up from his desk. 'Jane?' he asked, seeing the note in my hand.

'Yes, get me her address. I think you'd better get round there.'

Miles-Thomas stood at the door of the office. 'So sorry to interrupt,' he said, exuding languid disapproval. 'In ninety minutes my organization will be helping the fight against crime by reaching twelve million people in their front sitting-rooms. At your suggestion—' he fixed Biddle with an icy stare '—we decided to major on the Sincton murder. As we stand at present, much of the programme will be devoted to showing Her Majesty's Constabulary playing with itself. Unless you have a better idea, we had better go back to the interview between Andy Craig, yourself and DC Dexter.'

'I think you had better count James out. He has the small matter of an emergency call to attend to.'

'I don't believe it,' muttered Biddle.

'Jonathan, d'you have a mo?' One of Miles-Thomas's production assistants called him back into my office where they stood in earnest conference for a few seconds.

'Right,' said Miles-Thomas, returning. 'We're going for what we call a doorslammer. This emergency of yours. Can you put it on hold for an hour and a half?'

And I fell for it. I actually believed that I owed something to television. What, after all, would be the harm in our delaying if the result were a small parable of contemporary police work? Christ knew what they would find at Jane's flat, but the illusion of action would provide its own reward. Later I discovered that Miles-Thomas had a filmed report on the Oxfordshire rapist which could be used in the event of the ultimate disaster, namely our unravelling the Sincton case before the cameras were rolling. It was his fingertip instinct, he subsequently revealed in an interview with a media magazine, which persuaded him to stay with us as our plans crumbled around our heads.

'What exactly is a doorslammer?' I asked.

Miles-Thomas turned to his assistant as if I weren't there. 'Get a mobile unit up here, pronto,' he said. 'Work out a schedule allowing for a ten-minute OB before we come back to the station. Now—' he smiled at me '—I'll tell you exactly what we're going to do.'

It was for just such a moment that the *Crime Time* team had been waiting. Previous programmes had broken up the interviews and chat with heart-stopping incidents – plods jumping in and out of cars, slamming doors and driving rather too fast in their pursuit of Chummy – but, however shaky the camerawork, however loud the bleeped-out expletives, they had clearly been set up, recorded. The average TV viewer has an instinct for authenticity. The dream, for Jonathan Miles-Thomas and his team, was to catch the action live.

'A small amount of enactment will be required from you, Simon,' he told me, holding up a hand to forestall questions or objections.

'Andy will be interviewing you when the telephone will ring on your desk. In a very businesslike way, you take the call. It will be the Duty Officer.' The producer was talking in a low, soothing voice, as if he were coaching a child. 'You hang up, walk away from the interview. The cameraman—' he made a distracted, urgent gesture in the direction of his assistant, who made a note on her pad '—will follow you to James's desk. You'll tell him that there has been an emergency call. At this point Andy will ask if it has anything to do with the Sincton case. You'll tell him it has. Andy will then appear to be receiving instructions through his earpiece and will ask you if a cameraman can follow the officers attending the emergency. After a moment's thought, you'll agree.' He punched my arm gently. 'All right, Simon?'

'Bit of a fake, isn't it?' I asked uneasily.

'Not at all. It will appear utterly authentic. The cameraman then scurries off with James. Will he be going alone?'

'No. DC Smiley will drive the car.'

'Great. As long as there's room in the back for our man. We show the interviews, after which we return to the team heading for Jane's flat.'

'Right.' Even I could see that the potential for disaster here was unacceptably high. The car could crash. DC Smiley, an officer in whom I had never had the greatest confidence, could lose his way. Jane might appear on her doorstep, confronted by Dexter, Smiley and a breathless man with a camera. 'Can I help you?'

she would ask, as a nation of viewers shuddered with embarrassment.

'What happens if something goes wrong?' I asked.

'That's fine. This is what police work's all about. Presumably if the door's locked, they'll kick it down.'

'Yes, they'll have to go in.'

'Great,' said the producer. '*Excellente.*'

Robin brought the heel of his shoe hard against Jane's front door. With the first impact, the wood cracked. He stepped back and charged, shoulder first. The door gave, and he stumbled into her hallway.

He walked to the bedroom. Jane, still on the bed, turned towards him with cold fury.

'You bastard,' she whispered.

'I left you a knife,' he said.

'Don't be ridiculous.' Jane sounded weary, frightened. 'Let me go.'

He took the knife and was about to cut her free when he glanced down at her. It had been a strange twenty-four hours for Robin. He was under a lot of stress. He paused; then, hell's bells, he kissed her.

As Robin was later to remark in a press interview, an Englishman takes time.

Something odd had happened to my face. As I stared into the bathroom mirror moments before we went on air, I saw that a reptilian fold of skin seemed to have appeared out of nowhere to give me a sad, watchful look that I didn't feel was mine. This was not the face of a TV star; it was a character actor, a minor villain, a butler – a policeman.

Briefly, I thought about Paula, who would now be settling down to watch the programme of which, had I been more professional, she would have been the star. It was quite possible that she had made a fool of me. After all, if she was crazed enough to stalk Sincton for weeks, to tie him to a bed and leave him daintily fitted with a doughnut condom, stabbing him in the throat was hardly beyond her. Perhaps I had fallen for her semi-detached respectability. Murderers can live in East Sheen too.

Famous screen actors, I remembered, could express rage, passion or a broken heart with the smallest facial movement. I gazed in the mirror: rage, then passion, then a broken heart. My features twitched as if I had gone mad.

I'm told that when I first appeared on *Crime Time*, looming up glassy-eyed behind Andy Craig, I looked as happy and confident as one of the walking dead.

Craig asked me the prepared questions. As if some alien presence had hijacked my brain, I replied, dry-mouthed and hesitant, in the tortuous cliché of the undereducated.

'Now this Oliver Sincton was not British, was he?'

'No. He was of American extraction.'

'Could you tell us anything about Sincton which would help the viewers?'

'Well, Andy, he was something of a ladies' man, not unfamiliar with the celebrity circuit, and we have reason to believe that there were certain irregularities in his private life.'

'Are you saying he was deviant?' asked Craig, with that split-second glance at the camera which excluded me and included every viewer in the land. Behind the glass partition of my office, I noticed Miles-Thomas slumped in front of a small screen; he seemed to be asleep.

'Maybe not deviant so much as extremely active vis-à-vis the opposite sex. He used contact magazines to meet his lady friends.'

Great television. It couldn't have been going better. For Joe Punter, sadism is part of the TV diet. A famous actor drunk on a chat show, a candid-camera patsy watching his car roll over a cliff, a gibbering detective wrestling unhappily with the English language; this is the stuff of real life which gets the dinner overcooked and the programme discussed later in the pub.

More observant viewers may have wondered why, between stammered banalities, I would glance nervously at the telephone on my desk as if it were about to jump up and bite me. When it did finally ring, I reached for it and gabbled into the receiver, 'Excuse me Andy I better take this,' then turned to Andy and said, 'Hullo.'

'Jonathan here, Simon.' As agreed, it was Miles-Thomas on the line, talking me through my part. 'You're doing just great if you can relax a bit, all right? Now just say, "When was this?"'

I nodded importantly. 'When was this?'

'Just a bit more nodding, Simon. Lovely. A couple of beats, then say, "I'll get Dexter right on to it now."'

'I see.' I moved my head backwards and forwards like a robot.

'That's enough nodding, Simon,' said Miles-Thomas rather more impatiently. 'Let's get on with it.'

'Right,' I said. 'I'll get Dexter right on to it now.'

I hung up and, with a curt 'Excuse me a moment, Andy', walked out of the office, bumping like a blind man against the desk. As rehearsed, Dexter was busy at work on a report when I approached him.

'Word from the Duty Officer, James.'

'Sir?' And the bastard kept writing!

I swallowed hard. 'James?' You could hear the tremor in my voice. Dexter was making what they call in the business 'an entrance'. For a moment I was tempted to grab whatever ill-spelt gibberish he was jotting down and hold it before the camera.

'Sorry, sir. What was the problem?'

Here was the ultimate humiliation. James was a natural. As if he knew that the watching millions would recognize him for the way a policeman should be – young, concerned, *intelligent*, for God's sake – he was entirely at ease. He actually nursed me through our scene. 'You think it could be connected to the Sincton case?' he asked.

'Yes,' I said. 'It could be—' I hesitated, aware that I was about to blunder into mentioning Jane's name. 'Maybe it's—'

'Sounds urgent,' interrupted Dexter, as the cameraman almost shouldered me aside to get a better angle on his lovely dark features. 'I'll take Smiley and get over there, pronto.' Grabbing his jacket self-importantly, he strode over to Smiley's desk, tapped him on the shoulder and made his way out of the station.

Craig suggested, apparently thinking on his feet, that the camera might go with them in the car. Still stunned by Dexter's performance, I managed to say, 'Of course, Andy.'

We were back on an even keel now. The instant love affair between Dexter and the camera had steadied the programme, given it a focus, a hero. As Craig introduced our two interviews, I could relax at last. Miles-Thomas gave me an absurdly camp double thumbs-up. For the life of me, I couldn't see what he was so pleased about.

Laura was sincere, Coleman was oily. Without letting the dead hand of my screen presence descend once again on the programme, the producer cut directly, with a breathless voice-over from Craig, to a police car speeding towards a flat in Islington.

By a fluke of timing, for which Miles-Thomas would later take full credit, Dexter and Smiley were a minute from their destination, allowing James a few moments of over-the-shoulder tough talk which somehow managed to convey more about the case than the whole of my carefully prepared summary. Then, with a squeal of brakes that narrowly avoided propelling the cameraman from the back seat through the windscreen, they were there. 'Let's go,' said Dexter. Slam, slam.

Yes, Dexter's doorslammer; it was an instant TV classic.

The two men were standing on the landing outside Jane's flat by the time the cameraman had caught up with them. For a few seconds they were motionless, alert and dangerous, like real television detectives. James spoke softly into his radio, then, in his new TV voice, said to Smiley, 'We're going in. Try the door.'

Smiley leant gently on the door which, with a slight crack, opened. He looked significantly at Dexter and they entered the flat.

In the hall Dexter pointed to the sitting-room while he himself moved towards the bedroom. The cameraman naturally ignored Smiley and stuck with James.

He pushed the door open and stopped suddenly. The curtains were drawn. Something was happening in there. The microphone picked up the sounds made by Smiley who had gone into the kitchen. The camera followed James who, like a true performer, remembered his audience. He gave a backward glance and, for that instant, he was not just a police officer but a TV Everyman – shocked, amused, surprised, afraid, excited. To the left behind this close-up image, out of focus in the background, could be seen the face of a woman on the bed. And over James's right shoulder, during this moment which seemed to last so long, there was another, ghostly shape, pale and bony in the half-light, a pair of male buttocks.

'Who the bloody hell are you?' asked Robin.

At this point professionalism took over. The cameraman stepped to the left and panned away from Dexter, affording *Crime Time*'s family audience a view of Jane Goodenough, bound hand and foot, her nakedness only partially concealed by the unalluring nudity of Robin Nicholl.

There was a babble of voices.

'Get him off me,' said Jane, as if she were talking to one of her staff at the Ministry.

'Are you all right?' James was asking.

'Fucking hell,' said Biddle, standing behind me as, back at the station, we watched events unfold on-screen.

Jonathan Miles-Thomas gave an astonished little laugh. 'Keep 'em rolling,' he said.

'Jim, he's got a knife.' This was Smiley, blundering his way into the room, jogging the camera so that we were unable to see Dexter as he dived across the naked couple in an attempt to reach the kitchen knife by Nicholl's hand.

Robin was quicker, grabbing the knife and turning from Jane to Dexter. For a full half minute the two men grappled together on the bed while Smiley hopped around ineffectually. Robin slipped downwards, falling half off the end of the bed, and Dexter was able to grip his wrist, wrenching the knife out of his right hand. When Dexter reached for it, bringing it sharply against Robin's neck, the two of them froze, one on top of the other. The camera closed in on Robin as he lay helplessly in the V of Jane's legs for *Crime Time*'s supremely telegenic moment: Dexter, knife in hand, handsome and in control; Robin, naked, eyes shut tight in anguish and embarrassment, his mop of hair adorned, courtesy of Jane Goodenough, by a cute little pubic crown. It was unforgettable.

'You're under arrest,' said Dexter.

'Cut,' said Miles-Thomas.

We were one minute thirty seconds out. Andy Craig pushed past me to sit at my desk and waffle at the camera until he was given the wind-up sign. I remember little of what he said. DC James Dexter was mentioned several times; Detective Inspector Potter was not.

By now television's conquest of the station was complete. All pretence of police work was suspended while my colleagues gathered around the technicians

223

as they packed up, discussing the programme in a pathetic attempt to prolong the excitement. Amid much laughter and self-congratulation, Miles-Thomas and his assistants had left without another word to me or – a moment of small satisfaction – to Norman Biddle.

'Great TV,' he said, as we sat in my office, both of us obscurely aware that we had not benefited from the programme as much as we should have. 'Fast, exciting, unpredictable.'

'You did an excellent job,' I said. I felt sorry for Norman; from the distant look in his eyes, I could see that before him stretched an infinity of routine, unpublicized police work. His first real taste of showbusiness had left him hungry for more.

'An arrest on live television,' he said. 'Where do we go from here?'

'To the interveiw room? Nicholl's on his way.'

He sounded alarmed. 'You don't need me, do you?' he asked. 'I think I'd better talk to the Deputy Commissioner about a press release.' He stood up and stretched. 'At least we got our man,' he said.

'Maybe,' I said.

Joy was strangely subdued when I rang her. It's not every day that a family watches Daddy making his television début on a programme of unscheduled sex and violence. She told me that Mark and Dominic wanted to meet Dexter.

'So was it really Nicholl all along?' she asked.

'It fits. He was in the right place at the right time,' I said. 'He's certainly got a fair bit to explain.'

'But not Robin Nicholl, surely, Si? A killer?'

'Not a chance.'

Part Three

23

Down here it could be an open prison, or one of our more traditional boarding schools. There are classrooms, games pitches, corridors, serried ranks of rhododendron. During the morning the place is like a sepulchre; a frown of concentration hangs over it. Brains – tiny brains, for the most part – are being taxed. Strong hands, bred to grip beer mugs or punch faces, are grasping pencils and stabbing calculators. Later the Victorian red-brick buildings will echo to the sound of young male voices at play – ordered, optimistic, on their way to a bright future in Her Majesty's Constabulary.

Among the staff, secrets abound. A few are here for the joy of working with youth, for that moment when some simple, unlined face lights up with relief as, deep within a cavern of the mind, a penny drops. The rest have been diverted into this leafy siding after a professional mishap we don't like to discuss. Some are slightly bent, others rather too honest: none of us ever quite mastered the delicate balance between good and bad behaviour that is the mark of modern policing. We lost the conscience game, but were too set in our ways, or too afraid, or simply too lacking in ambition, to make the obvious move over to the other side.

Transferred to East Molesey. It doesn't sound good, does it? An instructor of trainee Dexters. Yet, frankly, it could be worse: I'm still on the inside looking out. I contribute to society. My pension remains intact.

The office where I now work is rather more agreeable than the fishbowl I inhabited back at the station. It

227

has walls made of brick, not glass; a certain privacy is allowed.

Nice view, too. There's a square of lawn under my window beyond which is a small pond with an island. Right now, there's no water, only green slime. Although it's late autumn, the weather still seems reluctant to do the decent, English thing. Sometimes I miss the evil smell of an urban summer.

A young man with a footballer's hair cut walks past the window, waving at me with a heartiness that's the merest whisker away from sarcasm. I'm not particularly popular here; they call me Peaky.

It's a mess, when all's said and done. I had hoped that, when I reconstructed the Sincton story, a pattern would emerge, a logic, maybe some neat little moral. In the end it was a murder that flattered to deceive: the career opportunities it appeared to offer in terms of promotion or fame never came off. Only a few of those involved were to emerge in credit.

Robin spent less time in custody than many of those who saw him arrested so memorably might have anticipated. Raised, like any good liberal, on stories of police brutality, he was pleasantly surprised to find that most of the questions he had to parry from fellow inmates, as well as prison officers, concerned his bedroom achievements rather than criminal matters. Bondage, was it, you kinky bastard? *Celebrity* bondage, seen nationwide. As the owner of the most comprehensively exposed buttocks in the land, Robin was the nick's Mr Personality. Incarcerated he may have been, but his ego was off the leash.

'What exactly were you doing?' Laura had asked, when she first visited him.

'I'll explain all that when I get out,' Robin said airily. 'Maybe you'll be able to use it in your next book.'

Taken aback by her husband's new-found confidence, she asked, 'You'll be out soon, won't you?'

'No problem,' said Robin, whose lawyer was already

conducting delicate, off-the-record negotiations to secure his client's release. 'The tape will clear me.'

Later that afternoon Superintendent Norman Biddle sat across the interview table from Robin and looked vaguely through the papers in front of him. 'What tape's that, Robin? I have no record of any tape here.'

'Inspector Potter. I gave him a cassette when I was brought in. He knows.'

'The inspector is on leave,' said Biddle. 'He's been told to rest for a few days.'

'Rest? What about my case?'

'I'm well briefed, Robin.' Biddle held up an authoritative hand in the direction of the door, where James Dexter was standing. 'The constable here knows the background.'

Still faintly embarrassed by his naked tussle with Dexter, Robin stared at Dexter. 'Bloody hell,' he said. 'This is ridiculous.'

'Now, Robin.' Biddle treated him to an ingratiating smile, a close relation to the expression he used when TV producers were in the vicinity. 'It's time we cut the crap and spoke frankly, man to man. We have enough evidence here—' he tapped my notes, which now included a few fatuous jottings of his own '—to send you down for the murder of Oliver Sincton and—'

'That's not what my lawyer says.'

'—and of course the rape of Jane Goodenough.'

'She *agreed* to be tied up.'

Biddle allowed this remark to hang in the air, as if they were already in court.

'All right, let's be sophisticated about this. Maybe she did agree – but that was the night before, wasn't it? The lady is quite adamant that when you returned the little game was over. Of course, it's a nice legal point. Can a masochist withdraw consent?' Biddle shook his head. 'Maybe a very liberal jury might understand your picking up a stranger, tying her up, going back to your wife, then several hours later returning to the stranger and, mistaking her protests for encouragement, jumping on top of her to complete what you had omitted to do the previous night, but they would need to be *very* modern-minded, would they not? I understand, of course, that this is the sort of thing that happens in certain circles, but you might have problems persuading the taxi-drivers and mums on the jury.'

'I explained what happened to Inspector Potter.'

'Between you and me, Robin,' Biddle smiled, 'I wouldn't put too much confidence in my colleague. He's been under a lot of strain recently, hasn't he, James?'

Dexter frowned. At that particular moment he had a lot on his mind. My temporary suspension from the case had, somewhat touchingly, alarmed him almost as much as Biddle's bumbling attempts to make a deal with a murder suspect. Then, every time he returned to his desk, the telephone rang with yet another absurd offer from a tabloid, chat show or advertising agency. No wonder he was confused. 'Quite a strain, yes,' he said.

'However,' Biddle continued. 'All may not be lost. I might just be able to help you.'

Robin rose to the bait. With the correct degree of co-operation from him, Biddle explained, the murder charge would eventually be dropped for lack of evidence. As for the question of Jane's rape, that could be, to use one of the superintendent's favourite terms, 'finessed'. All that would be required of Robin was a further month in custody, followed by a deep and binding vow of silence.

Robin thought about the proposal. On the one hand there was the truth, his debt to Ollie. That, given Sincton's behaviour, no longer weighed too heavily. On the other there was the risk of conviction, the certainty of unwelcome publicity, particularly in the area of his wife's working methods. It was not a difficult decision.

The month in jail, of course, was an essential part of the plan. *Crime Time*'s next edition would include a triumphant cameo role for Norman Biddle, standing beside that national hero James Dexter, sharing his glory. After that it was in everyone's interest that the case quietly be allowed to fizzle out.

Almost uniquely among my fellow instructors, I'm no believer in conspiracy theories. My experience of twenty or so years in the force has convinced me that careers are destroyed not by the hidden hand of evil in high places, or by sinister cover-ups, but by sloth, incompetence or, most frequently of all, rank stupidity. There are, however, exceptions.

The day after *Crime Time*, I received a call from the Deputy Commissioner. He congratulated me on the satisfactory outcome of the case.

I told him that there was more to come. 'I don't believe Nicholl is our man, sir,' I said with misplaced pride.

'No?' The Deputy Commissioner paused. 'You don't think you're becoming rather . . . over-involved?'

'In what way, sir?'

'I know that it's exciting appearing on television but there are other crimes going on out there, Simon.'

It took my breath away. Surrounded by starstruck fools, I was now the one accused of succumbing to celebrity fever. 'I believe there's something important going on, sir,' I said.

'Simon, I want you to take some leave. You can't have seen much of—' he hesitated '—Joy and the kids recently.'

At first I hadn't understood. Leave? Now? I told him I would take it in a few days' time.

'You looked very tired on television.' A certain feigned awkwardness, a gruff concern, had entered his tone. 'I'd like you to spend seven days at home with the family.'

I explained, perhaps in rather too much detail, about how my face was unsuited to television, how Miles-Thomas had set me up as *Crime Time*'s straight man.

'Yes yes,' he said, like a man whose very worst fears had been confirmed. 'But it's always a good idea on these occasions to recharge the batteries before they go flat. I do it myself sometimes.'

'Now seems a bad moment, sir.'

'A week, Simon. I have to insist,' said the Deputy Commissioner, adding, as if I should be pleased, 'I'm asking Biddle to stand in for you.'

Still, even with Biddle moving in, I saw nothing wrong. In whose interest was it to sabotage the investigation? There was no money at stake. And what was a week? Under normal circumstances, I would have taken the leave, then returned to the job to spend a few moments fitting up Robin Nicholl so that, with the right judge and jury, we had a chance of getting lucky in court. End of story.

Unfortunately for me, circumstances were no longer normal.

My wife had decided that I was a hero. 'You came over really well,' she said, comparing my television performance favourably even to that of our star, James Dexter. 'You were a real human being,' she said.

And I confided in her. Robin was innocent. I now knew what had happened, although the question of who actually wielded the knife remained unanswered. I explained why the time had come for me to walk away from the investigation. No-one was interested in the truth. To risk my career for the worthless shade of Oliver Sincton was an entirely futile gesture.

'There is such a thing as justice,' she said.

Joy and the path of justice versus a quiet life, survival even; it was finely balanced. Then Dexter let me down badly by taking a moral stand.

He appeared on my doorstep late one evening,

232

looking ill at ease, like someone afraid of being caught consorting with the enemy. I invited him in and we talked in the rock garden.

Norman Biddle had made a serious miscalculation in his dealings with James Dexter. Biddle thought that, just because Dexter was a TV natural, he would embrace TV principles – that is, no principles at all. He assumed celebrity was enough to keep James happy.

'They're closing the case, sir,' he said. 'Running it until the next *Crime Time*, then dropping it.'

'What about Nicholl?'

He told me about the deal with Robin.

'And the tape?'

'No-one seems interested any more,' said James. He reached into the pocket of his jacket.

'Thank you, James. I'll say I took a copy before I went on leave.'

He stood up nervously, as if the full significance of his action had just occurred to him.

'You could do me one more favour,' I said. 'Do you have the news video of Suzi Ashbourn's death?'

He nodded.

'Could I borrow it for five minutes? There's something I want to check.'

'Yes, sir,' he said. 'There's something else you should know, sir.' Dexter looked truly miserable. 'It's that Paula Matthews.'

No, in the end it wasn't Dexter, or Joy, or even the tattered remnants of my professional integrity that propelled me forward at this point. It was the death of Paula.

Of all the accidents that littered the trail of Ollie Sincton (bodies falling from the sky on to pavements, legs flying through the air at a county show), Paula's was the most absurd. In spite of my specific instructions, she had not let sleeping dogs lie.

While I was waiting for Nicholl to be brought into the station after his arrest on *Crime Time*, I had received a call from her. She seemed cheerful, particularly when I told her that there was no reason for her to be implicated in the case. 'What do I do now?' she asked.

'You go home and stay out of singles bars,' I said.

She called the station two days later, asking for me and getting Biddle. She wanted to know what was happening. She felt awkward, as if she should be giving evidence. That poor man Nicholl, she was sure he had nothing to do with it. Maybe it was the prospect of her return to everyday life in East Sheen, maybe she wanted a small share of the publicity action. That was stupid, as was her assumption that Norman Biddle and I were working on the same team. She told him everything.

It took them two days to get her, and her death had a suitably domestic banality to it. Crossing a road near her house, laden with groceries, she was hit by a speeding car. She died later in hospital. Bad luck? Coincidence? Even Dexter couldn't buy that. She hadn't known much, but someone had decided to be on the safe side.

I felt bad about this. I should have been firmer. Paula, after all, was an outsider in the game; she didn't know the rules. Presumably, with my proven record of corruptibility as one of life's professional survivors, I was thought to be less of a problem.

It was odd, later that night, sitting between Dexter and Joy, watching in my own front room the death of Suzi Ashbourn. Normally I'm against policemen bringing their work home with them, particularly when it is as unpleasant as Suzi's last show, but there was no alternative. I needed Joy's expertise.

It was clear from the film that a zany suicide bid was not what Suzi had in mind. She must have been waiting for her prince. Then, at the moment he appeared in the royal tent for the gun parade, she made her move. In her addled state of mind, crazed by love

234

and drugs, the last thing she would be expecting was that those nice shiny toy guns would belch forth flame. She just wanted to see her prince.

The cameraman, a true artist, had followed her trajectory through the air, then panned slowly around to the royal tent. White-faced and smiling, the prince was escorted away from the unpleasantness by burly detectives in his entourage. Other members of the royal party rose to leave.

'There.' Freezing the film, I turned to Joy. 'Who do you know among the prince's friends?'

My wife crouched in front of the television screen. 'That's Lady Firbank, the dress designer who's a cousin of the Queen. Then there's Charles Fortescue who was at school with the prince's brother. That's, you know, the chap who races cars and who went out with Princess Stephanie of Monaco. Then there's Lord Firbank who goes to Mustique a lot. Next to him is Lady Sarah—' I was impressed. Those hours and days spent reading the gossip columns had not been wasted; when it came to identifying the vacuous, well-fed faces with which our royal family likes to surround itself, my wife was a champ.

'What about him?' I pointed to a tall, dark-haired man who stood at the back of the group.

'Don't know that one. A detective, maybe.'

'D'you recognize him, James?'

'Never seen him, sir.'

Now here was something strange. I have a bad memory for faces – something of a disadvantage for a detective, I agree – yet this man was familiar to me. At first I assumed that those bland public-school features had stared at me from one of Joy's magazines but, if Joy didn't know him, then I must have seen him during the course of my investigation on an occasion when I was without Dexter, when I was working alone.

Doorstepping is not my style. Once you reach the rank

of detective inspector, you have people to do your loitering for you, but right now I found myself without staff, so I had no choice. The evening after my home-video show, I stood in a doorway in Whitehall, jostled by pasty-faced, evil-smelling commuters as they hurried for their trains. My man, being one of our more dedicated civil servants, did not emerge from the Ministry of Defence until almost seven o'clock.

'Christopher Hudson-Black?' I stepped forward.

At first I thought I must have the name wrong. He looked at me, uninterested and without the faintest glimmer of recognition. I might have been a dosser asking for the price of a cup of tea.

'It is Mr Hudson-Black, isn't it?'

He stood there, like a head boy, tall, smooth-faced and slightly reproving. In spite of the heat, he wore a dark blue overcoat which added to his air of youthful authority. 'Who wants to know?' he asked.

'Detective Inspector Potter. We have met.'

'Ah yes. You paid my late lamented colleague a visit after her friend was killed.'

'That's right.'

'I understood that had all been cleared up.'

'Not quite. I just need five minutes.' I smiled as he glanced at his watch. 'It really is rather important.'

As we walked down Whitehall Hudson-Black acted, presumably for the benefit of any other civil servant who may have seen us, as if we were colleagues on our way to catch the same train. Even so, we must have appeared an incongruous couple, him in his military coat, dark suit and black shining shoes, me in slacks of apologetic beige (even in mufti, I'm one of nature's policemen). His talk was mainly of Jane Goodenough's unplanned exposure on *Crime Time*, word of which – although she was never named in the programme or in the press – had spread around the Ministry. He had always thought that she was too good to be true, he said. I made some non-committal remark about few of us living without the odd skeleton in the cupboard. Hudson-Black seemed not to hear. 'I believe she's resigned from Ag and Fish,' he said with an unendearing chuckle.

We found a pub in which office workers strung out their working day over whiskies and gins before returning home. I bought us both a Scotch, which we took to a corner table.

'I'm not sure if I can tell you much more about Jane,' he said and, for the first time, I detected an uneasiness about him. 'Her private life was a closed book as far as the rest of us were concerned.'

'Tell me about the connection between the Ministry and the palace.'

Breeding counts for much on these occasions (I see Sincton exuding a protective sheen of lubricant like some small threatened reptile, I see Robin unable to prevent the tell-tale blush coming to his cheeks, I see Biddle blustering in foul-mouthed impotence). Hudson-Black took his time before replying, 'You're working alone now, are you, Inspector?'

'I'm simply trying to find out who killed Oliver Sincton. What we do with the information is another matter.'

Hudson-Black looked at me directly, as if he had decided, for some pragmatic, self-serving reason, to help. 'I'll tell you what you should already know,' he said, and I noticed how almost every remark he made seemed to bear a concealed insult. 'There's a formal link, covering security matters beyond the normal ambit of your good colleagues and yourself.'

This was news to me but I nodded knowingly. 'A formal, secret link?' I asked.

'There's no great secret; we simply don't discuss it with Joe Public.' He paused for emphasis. 'Beyond that, there are less stratified, more personal contacts. We help one another out sometimes.'

'Which was why you were at Windsor the other day.'

'Windsor? I'm not sure I could comment about that.'

'You were seen there on the day Suzi Ashbourn died.'

'I keep in touch. I have friends at Windsor.'

'Jane Goodenough knew about that.'

'Knew about it?' Hudson-Black laughed. 'She was the royals' principal contact at the Ministry. How else do you think she got the job? Her father was an equerry for a few years after he retired. It was intimated that her involvement would be welcomed. Daddy had put in a word.' An edge of petulance had entered his voice. 'Certain networks still pertain. You're not frightfully well briefed, are you?'

'You realize that she had an affair with your Mr Davies.'

He winced at the thought. 'Doesn't surprise me,' he said. 'He's randy. She's ambitious. They were made for each other.'

'Did Jane confide in you about Sincton and Suzi Ashbourn?'

'She was not the confiding type.'

'So she spoke to Davies.'

'I'm not sure I could comment on that.'

'As time went on, it became clear that there was much upon which Hudson-Black was not sure he could comment. Yet, as he played the part of the hear-no-evil, see-no-evil functionary, I sensed indecision. With a little more courage, he could sabotage Davies's career, but then, just for a moment, he would have to place himself in the firing-line, never an acceptable position for a Whitehall man. I had hoped that what small information I possessed would encourage him to open up, if only to protect his own back, but Hudson-Black was an organization man, alert to the maverick, the loose cannon, to the man who, for whatever reason, has gone native or has decided to hunt alone. Now I had to move fast; he was certain to file a report on my renewed interest in the Sincton case.

As he stood to leave, I said, 'We've decided not to go public with the contents of the tape.'

'Tape?' he said. 'Remind me about the tape.'

So, walking slowly towards the river, I told him about the moment of low cunning which had cost Oliver Sincton his life.

Naturally, Sincton had known better than to put his trust in a girl like Suzi Ashbourn. He regarded himself, after all, as something of an expert on bimbo psychology. She may have abandoned all forms of conventional morality years ago, her behaviour in virtually every department may have suited Ollie's purposes, but she was not reliable. There was always that risk of one small spark of decency, that little coal of warmth which could send the sweetest deal up in smoke.

Suzi and the prince; in retrospect, it was inevitable that, just when it was least convenient, she would be overcome by some inconvenient pang of responsibility, or love, or loyalty, or even guilt. Sincton knew these girls. He took the sensible course, leaving a second microphone in her neat little handbag so that, even when Suzi decided to censor her royal love scene, their hot, explosive encounter was still wafted across the warm night to where Ollie sat eagerly taping it all.

'Not that it was particularly shocking,' said Hudson-Black.

'In a sense, no.'

Sincton must have thought that his ship, at last, had come in. Perhaps, being foreign, he never quite understood the relationship between royal family and loyal subjects. In what he had described as 'the ultimate celebrity show', certain conventions still applied. A spot of irreverence here (blurred shot of some peek-a-boo princess in a bikini, *sotto voce* jokes about royal weaknesses such as swearing or an affection for good wine), the occasional criticism concerning the astonishing cost to the country of keeping the show on the road or its unfortunate choice of hangers-on, but nothing that went too far, nothing that might possibly put the whole circus in jeopardy.

A royal holiday romance was ideal, and so was Suzi Ashbourn. Attractive, young, ill-bred enough to represent no kind of threat to the princess but not so vulgar that the prince could be accused of a serious lapse of sexual taste, she was the perfect fall-girl. Above all, she could be relied upon to tell an acceptably lubricious version of events to the press. An injection of containable scandal: it was just what the royal plot needed.

By the time we had reached the station, Hudson-Black was looking more thoughtful. Belatedly realizing that it was within my power to derail his career, he suddenly seemed reluctant to see me go.

'What happened to the tape?' he asked.

I decided to lie. 'We'll be treating it as Exhibit A,' I said.

'Some would say that was irresponsible.'

'Maybe they would.'

I left him at the station. Soon he would be on the telephone to Davies but I no longer cared. I had what I needed.

Jane, of course, was not at her flat. On reaching home, I rang round, tracking her down without much difficulty. While her father was on his annual fishing holiday in Scotland, she was staying at Roseclare. Over the telephone she seemed subdued and, for a moment, I felt sorry for her: losing two jobs in a month and appearing on national television naked and strapped to a bed was tough on anyone, even Jane. All the same, I kept the small talk to a minimum and we agreed to meet the next day at Roseclare.

There are times when it's almost impossible to look on the bright side. Before me I see a wasteland of misery and frustration; Peaky Potter confronted by year after year of cropheaded idiots, most of whom have joined up for the chance to drive fast and hit people, introducing them to the investigative arts which served his own life so badly. Like the older instructors, I'll become odd, at first cranking up my own peculiarities to get me through the day, then becoming the genuine article, a sour, eccentric former policeman.

That night I told Joy everything I knew. We sat up late in the sitting-room, just talking. She, with unnerving foresight, was considerably less optimistic about the outcome of the Sincton case than I was. We laughed at the way it had all turned out, a saga of infidelity and bad behaviour that had only become fatal when two people, alone in a bedroom, had failed to do the indecent thing expected of them.

At some point – perhaps it was the mention of indecency – I asked about her and Gary. She laughed with genuine surprise. The idea of going to bed with him had never occurred to her, she said. 'How could you think such a thing?' she asked. 'I may give you a hard time but I do love you.'

'Whatever happens?'

'Whatever.'

I believed her then, and I still do. These days she's out on the town two or three times a week, taking advantage of my more regular hours. She dances the new dance, drinks the new drink, flirts with the Gary of the moment. Then she comes home to me. It's fine; I trust her.

Jane Goodenough, I discovered the following morning, had not been changed by her exposure. When she greeted me at the front door, thoughts of when I last saw her – gasping as Dexter and Robin rolled around between her legs – seemed no more than a shaming memory. Background is a wonderful thing.

'The car's parked down the road,' I explained.

Jane nodded. 'Fine,' she said.

The sitting-room, into which she led me, was gold in

241

the late summer sun, but there was dust on the tables and a smell of mustiness in the air. Jane was pale, but appeared relaxed. From the way she talked to me, I might have been an insurance salesman.

'Yours, I believe,' I said, taking the cassette from my jacket pocket.

'Ah. The famous tape.'

'Why was it in your flat?'

'Ollie had this odd faith in his own charm. He was so clearly using my father for information when he was meant to be helping with the autobiography that one day Daddy suggested he confided in him. Man to man. After all, Daddy knew a lot about the way they operate at the palace.'

'He showed him the cassette?'

'He was American. He didn't understand the way things worked. Daddy gave me the copy of the cassette and I spoke to Davies.'

'Shall we hear it?' I laid a radio-cassette that I had borrowed from my son Mark on a low table between us. 'Refresh our memories,' I said, picking up the tape and inserting it into the recorder.

Jane sighed, arms folded. 'If we must, Inspector,' she said.

Listening to that well-known regal voice, punctuated occasionally by Suzi's breathy questions, it was difficult not to smile. They really did discuss vegetarianism, his work on behalf of the Wholefood Foundation, her rather less significant efforts for the whales. This, I imagine, was better even than Suzi's dreams. She liked a serious talk in bed; so often, in the past, her explanation of Whalepeace or the FurFighters campaign would be interrupted by an insistent (talk about *rude*) hand on the top of her head. Here it was conversation, words, really magic.

After a while, the prince fell quiet as she chattered on about the terrible time being had by the blue whale, how she never touched a tuna sandwich after she heard what they did to dolphins which were just incredibly intelligent and beautiful animals, like sensitive you know, what must they think, you wouldn't catch dolphins blowing each other up or chopping down the rainforests, it made her ashamed to be human. That's very true, Suzi, said the prince.

There was just one moment of awkwardness. Aware that, nice as the conversation was, saving the planet was not the main reason for their meetings, Suzi broke off mid-gush and made some sort of move (a hand on the royal thigh, perhaps, slender fingers running through the royal locks). Would he, you know, they could, she'd like it because, well, she found him very . . .

'Suzi.' There was a poignant pause, filled only with the sound of our girl rummaging around hopefully. 'Suzi, I don't want to do bodies, OK?'

Do bodies. Yes, he really did say that.

'Oh,' said Suzi, surprised and even slightly hurt. This was something of a first for her. 'Don't you like me?'

'I do like you very much. I find much of what you say absolutely fascinating.'

'Well, then—' There was a silence on the tape, during which Jane stared out of the window. Clearly, Suzi was persisting in a way which discomfited the prince.

'No!' He sounded panicky now, a strangulated tetchiness entering his voice. It wasn't her or anything like that, he explained. It was just that he didn't like it, that was all. He just found that he wasn't interested any more. It was no use trying. Anyway, he found it all a bit of a bore.

'Oh.' Suzi had been unable to hide her disappointment.

'I really must ask for your discretion in this matter.'

'Of course.'

And so they went back to discussing the vegetarian way of life.

That was it. A member of the royal family who wouldn't do bodies, who found it all a bit of a bore. Did it matter? It never had in the past.

'So Suzi was set up,' I said to Jane, as the magical tryst droned to its exclusively verbal conclusion. 'She was there to prove that the prince was just a regular, adulterous guy like everyone else.'

'There were rumours in foreign magazines that he was gay or something. It was felt that this kind of coverage was inappropriate for the royal family. So—' Jane might have been discussing the minor details of a defence contract '—a well-publicized fling with some plausible tart was thought to be the answer.' She brushed something off her dark blue skirt. 'The Ashbourn girl was ideal.'

'You didn't get Sincton to set it up.'

'It wasn't necessary. As usual, he told me who he was seeing. When he mentioned Suzi Ashbourn, I had her looked into. Setting a trap for Ollie was never difficult. He was always such an innocent.'

'But indiscreet.'

'He just had to tell. He couldn't resist it. Within moments of arriving home from Mustique, he was boasting to me about his biggest project ever. I spoke to Hugh Davies. We agreed that something had to be done. So I borrowed the flat off the Ministry and installed him there. He was under surveillance.'

'No more than that?'

'I thought not. Obviously I was wrong.'

The extent of Jane's implication in the death of her former lover, I never fully established. My guess is that, like a true civil servant, she was an expert at blind-eye management, at knowing precisely which questions not to ask. Now, with an openness which at the time I found surprising, she told me what had happened to Oliver Sincton.

He was, it seems, being eavesdropped around the clock. It was known at the Ministry that, sooner rather than later, he would have to be stopped. Already he had tried to sell Suzi's story (the true account, that is, not the phoney romance she believed he was working on) to a couple of newspaper editors. They, being well trained in royal matters, turned him away and reported his activities to their contact at the palace. At the time of his death, Sincton was talking to an agency which specialized in syndicating stories to the foreign press.

'Why didn't anyone talk to him – try to put him off?' I asked Jane.

'We put a couple of anonymous calls through. He thought they were a joke. Even on that last night, Ollie never seemed to realize that this was real, not a soap opera.'

He played into their hands. That evening at the Groucho, Jane had spent much of their meal together begging him to drop the Suzi Ashbourn story, but it was too late; he was now in the grip of some sort of wild fantasy, a money-making scam that would also show the monarchy to be a fraud, a puppet-show. All the same, he must have had an idea that he was living dangerously. There was no other explanation for his strange conversation with Robin as he left the club.

Enter the ultimate *dea ex machina*. Paula, the good girl turned bad, the avenging angel, the slightly disappointed writer. Weak and randy fool that he was, Ollie had to take her home. Meanwhile Jane was ringing Davies to tell him there was nothing more she could do to change Sincton's mind.

It was not the last call Davies received that night. Three hours later one of the men in the small listening room at the Ministry put in a routine report. Their American friend had been up to some muckiness, had picked up a rough individual who, to judge from the sounds coming down the line from Half Moon Street, had left him in a highly vulnerable, possibly even helpless state.

Davies took some sort of executive action. It's

possible, of course, that he drove up to London, used his key to enter the flat and ran Ollie Sincton through the neck with a kitchen knife, but that degree of involvement hardly seemed his style. I imagine a languid, yet precise instruction was issued to some Ministry operative specifically employed for such unsavoury commissions. As Jane said, either way he was guilty.

I had asked her to get Davies down to Roseclare at midday. It was now eleven-thirty. She seemed to understand what was required of her: an interview with her former employer in which she would ask for her job back, discussing Sincton's murder in enough detail for him to incriminate himself. I would be next door, listening, noting and recording.

I sat in Goodenough's dining-room at a shiny mahogany table, facing the door leading to the sitting-room. Yes, I honestly thought that my persistence had been vindicated, that I was about to place a firm line at the foot of the list of casualties which had followed Ollie's death. A car drew up outside. The bell rang. Jane went to the door and I heard voices. I sat poised and cool, the detective at work.

A door opened behind me.

'Hi, Simon,' said Superintendent Biddle.

There was no-one I was less pleased to see making his entrance at this critical point.

'Norman,' I said drily. 'What a surprise.'

He was still standing in the doorway, milking the moment like an incompetent *farceur*. 'We thought you were at home,' he said at last, running a finger down the edge of the dining-room table.

Briefly, foolishly, I thought it was coincidence that had brought him here. 'I've cracked it, Norman,' I said. 'Our man's on his way. Shift the car and you can be in at the death.'

'Thanks, Simon,' he said. 'But Hugh won't be coming.'

I looked at Jane, who at least had the good grace to appear embarrassed by her betrayal.

Biddle was now in front of the dining-room window. After the summer's drought, the lawn was cracked and yellow. 'We've been in touch with Davies for some time. At the top level.'

'You knew he did it?'

'A while ago we were made aware that this was more than just another murder. There were security implications.'

I laughed. 'A limp dick in the palace? It's hardly going to cause a revolution.'

'The feeling is that it's essential for at least one of our great institutions to be entirely and unquestionably sound. Our royal friends may not be tremendously bright or hard-working, and they may be unexceptional in virtually every way, but they're there. They're born, get educated to an acceptable level, sow an acceptable amount of wild oats, marry an acceptable wife or husband, and die at an acceptable age. Not very exciting, but it's important. It gives the nation something to look up to, to depend on. Surely even you can understand that.'

'I can't for the life of me see why it matters if one of them has lost interest in women.'

'That was discussed, I gather. The view was taken that the timing was wrong; it was too early just to . . . give up. And what about the princess? So it had to be finessed. Fortunately—' Biddle smiled smoothly at Jane Goodenough '—there are structures in place for handling this kind of eventuality.' He picked up the tape that was on the table and, with a magician's flourish, put it in his top pocket.

'The show must go on,' I said.

'If you like, yes. A certain pragmatic, expedient approach is . . .' He trailed off as if the necessity of spelling out the obvious was becoming tiresome to him. 'For Christ's sake, he was only a kinky American.'

247

'Other people died.'

'They wouldn't have if you hadn't been so ridiculously persistent – you and that dolt Nicholl.' He gave a sort of comic wince. 'What happened to you, Simon?' he asked. 'You used to be so sensible.'

'It was you who got us on to *Crime Time*.'

'That was before I was aware of the big picture.'

'Don't tell me the TV people knew about this too.'

'Good lord, no. We're not mad. It was decided that, so long as we kept Suzi off the air, there was no problem. It would be fun.'

'Thanks,' muttered Jane.

'All in a good cause,' said Biddle, turning to her with a shrug. 'You know that you'll be looked after once the dust has settled.' He was standing in front of me now as I sat at the table. 'It's Simon here I'm worried about.'

Call me naïve, but I was really not prepared for this. 'Go on,' I said.

'I'm afraid that the Investigations Unit have been going through your files. I can't believe how careless you've been, Simon. It doesn't look good.'

So that was it. They had me as trussed up and helpless as Sincton had been on the night when the Ministry came to call. The informal arrangements, the minor kickbacks and indiscretions upon which my career had been built had now been carefully uncovered. They even, I subsequently discovered, found evidence to suggest that I had fixed up Franky Dimond in order to win my future wife. Individually, these off-the-record agreements looked unwise; together, they were a death warrant.

I returned to the station later that day to find that my office had been denuded of all my papers. Innocent to the last, Dexter seemed utterly bewildered by this development.

The deal that was put to me was simple. Forget the Sincton case and there's a job for life at East Molesey.

Pursue it – a pointless act of heroism in a dubious cause – and I would be making an appearance before the Police Complaints Commission. Either way, my career as a detective was over.

I thought of Joy, the kids, of the professional future of a disgraced copper. What would it be? A shady security job? Some sheet-sniffing private-detective work? Forget it. I was tired of Oliver Sincton. East Molesey it was.

Even now, the past won't leave me alone.

While in custody, Robin had his second great idea, a better concept even than Max Beanbag. He and Laura would rebuild their marriage in a proud, open and, above all, public way. It was a story with everything: obscurity and success, love and deviance, death and renewal. Claire Nash, who was prepared to handle the project so long as she only appeared in its pages under deep cover, sold it to Laura's publisher for a serious six-figure sum. It was agreed that a pre-publicity splash in the form of a media blitz on Robin's release was advisable. They would make a lovely pair: the modern couple under fire, players in a fable for our times.

Last night Robin appeared on television, the star guest of *How Was It For You?*, a late-night chat show on which celebrities are invited to discuss matters of considerable intimacy for the benefit of the viewing public. According to its host, the famed sexologist Dr Julia Grey, Robin's belated bolt for personal freedom was the year's most relevant comment on the current state of interpersonal relations.

'So let me get this right, Robin,' she said, smiling behind her large, honest spectacles. 'You felt that you were missing out in some way, that you were on the outside looking in, that an adventure with this person you met in a wine-bar was an expression of that part of your nature which had hitherto been suppressed, right?'

'Erm, gosh.' Robin writhed in the studio chair, which seemed to be a couple of sizes too small for him. 'I don't know about that. It just seemed a good idea at the time.'

Dr Julia's audience loved Robin, this lanky, endearing embodiment of the English way of sex. He understood their frustrations, the endless unhappy tussles with their baser natures, and yet he had come through. Here he was, sharing it all with them on national television.

'Every marriage is different,' Robin said, 'and ours had been going through a rocky stage. I'll spare you the details but . . .'

Few details, of course, were spared during the programme; this was a touching, human story on which Dr Julia finally conferred her blessing. It was entirely valid, she said. Was it true that he was writing a book?

'Yes, it's about the modern way of marriage. My wife's contributing a foreword,' said Robin.

So Robin seems to be on his way to a new career as the acceptable face of adultery although, to me, his explanation of the night when he strayed so publicly from the path of fidelity remains utterly unconvincing. The truth, I believe, is simpler: he took, as usual, the line of least resistance. Everyone was at it and now so was Robin.

The sky did not fall in. Civilization did not crash around his ears. His marriage did not, after all, curl up and die as he made love to Jane Goodenough. No. Instead, a policeman blundered in, followed by a cameraman; there was a fuss, after which his marriage bloomed once again. Such were the fruits of sexual adventure.

With touching but dangerous loyalty, James has taken to calling by at the house. He gets on well with Joy and, despite turning down the chance to replace the hopeless Andy Craig as presenter of *Crime Time*, he's a hero to Mark and Dominic and has signed their autograph books in the familiar handwriting that would not disgrace a keen but backward twelve year old.

James's feelings towards me are, by his standards at least, complex. Sensing, quite rightly, that the force has not played fair with me, he's puzzled by the ease with which I appeared to lose interest in the death of Oliver Sincton. 'What was all that business about the Windsor video, Simon?' he'll ask, the Christian name causing him problems as always. 'False trail,' I reply, like a pensioner slightly bored with discussions of the past. 'One of life's little mysteries.'

He was remarkably bitter about the celebrity accorded to Robin Nicholl on his release and, for a while, took to insisting plaintively that to be caught and filmed on top of a naked woman you have tied to a bed, then to grapple with a police officer with a knife in your hand, should surely make you guilty of something. I considered explaining to him precisely what had happened, perhaps even giving him the tape I kept at home, but then I thought better of it. By now I had developed a certain affection and respect for James Dexter; he didn't deserve to be in the firing-line.

That tape. It's not, sad to say, Suzi's vegetarian discussion with royalty – evidence which, I imagine, Biddle shredded, burnt and scattered in the Thames within hours of repossessing it at Roseclare. This tape is my cassette – or, to be more accurate, my son Mark's.

Norman Biddle, it turned out, was rather better at betraying his colleagues to further his own career than he was at standard detective work. While picking up the royal tape, boasting all the while of connections with palace and Whitehall, the superintendent failed to notice that, on a chair beneath the table, a second cassette was running on Mark's little recorder, turning and turning like a rope around his neck. It's all there, the entire conversation, interrupting, somewhat incongruously, a programme of Top Forty hits that my son had hoped to keep.

I would like, at this point, to acknowledge the help of my beloved wife Joy in the preparation of this reconstruction. It was she who expressed the view that it was my civic duty to set down my version of events and to send it, with Biddle's unwitting confession and incrimination of Hugh Davies, to the Director of Public Prosecutions.

On the island surrounded by the dry, green pond outside my office are some tall poplars in which there lives a flock of green parakeets. They wheel high over this establishment, screeching and squawking and generally proclaiming their foreignness to the people of East Molesey. No-one knows where they came from, the parakeet not being indigenous to these parts, but somehow they survive here. It's been a good summer for them, as dry and hot as home, wherever that may be, but now they sit there in the trees, complaining loudly. The weather's on the turn; I think it's going to rain.

End of

EXHIBIT A

The Ruins Of Time
by Ben Woolfenden

'So powerful is this novel that the reader is mesmerized
into believing that he is taking a journey through the ruins
of time that is his very own'
BERNICE RUBENS

Reluctantly drawn to his father's fanatical research into
the family past, Tom Crane falls victim to the same clues
that once dogged his parent – old photographs, unsent
letters, and a strangely compelling Victorian painting.
With the old man's death, Tom must shoulder the burden
of the search to uncover the sorrows and tragedies that
haunted his father and which are now his own
inheritance.

This compelling, atmospheric and many-layered novel
marks the début of a remarkable talent.

'A novel within a novel which has a mesmerizing
intricacy . . . it is a joy to read'
TODAY

'Cleverly structured and stylishly understated'
BARBARA TRAPIDO

0 552 99500 2

BLACK SWAN

The Music Programme
by Paul Micou

'Evelyn Waugh is not dead; his spirit lives vividly on in the dark and measured hilarity of Paul Micou's first novel'
JAN DALLEY, OBSERVER

All is not well at the Timbali headquarters of the Music Programme. The imminent arrival of U.S. Congressional envoy *Charles 'Crack' McCray* threatens the Programme's funding. The panicking employees try to pull themselves together to form a united and competent front: Englishman *Dr Humphrey Lord*, Assistant to the Supreme Director, Late Baroque, finds himself in the front line of the Programme's defence. *Dan O'Connor*, putative Irishman and prized speechwriter, hopes not to be too distracted from his passionate pursuit of the French Ambassador's teenage daughter. *Wendell 'Skip' Skinner*, American jazz trombonist, nearly sinks the ship with a characteristic drunken gaffe. *Ludvik Kastostis*, the MAXIMALIST composer-in-residence, dashes recklessly to the end of his latest, loudest work, *Flamedance of Euphorion*, hoping to have something – anything – to show for himself. And somewhere, above it all, looms the mysterious, reclusive figure known only as the 'Supreme Director' . . .

'The last writer to enter so funnily into the spirit of Africa was – best of all compliments – Evelyn Waugh'
DAVID HUGHES, MAIL ON SUNDAY

'Micou's dazzling, hilarious début is good news for those of us who have been waiting for someone to come along and show that humour and emotional chaos go together like good splinters and fingers'
JONH WILDE, BLITZ

0 552 99381 6

BLACK SWAN

A SELECTED LIST OF OTHER BLACK SWAN TITLES

☐	99186 4	A KIND OF LOVING	Stan Barstow	£5.99
☐	99434 0	GIVE US THIS DAY	Stan Barstow	£4.99
☐	99531 2	AFTER THE HOLE	Guy Burt	£4.99
☐	99348 4	SUCKING SHERBET LEMONS	Michael Carson	£5.99
☐	99465 0	STRIPPING PENGUINS BARE	Michael Carson	£5.99
☐	99524 X	YANKING UP THE YO-YO	Michael Carson	£5.99
☐	99477 4	THE MAN IN THE WINDOW	Jon Cohen	£5.99
☐	99487 1	JIZZ	John Hart	£5.99
☐	99169 4	GOD KNOWS	Joseph Heller	£3.95
☐	99195 3	CATCH-22	Joseph Heller	£6.99
☐	99538 X	GOOD AS GOLD	Joseph Heller	£6.99
☐	99204 6	THE CIDER HOUSE RULES	John Irving	£6.99
☐	99209 7	THE HOTEL NEW HAMPSHIRE	John Irving	£5.99
☐	99369 7	A PRAYER FOR OWEN MEANY	John Irving	£6.99
☐	99205 4	THE WORLD ACCORDING TO GARP	John Irving	£6.99
☐	99567 3	SAILOR SONG	Ken Kesey	£6.99
☐	99384 0	TALES OF THE CITY	Armistead Maupin	£4.99
☐	99086 8	MORE TALES OF THE CITY	Armistead Maupin	£5.99
☐	99106 6	FURTHER TALES OF THE CITY	Armistead Maupin	£5.99
☐	99239 9	BABYCAKES	Armistead Maupin	£5.99
☐	99383 2	SIGNIFICANT OTHERS	Armistead Maupin	£5.99
☐	99374 3	SURE OF YOU	Armistead Maupin	£4.99
☐	99381 6	THE MUSIC PROGRAMME	Paul Micou	£4.99
☐	99461 8	THE DEATH OF DAVID DEBRIZZI	Paul Micou	£5.99
☐	99501 0	ROTTEN TIMES	Paul Micou	£5.99
☐	99500 2	THE RUINS OF TIME	Ben Woolfenden	£4.99